Berkley Prime Crime titles by Kate Parker

THE VANISHING THIEF

THE COUNTERFEIT LADY

THE ROYAL ASSASSIN

THE
ROYAL
ASSASSIN

KATE PARKER

BERKLEY PRIME CRIME, NEW YORK

BERKLEY
PRIME
CRIME

An imprint of Penguin Random House LLC
375 Hudson Street, New York, New York 10014

This book is an original publication of Penguin Random House LLC.

Library of Congress Cataloging-in-Publication Data

Parker, Kate.
The royal assassin / Kate Parker.—Berkley Prime Crime trade paperback edition.
pages ; cm
ISBN 978-0-425-26662-5
I. Title.
PS3616.A74525R69 2015
813'.6—dc23
2015003055

PUBLISHING HISTORY
Berkley Prime Crime trade paperback edition / July 2015

PRINTED IN THE UNITED STATES OF AMERICA

10 9 8 7 6 5 4 3 2 1

Cover illustration by Teresa Fasolino.
Cover design by George Long.
Interior text design by Kristin del Rosario.

Penguin
Random
House

To Corey, Adrienne, and Jennifer
You still keep me on my toes

CHAPTER ONE

"GOOD morning, Miss Keyes. Is Miss Fenchurch here?"
The familiar baritone of the Duke of Blackford reached me from the front of my bookshop. I jerked my head up to face the door of my tiny office. The metal tool I was using to pry open a crate of two-shilling novels slipped and jabbed my hand. I sucked on my injured finger, tasting blood mixed with ink and coal dust from the boxes, and felt my cheeks burn with embarrassment.

I didn't have a mirror, but I knew my auburn curls were springing loose from my topknot. I was filthy and in no fit state to be seen by anyone. My assistant, Emma Keyes, was seeing to customers while I dealt with the shipments of new books and illustrated weeklies, which filled the office and back hall to overflowing.

I shouldn't have been surprised that on a day when I looked like something Dickens, the neighborhood cat, left on my doorstep, Blackford marched back into my life. *Blast*.

"She's in the back, Your Grace."

I'd given Emma orders not to let anyone see me. *Traitor.*

A moment later, the duke appeared in the doorway with a cheerful "Good morning, Georgia." He strode forward around the various stacks of periodicals and books, somehow squeezing past without a single smudge clinging to his immaculate trousers. Whipping out his pristine handkerchief, he pulled my finger out of my mouth and wrapped up the injured digit. "I can't have you getting blood poisoning. We have a problem and I want your help."

The words "I want your help" coming from Blackford's lips would lead me to cross deserts in August and fly to the moon in a hot air balloon. Unfortunately, with Blackford, those were real possibilities.

The hint of excitement, of danger, that the duke carried with him made him irresistible to me. The fact that he was handsome and incredibly self-assured added both to his allure and my frustration. Blackford was a duke. I was middle-class. My dreams had no hope of coming true.

He looked me over and scowled. "Have you gained weight?"

Leave it to the duke to dissipate the warmth he always created in me when he held my hand. "No. I wore my work corset and this drab gown this morning because I'm checking all these boxes of books and periodicals against the shipping papers. This is my business. I don't trust my suppliers. And I will not be shortchanged."

I pulled my hand away, still wrapped in his handkerchief. "I'm sorry I'm not dressed to receive Your Grace for tea."

"I'm not here for tea, Georgia. I'm here for assistance."

Blackford needed my help. Of course he did. There was no other reason a duke would call on a middle-class shop owner. And the only time he needed my help, and the help of the Archivist Society, was when a crime had been committed that affected the ruling class. "What is the crime?"

"Murder." The duke stood before me amid the clutter and dust, unsullied, unwrinkled, unflappable. His posture was regal and his dark eyes mesmerizing.

His presence made my heart beat faster. At night, I often dreamed of the time when he kissed me. Well, I started it by kissing him. My face heated despite the pleasant breeze coming through the window, knowing he must not have felt the same way. His response to what I thought was a glorious moment was to disappear from my life far too often during the next year. This last trip, to the continent on his own business as well as to stop intrigue in Her Majesty's family, had lasted nearly three months.

However, I was determined to cling to my dignity. My office may have been tiny and crowded with new stock, but it was mine. Georgia Fenchurch of Fenchurch's Books was hostess here, not Queen Victoria. I removed two cartons from a chair and lifted it over some boxes.

Blackford snatched the chair from my grasp and set it down in the only free space on the floor. "Sit down, Georgia." He used his no-nonsense tone that made most people jump to do his bidding.

"You sit on the chair. I'm already filthy."

"I won't sit while you stand."

I appreciated that he was always a gentleman. "This stack of cartons will do nicely for my chair." I maneuvered my feet and my skirts into a tight gap between piles of scholarly tomes and perched on a container of the newest fiction, including the latest by Mrs. Hepplewhite. A copy of her gothic novel would go home with me that night.

Once Blackford sat, pride made me lift my chin and look down my nose at him. "You have my full attention."

Blackford picked up a copy of one of the many periodicals we stocked. I couldn't see if this one covered the queen's record-setting length of reign or the engagement of the son of her cousin to a fetching young Russian royal. Inexpensive illustrated editions touching on either event sold as soon as they appeared on shop shelves. I made sure they were instantly available in my shop. "Who buys this trash?" he asked.

"The people who pay my bills. And if you aren't going to come to the point, I need to get back to work."

He shook his head but he stayed in the chair.

I lowered my voice. "Who was the victim? Where did the crime take place? And why are you involved?"

He waved the periodical at me. "The victim was the Russian bodyguard of this Romanov fiancée of the Duke of Sussex, the queen's cousin. The guard's body was discovered on a train returning from Scotland. There are international implications because of where the train originated."

"How is Her Majesty?" I asked. I knew she was at Balmoral awaiting September twenty-third, the day when she'd become our longest-serving monarch.

"Well and wanting a quick solution to this problem. Tsar Nicholas and his family are visiting her, and the Russians see anarchists under every bed."

"It's only been fifteen years since their tsar was assassinated. I'd be edgy, too."

"They should be. Scotland Yard has detected anarchist activity in the East End. But there's no reason to believe anarchists killed the guard to Princess Kira."

"Princess? I thought she was a grand duchess."

"The press never gets titles correct. She's a great-granddaughter of Nicholas I but not in the direct line of inheritance. Her grandfather was a younger son. Therefore she is styled Her Highness, Princess Kira." He brushed away the issue of her title with a small motion of one hand. I couldn't help but stare at his still-pristine fawn leather gloves. I was dirty from the moment I walked into this paper-and-ink-filled space.

"Never mind her title." He frowned at me. "The problem is Scotland Yard fears something worse will happen on British soil."

"You mean to the princess? Because one of the Russian soldiers has already been killed?"

"To the princess, or to the tsar and his wife and daughter, who are in Scotland at this very moment. Scotland Yard also has to worry if a member of our royal family is an assassin's target."

"Why kill a guard who'd left the queen and tsar and was coming to London? That doesn't make sense. Unless the guard had enemies here. Do we know anything about him?"

"Very little. He was an older, married man with a wife and children in St. Petersburg. He was chosen for this position because he was settled and trustworthy. They couldn't allow anyone young and dashing to be that close to the princess. The rules of propriety, you know."

"His poor family." I pictured them in a hovel in the snow. Except for the royal family, I pictured everyone in Russia living in poverty in year-round snowdrifts. "What was his name?"

"I don't know." The duke pulled off his gloves and set them on his knee. Then he reached out and took my uninjured ink-smudged hand. "This is going to be a difficult investigation because the Russians are insular. Standoffish. They don't want our help in finding the murderer. As far as they're concerned, the killing was done by anarchists. They want Scotland Yard to round up all known anarchists and hang them."

Between the thrill of Blackford's large, warm hand touching mine and embarrassment over the filth on my skin, I barely managed to pay attention to his words. "Why?"

"Because they're anarchists."

I looked at him in amazement. "We don't do things that way in England."

"You see the problem."

"Lack of cooperation from those who knew the victim best." Then it hit me. "You're involved because the Foreign Office is involved. I suppose the Russian government objects to everything Scotland Yard asks or does."

He nodded. "We're going to need a different approach. Do you speak Russian?"

"Are you joking?"

"How about French?"

"I speak it like an Englishwoman, but I read it very well."

"Good. And I see a typewriter on your desk. You must know how to use it."

"For bills and orders. Nothing more." Where was this going, I wondered.

"We need you to go undercover again. As Princess Kira's English secretary."

"No." My business hadn't fared well during my last undercover assignment. As much as I objected that time, playing the part of Blackford's paramour had had its benefits. I didn't see any good coming from being away from my bookshop a second time as a secretary.

"Georgia. Relax. Emma will be here looking after the shop. You'll spend every night at home. Your middle-class clothes and life will be part of your disguise." He smiled at me. Wolves must smile like that at their prey.

"What about the Archivist Society's current investigation? I'm sure you know what we're working on, and you know we try not to split up our resources on two investigations at once."

"You'll have to make an exception."

"Why? We need to find out who robbed the home of the Marquis of Shepherdston. The thieves used dynamite and blew up part of the house before they killed one of his footmen. They're much more dangerous criminals in my view."

"That's only your view."

I pulled my hand away. He was being deliberately stubborn. Since the day the duke and I had met, when he tried to stop the Archivist Society from following leads in an investigation, he'd made it his business to know every case we worked on. I felt sure he'd suggested to the marquis that he employ the Archivist Society. We were now hard at work on an investigation, parallel to Scotland Yard's, on this burglary.

So far, neither effort had uncovered anything useful.

"Don't deny you know the Archivist Society has been asked by the marquis to find out who blew up his bedroom and shot his footman." I raised my eyebrows, daring the duke to lie to me.

"They blew up his safe. The bedroom was a casualty of the bomb."

I grumbled under my breath at Blackford's cavalier attitude. "Nevertheless," I insisted, "they took the contents of the safe and some valuables from the rest of the house and the marquis has hired us to find the robbers and get his goods back."

Blackford lifted one shoulder in a shrug. "He's hired the Archivist Society. He hasn't hired you personally."

"I'm certain the Archivist Society has members who fit your needs better than I would." Fenchurch's Books was my livelihood, and I'd had to abandon it for almost two weeks during a previous investigation with the duke. Lacking a husband or family, I had to look out for myself. Such was the fate of a spinster.

"But none I want to work with. I am well-known to the Duke of Sussex. He will be around the princess a great deal, and I will accompany him as a friend and as Whitehall's representative."

Here it was. A chance to work closely with Blackford again. Despite my hesitation to leave my shop, I felt excitement flooding my veins.

"I've already planted the seed in Sussex's mind that his fiancée needs a secretary who can also assist her in learning our language. The princess has been sheltered. She's very shy and knows practically no English. She does, however, speak passable French."

"About the level of mine." I looked him in the eye. "You've already arranged to have me hired as this woman's English teacher, haven't you? You did this before you asked me or spoke to Sir Broderick about the Archivist Society taking on this case. Blackford, you have to stop forcing people to do your bidding."

"It's not my bidding. It's Whitehall's. I merely assist."

"We're not your slaves."

"Serfs."

"What?"

"Serfs. In Russia, peasants are called serfs. You'll need to know that."

"We're in England. We call them slaves. I am not a peasant and the Archivist Society does not like being used this way."

By this time, even someone as self-assured as the duke should have noticed the steam rising from my head. He held both of his hands palms out toward me. "Georgia, I apologize. From here, I'm going to see Sir Broderick and ask him to arrange a meeting of the Archivist Society for tonight. I do not mean to take you and the society for granted. But you're amazingly talented and I enjoy working with you."

I hoped he meant me and not the entire Archivist Society. I gave him a gracious nod and replied, "We are always eager to help Her Majesty and the government. And of course you," I added, making my last words sound like an afterthought. My lack of assurance where the duke was concerned made me prickly.

"Good, because I can't imagine how we'll be able to discover why this Russian was killed unless you help."

Acting as Princess Kira's secretary, I'd see him almost daily. Thoughts of his constant proximity made me feel flushed. Aloud I said, "Aren't you interested in who killed the guard?"

"No. *Why* is more important. If it was an anarchist, why kill only the guard? If this is part of some Russian insurrection, why kill the guard on the train and not one who was protecting the tsar in Scotland? If the murder was a personal vendetta, why wait until the guard was in England?"

"You think the princess is the target?"

"Or the princess and the Duke of Sussex. Or her hosts in London, the Duke and Duchess of Hereford."

"Should I be armed while typing?" I couldn't resist asking in a dry tone.

Blackford took me seriously. "No. Scotland Yard is keeping an eye on Hereford House, the duke maintains a full staff, and the princess has a chaperone who could hold off an army of anarchists with her temperament alone."

What was I getting myself into? "Do I have to pass an interview with the chaperone or the duchess?"

"The duchess is a friend. We have this worked out between us, and the chaperone has no say."

I stared at him as if he'd overlooked an important point. "If she can hold off an army, what is one hired secretary?"

"Officially, you work for the duchess. She is lending you to the princess."

"How long have I been working for the duchess?"

"Not long. The princess and Sussex stopped off for a short visit on their way to London, so we'll go this afternoon and introduce you to the duchess before the princess arrives."

"How long do we have to set this up?"

"Two days. The princess is in a hurry to reach London."

"Why?"

"Princess Kira is a painter. She likes to paint street scenes."

"I'll have to get hold of Frances Atterby and learn if she's free to help run the bookshop again. You're certain I won't have to run all over England with this princess?"

"Yes." He gave me a smile that reached his eyes and took my hand again. "I'm not an ogre, Georgia. I know how much your bookshop means to you."

"But if the princess takes off for someone's country estate, you'll expect me to go along." I knew how the duke's mind worked.

"She doesn't want to leave London with all these new sights to paint. And all the major art galleries are in London."

I'd only have two days to research painting so I'd have some idea what the princess was talking about. In French. I'd have to step carefully or I could blunder badly. "Won't she want to paint in the countryside?"

"Her family's kept her on their country estate most of the year. She's had little opportunity to visit St. Petersburg, and she wants to live in a big city. London will be new and exciting for her."

But why was she staying with the Herefords? Then I remembered. "The Duchess of Hereford is a well-regarded painter, isn't she?"

"Yes."

"That explains why the princess is staying with her."

"The Herefords are young enough not to bore a young lady and cosmopolitan enough not to make her think all Englishmen are provincial louts."

"So everything is focused on this princess and no one cares about the guard who died." I pulled my hand away and folded my arms over my stomach. I would have tapped my foot but there was no room between the boxes. I hadn't met the princess but so far I'd not heard anything to make me like her. My sympathies lay with the guard's family. I was seventeen when both my parents died. Their murder still haunted me.

"We care because we need to know why he died. Scotland Yard has very little evidence to link anyone to the killing."

"So the murderer will go free."

"Hopefully, we'll catch him before he kills again." Blackford looked squarely into my eyes, knowing he'd said the words that would make me go along with this investigation.

BLACKFORD RETURNED TO the bookshop in the afternoon to escort me to the home of the Duchess of Hereford. I couldn't think of any reason why he always used the ancient carriage given to his family by the Duke of Wellington for services rendered at Waterloo unless it was to aggravate me. Sitting high off the ground, I found it difficult to climb in and out of it even with assistance. In short, I was at a disadvantage. I appeared foolish.

I glanced over at an urchin who was hawking a free broadsheet, and my aggravation grew. My shop stocked dailies and weeklies that we charged customers for. I didn't like free competition on my doorstep.

"Miners' strike. Show solidarity," the boy bellowed at us, a page held high in his ink-stained fingers. I was about to shoo him away when he smacked the duke in the chest with a copy.

The duke glared as he took the paper and then gave me a hand up before climbing into the coach after me. "Well, at least the price is right," he muttered and tossed it aside. "Solidarity, indeed."

An image of the unsullied duke manning the barricades with the grimy miners brought a smile to my lips.

Once we were under way, he glanced across the carriage at me and said, "You cleaned up nicely."

I was wearing my newest white shirtwaist with a blue skirt and clean white gloves. Emma had tamed my hair into a proper coiffure under a wide-brimmed straw hat. I was surprised he noticed. "Thank you."

His grin widened. "I rather liked you covered with ink and, what was that, coal dust?"

"Yes," I hissed out through clenched jaws. No woman wants to be reminded of her less-attractive moments.

"It gave you a certain dangerous disguise."

Heat rose to my cheeks. "Could we focus on the case at hand, please?"

His expression was instantly serious. "Of course. The Duchess of Hereford has two charming young children, a talent for painting, and a well-run home. She's a decent employer but she expects punctuality and meticulous work."

"How old is she?"

"Perhaps a few years your senior."

We stopped on Park Lane in front of a beautiful redbrick home that probably had been built during the early Georgian period. The front garden was full of roses, and well-tamed greenery bordered the walkway to the front steps.

When the duke helped me down, I slipped on the top step of the carriage and nearly knocked him over. Fortunately, the muscles I felt through his silky wool suit jacket were up to the task of saving my dignity. The shock of the near tumble didn't speed my pulse as much as feeling the marble inside his sleeves.

I walked toward the front door with a heated face, then stopped on the path. "Blackford, you didn't tell me the Herefords are your next-door neighbors."

"Yes. Hereford and I have known each other since we were in our prams."

A butler answered the footman's knock, took Blackford's card, and led us into an immaculate formal parlor done in blues and creams. I walked around, admiring the paintings on the walls. One in particular, showing a young boy and a younger girl, captured my attention.

"I painted that portrait of my children two years ago," came a voice from behind me.

I turned and gave a deep curtsy. "It is beautiful, Your Grace."

She'd already turned to Blackford, calling him Ranleigh. He in turn called her Lady Beatrice. She was tall, thin, and graceful, with a low-pitched speaking voice. The sort of woman Blackford needed to marry.

I was depressed already, and I hadn't yet learned what my duties would be.

The duchess sat down, offered us tea, and on our refusal said, "The princess will be arriving about noon the day after to-morrow. It would be good if you were here a little early, Miss Fenchurch, to appear part of the household."

"I'm going to use the name Georgia Peabody, if you don't mind," I said. "I don't want anyone connecting my work here with Fenchurch's Books."

"Of course. Miss Georgia Peabody, then. Do you speak any languages?"

"I speak some French. And I read it very well."

"And you type?"

"Yes, Your Grace."

"And your handwriting?"

"Clear, but not flowery." I wanted her to understand I was from the middle class. I didn't have time to deal with anything above utilitarian.

"Excellent. Let me show you the rooms you need to be familiar with. Then we'll sit down and put our heads together on what we know and what we need to know."

She was businesslike. I thought I might like working with her.

"Where is Hereford?" Blackford asked.

"He took our son and left this morning for our estate. He said if we're going to have a Russian invasion in his house, and a female Russian invasion at that, he was leaving."

Blackford laughed. "Sounds like Hereford."

The duchess did not look pleased. Leading us down a corridor, she opened a door on a pleasant morning room with a lovely view of the back garden. On a desk by the window was a typewriter. She showed me where I'd find ink and notepaper and typewriter supplies. "You'll work here and have your lunch served to you in this room. There's a cloakroom and a retiring room by the back door. This way, please."

She showed me where I could use her modern "facilities" and hang my coat. There was a table by the coatrack already holding a small hat and a pair of darned gloves. "My daughter's governess's," the duchess said by word of explanation and led us back to her beautiful parlor.

Once we were seated, she said, "You'll be expected to be here from ten until five. Servants talk, and they'll quickly figure out if you're not who you say you are." Then her attitude softened. "Try to be as indispensable to the princess as you can. I've been told she could be in grave danger, and I have no idea how to respond. I've also been told you're very resourceful."

"I try to be. How much do you know about the princess?"

"She's nineteen. She has an excellent talent for painting. I'm told there was much searching in the Almanach de Gotha to find a good match for her. Someone who would tolerate her painting. Sussex adores her talent and is a good match for her, being a third-generation descendant of a ruler just as she is."

"The Almanach de Gotha?"

"The stud book for all the royal families in Europe," Blackford told me with a hint of a smirk.

Oh. Of course there would be one. I couldn't imagine why the duke found it amusing, however. He was in Debrett's, the British aristocratic equivalent. "Are they fond of each other?" I asked. "The princess and Sussex?"

The duchess looked blank. "I suppose they will be."

I wasn't sure if that was an encouraging statement. "What do you know about her as a person?"

She gave me a rueful smile. "Not much that would be helpful to you. The tsarina wrote the queen about the girl's artistic talent and then the princess herself sent the queen a painting. It was— breathtaking."

"How long will she be staying with you?"

"Until she returns to Russia. I don't know how long she plans to remain. Sussex will be a constant visitor. He seems more smitten than she is and wants to win her over."

"Win her over?" This sounded like a complication.

"Perhaps that's the wrong phrase." The duchess thought for a moment. "She's perfectly willing to marry him, there's no trouble there. It's just that Sussex is in his late thirties. He should have married some time ago, but he's so boyish, no one thought to marry him off until he inherited the title three years ago. It appeared to everyone that his sickly father would outlive us all." She gave a small shrug. "His mother has always been the dominant one in the family and has blocked every effort to find her son a suitable wife. The dowager duchess would keep him tied to her apron strings until he was sixty if Victoria allowed it."

If I were Princess Kira, I'd be running in the opposite direction. "She plans to stay weeks? Months? Until the wedding?"

The duchess's eyes widened at the thought. "Oh, I hope not. The wedding is scheduled for next spring. Before the Jubilee celebration. Surely she'll leave by November and return in April. I think the princess is due to stay at Osborne with the queen for a short time before the wedding. Windsor Castle would be more convenient, but Victoria prefers to spend the spring at Osborne."

This investigation could keep me away from the bookshop for two months. I shot a dark look at Blackford, who'd sat silently through our conversation. The smile he returned was enigmatic.

For a moment, I was sorry he'd come back into my life.

CHAPTER TWO

THAT evening, Emma Keyes walked with me to Sir Broderick's along the busy pavement. Families strolled together while enjoying the seasonably nice weather and speedy walkers rushed home to dinner or evening pursuits. The roads were clogged with carriages and hansom cabs, wagons having already returned to be reloaded for the next dawn.

I noticed that several male heads turned when we walked by but knew their glances weren't for me. Emma had been an attractive child who'd blossomed into a beautiful woman. Mercifully, she'd also been born with brains and good judgment. Otherwise, no woman could have stood her.

When we arrived for the Archivist Society meeting at Sir Broderick's large town house, Jacob, his assistant, opened the door. He took our cloaks and said, "We're meeting in the parlor."

Emma froze on the second step heading upstairs as I turned to face the young man at the bottom of the staircase. "Not the study?"

He grinned. "Mrs. Hardwick and Sir Broderick have the room cleaned up ready for company, so we're using it tonight. Go on, take a look."

We always used the study. I rushed around the elevator with Emma on my heels and threw open the door. When I came to a surprised stop, she collided with me, and we both took a few steps into the room.

The parlor appeared just as it had a dozen years before when Sir Broderick left the house on his feet for the last time. Now he sat in his wheeled chair in front of the roaring fire smiling at us. "Come in and have some tea. Blackford will be here shortly and then we can start."

I walked over to where Mrs. Hardwick had placed the tea service and a plate of Dominique's scones. "You've worked a miracle," I told her. "He hadn't used that elevator to come down here until you arrived."

"He probably wasn't ready to use it until now," she replied. She was a square-faced woman with gray streaked in her light brown topknot.

"I've known him since before the accident," I said. "And I believe you've instigated this marvel."

She smiled at my words and her face lit up with kindness, making her beautiful. Sir Broderick was lucky to have hired her as his housekeeper. Luck he deserved.

I took my tea and a scone and sat next to Frances Atterby. "Dominique hasn't lost her touch with scones," she told me.

I took a bite. The flavor made my eyes close in rapture. When I opened them again, I took another look around the room. The new fabric on the chairs and sofas was smooth and crisp, and the draperies had been hung so recently they lacked faded patches from the sun or soot from the fire. Sir Broderick and Mrs. Hardwick must have spent the past few weeks redecorating this room without telling any of us.

"What's the new case about?" Frances asked.

"If things end up as Blackford wants them, I'll need you in the bookshop again. Emma will be there to help."

"Good. My son's wife has a sick relative in the country and she thinks I would make a fine nurse."

"You would."

"Can you see me in the country, tending the sick and gathering eggs and milking cows? She forgets I ran that hotel with my husband before she was born. I'm a Londoner, and my family is here." Frances finished her scone and nodded firmly, her jowls wobbling.

"I'll claim you as my sister if it'll help." Adam Fogarty stopped his ceaseless pacing behind our sofa.

"Ah, Adam, you'll always be a brother to me," she responded. "How's the leg?"

"Better. The weather's been fair. So, what's our case?"

"The Duke of Blackford is presenting it," I told him.

"Not more spies." I detected a groan in his reply.

"Anarchists this time."

"Worse," he said and continued his stroll around the room.

At that moment, the duke walked in followed by Jacob. We all, except Sir Broderick, rose and gave Blackford a low bow or curtsy. He bowed to Sir Broderick and then gave the room a bow. Then he sat down near Sir Broderick but away from the scorching heat of the fire. Mrs. Hardwick brought him a glass of whiskey.

The preliminaries out of the way, Sir Broderick said, "I called this group together tonight to plan our investigation into the murder of a Russian imperial guard in a British railway coach and to implement our protection of the princess he was assigned to bodyguard. This princess will be marrying the Duke of Sussex, the son of a cousin of our queen."

"He was the only bodyguard?" Adam immediately asked.

"Yes."

"Is that usual? To have only one guard?"

"She's of low rank in the royal family, and once she arrived in Britain, the Russians expected us to protect her."

"What does the princess say about the attack? The guard should have been right there with her." Adam Fogarty scowled, clearly puzzled.

"He wasn't. They were in a station and he stepped off the train for a few minutes. His body was found in the luggage carriage. The tsar leaves Balmoral for home shortly with the tsarina and the rest of his guards and household. The queen has promised we'll do everything we can from this end to catch the murderer." Blackford glanced around the room at each of us. "Her Majesty expects a quick but thorough investigation."

"She wants results," Sir Broderick muttered.

"Was anyone seen with him?" Fogarty reverted to his police sergeant training whenever he began asking questions.

"Porters, ticket collectors, and stallholders were all questioned. No one saw anything. You'd think a man in a Russian Imperial Guards uniform would stand out in Yorkshire," the duke said.

"Was the platform busy?" I asked.

"Yes. The train the princess and her entourage rode on headed to London stopped at the same time as a train bound for the queen and Balmoral. It's a small station. The railroad arranges the schedule so no other trains pass the area near that time. Government ministers and servants were on the platform trading gossip and intelligence about the state of things in the queen's household. They were all focused on getting their own questions answered in the few minutes before the trains pulled out in opposite directions."

"Have questions been asked of those arriving in Balmoral?" Frances asked.

"Yes, and no one noticed the guard."

"How was he killed, and was anything taken from the body?" Emma asked.

"He was stabbed from the front. One strike to the heart. Quick and clean. One of his epaulets was torn off in a quick, brutal struggle and a button was missing."

"Was the killer marked by the guard?" Emma asked.

"Possibly. There was blood on one hand, but it may have been the guard's."

"Did they find either the epaulet or the button?"

"No. If they weren't lost amid the piles of baggage, then the killer must have taken them with him. Possibly accidentally. If this was deliberate, it sounds like the anarchists. I can't think of anyone else wanting this type of souvenir," Blackford replied.

"What about blood? Shouldn't the killer have ended up all bloody?" I tried to picture the scene. Someone in the railway station or on a train should have noticed blood on a passenger.

"There was a pool around the guard on the floor of the railway carriage, but his uniform may have kept the killer from being sprayed with it. Russian uniforms are thick. When he was found, there was more blood on the inside of his coat than the outside. His tunic was soaked with his blood."

I studied Blackford after he told us this last piece of information. "So the blade was long?"

"Long and thin. Easily hidden."

"Someone obviously came prepared to kill. I wonder if he came up on the London train." I glanced at Blackford to see if he was thinking the same thing I was.

He shuddered. "Otherwise, the murderer had been in Balmoral with the queen."

"Were any tickets sold at that station in Yorkshire for either train? Or after they left, did the conductors find any passengers without a ticket?" The killer had to go somewhere after the murder. If he came up from London and wanted to go back there . . .

"No, but they did report that a stranger bought a ticket to London on the next train through the station. A stranger without luggage," Blackford told me.

"Did they get a description?"

"Tall, bearded. He reportedly looked like a tramp and said very little."

Looked like a tramp? I imagined anarchists dressed this way.

"Where was the luggage carriage on the train in relation to the coach for the princess?" Adam Fogarty asked.

"They were next to each other, so the guard wouldn't have been on the platform long. Which probably cut down on the number of people who might have noticed him."

"So far, we know little about the princess and less about the dead guard," I told them. "Your Grace, could you get us any information that Scotland Yard has uncovered on either one?"

"The guard's name is Lidijik, Semyon Lidijik. He's been in the guards eighteen years, married, two children. They live in St. Petersburg, but he and his wife come from the country estate owned by the princess's father, Prince Pyotr Romanov. Lidijik didn't seem to be the kind of person anyone noticed. Not particularly ambitious. He was an adequate soldier. No known enemies."

Blackford stared me in the eye. "You see, Georgia, I am paying attention to the victim."

"Thank you, Your Grace." Once again he surprised me. Ordinarily, he considered the needs of Whitehall before he gave the victim a thought. His ability to amaze me was one of the many reasons I looked forward to working with him.

"I plan to see Sussex on his return and get him talking. He was on the train, he's spent time with the princess, and presumably he saw her bodyguard. Hopefully he noticed something."

"Something he doesn't realize is important?" Emma asked.

Blackford made a quick face before he spoke. "Poor Sussex will never realize the importance of anything. The trick is just to get the man talking. And then to keep listening."

"This is outside the realm of our normal sources of information," Sir Broderick said. "Have the Scotland Yard detectives interviewed any of the government ministers who were on the train? Did they see anything?"

"The passengers continued to London on the train with the body and have been questioned. I spoke to one of them, Lord Tayle. He and the other ministers were in separate railway compartments from the carriage the princess rode in. He got out at that rural Yorkshire siding where they take on water and coal when they're making the run between Balmoral and London. The northbound train arrived about a half minute later, and he searched out Lord Rogers to ask him to continue trying to discuss an unpopular measure with Her Majesty. The queen often refuses to discuss bills she doesn't approve of."

Blackford shook his head. "Tayle was so focused on his task that he didn't notice any strange activity. No one in a Russian uniform. He doesn't think the princess or Sussex got out of their carriage, but he's not certain."

"We have no eyewitnesses and little evidence despite a very small window of opportunity," Sir Broderick began. "Any suggestions on how we should proceed?"

"I've already set up with the princess's hostess, the Duchess of Hereford, for Georgia to act as their secretary and to tutor the princess in English. Georgia will be able to talk to the princess as well as observe any dangers around her." Blackford smiled, knowing any plans would now have to be made around his scheme.

"Will she have to go away again?" Frances asked.

"Only from the bookshop. She'll have her evenings and Sundays free, and she'll be able to live at home," the duke assured her.

"Where does this leave us with the investigation into the explosion and robbery at the Marquis of Shepherdston's? We did promise to look into that first," I reminded them.

"You'll be on the Russian investigation full-time," Sir Broderick said, "but the rest of us can work on both. And I can call on more members of the Archivist Society to help with both investigations. It will stretch us in two directions for a while, but I'm sure we're up to the challenge."

Wonderful. Sir Broderick and the Duke of Blackford seemed to think as one. What was it about powerful men? "Have we learned anything new in the Shepherdston investigation?"

In response, Sir Broderick said, "Jacob, would you bring Mary in, please?"

Jacob returned in a minute with a slender young woman who was no bigger than a boy. Mary! I remembered her immediately. She'd been a maid for the Gattengers until her master's arrest for murder and treason brought her to the attention of the Archivist Society. After the Gattenger house was closed up, she served as a maid in our borrowed house in Mayfair while I pretended to be Georgina Monthalf, lover of the Duke of Blackford.

We made sure Mary never learned the true identity of Georgina or her lady's maid, Emma.

"This is Mary Thomas," Sir Broderick said. "She wants our help in finding those responsible for the murder of her brother, Robert Thomas, a footman for Lord Shepherdston."

"Yes, please. He was all the family I had left, and I miss him. I can't pay you much—" She dabbed at her brown eyes.

"Don't worry about that," Emma said, brushing the thought from the air with one hand. "We're happy to help. I remember you from last year. You were a maid in our house in Mayfair. I was the lady's maid."

"And you're part of the Archivist Society? You let servants help you?" Mary sounded equal parts amazed and overwhelmed as she gazed around the room.

When she spotted the duke, she gasped out, "Oh, Your Grace," and took a step back.

"It's all right, Mary." Blackford spoke in a surprisingly soft voice.

"I'm really a clerk in a bookshop." Emma raised her voice slightly to get the girl's attention. "I played the role of a lady's maid for that investigation. In the end, we found out how your mistress died and saved your master from the gallows."

The girl's sad eyes showed their first spark of hope. "I'm glad. They were a nice couple. I hope you can help me that way. Nothing will bring Robert back, but I'd like the evil man who shot him to pay for what he did."

I'd lost my family at seventeen, and Mary didn't appear much older. My heart ached in sympathy for her and for the child I had been. "You have our condolences on your brother's death. Do you want to stay and hear what we've learned so far?"

"Yes, please. Your Grace?" Mary asked, taking a small step forward.

Blackford nodded.

Sir Broderick gestured toward a chair. Mary sat on the edge as if afraid at any moment we'd shout at her for sitting.

At a nod from Sir Broderick, Grace Yates, Archivist Society member as well as Lord Barnwood's secretary and librarian, said, "We've learned the identity of everyone who entered the marquis' home in the ten days before the explosion. The only people who were not regular visitors were a firm of interior decorators removing wallpaper. But the marquis has used the same firm for years."

"Scotland Yard's analysis said too much explosive was used on the safe, causing the heavy damage. There aren't many who can blow a safe properly. They think this was the work of new villains. Amateurs," Adam Fogarty told us.

"But one of them appears not to be an amateur with a gun," Sir Broderick said. "When the footman, Robert, stood between the two men and freedom, the taller man shot him through the heart and escaped. Expert shooting." He grew silent for a moment.

I glanced over at Mary. She stared at the floor, her lips pinched closed.

"If the lady's maid hadn't been sent to fetch her mistress just before the explosion, she never would have had a good view of the two burglars or the shooting. Too bad the villains wore masks."

"Masks?" Mary looked up, her eyes widening.

"Yes, half masks such as are worn at a ball, plus caps pulled low on their heads," Sir Broderick explained.

"The lady's maid isn't involved?" Emma asked.

"Unlikely. She's been with the family for years. Scotland Yard's report included the woman saying after the shooting, 'The shorter man shouted something to the shooter in a foreign tongue.'"

I looked at Sir Broderick when he surprised us with this news. "Any idea what language he was speaking?"

"None. Mary, when was the last time you saw your brother?"

"It had been more than a week before—" She took a deep breath before she could continue. "I'd rarely been in the servants' hall at Shepherdston House, not in months, so I'm afraid I can't help with the investigation."

Sir Broderick nodded and then looked at each of us in turn. "It's getting late and we'll all be busy tomorrow. Thank you for coming, Miss Thomas. We'll find the man who shot your brother. You can count on us."

"And we'll find you at the Duke of Blackford's household, miss?" Adam Fogarty asked.

She slipped on her coat as she said, "Yes, I'm a parlor maid there."

"Wait with the coachman, Mary, and we'll get you home," Blackford told her.

Once she left, Sir Broderick said, "Let's get back to the problem of the Russian princess."

"I'll be glad to check on security with the patrolmen," Adam Fogarty said. Chances were he knew most of them and they'd introduce him to the rest of the bobbies.

"Jacob, I want you to question the Russian embassy about the guard and the details of his burial. Say you're from Whitehall, sent by a minister to ask if any assistance is needed. Find a clerk who'll talk to you." Sir Broderick turned to Blackford. "I know it's a long shot, but it's worth the effort."

"Anything else?" Emma asked.

"Not yet," Sir Broderick replied. "We don't have the resources to track a killer who might have come over from Russia and returned home already. I suspect there won't be much for us to do on this investigation."

I'd be glad to quickly return to my bookshop, but I wished I could spend more time with the duke.

As we prepared to leave, Sir Broderick said, "Would you please stay a moment, Georgia?"

I nodded to Emma, who followed the others into the hall while I returned to sit uncomfortably close to the fire, which was still burning fiercely behind Sir Broderick. The heat counterbalanced the cold that had settled over me when he asked me to remain.

His appearance in a room he'd not visited since the attack that left him in a wheeled chair told me those events couldn't be far from his mind. And Sir Broderick was the sort who, if he thought about something, would take action. "What have you learned?" I asked.

"We know that the owner of the property where your parents died was indeed in Egypt when the attack happened, but he's currently in London. I spoke to him recently. He's always admitted he'd been on his estate only a few weeks before the atrocity that claimed your parents' lives and my health." He slapped his hands on the arms of his chair. "Now that we know the villain's name, I asked him if he knew Count Farkas. It turns out at that time the man was his houseguest."

Count Farkas. The sound of his name made me feel ashamed. If I'd been smarter, faster, stronger, perhaps my seventeen-year-old self could have saved my parents' lives and protected Sir Broderick from the building collapse that destroyed his legs. But as angry as I was at my own failure, I was furious at the man who killed them in his search for a Gutenberg Bible. I wanted to catch Count Farkas and watch him hang.

Setting aside my anger with a deep breath, I said, "No wonder the count knew about the cottage where work was ongoing. Had he known it would be empty of workers?"

"Yes. The owner told Farkas he was abandoning work until

he returned from overseas." Sir Broderick gripped the large back wheels of his chair, his eyes blazing with pent-up frustration.

I leaped up and began to pace the room. The space was too small and too crowded to contain my furious steps. "He had the perfect place, out in the country, undisturbed, where he could torture my parents for information about his Bible."

I'd kept an eye out for my parents' killer for a dozen years before I spotted him from an omnibus over a year before. I'd given chase but lost him on the crowded pavement. After that, I'd redoubled my efforts to find him despite Sir Broderick's doubts.

Since then I'd received taunting letters from the killer and spotted him a second time, leading to the discovery of his name. Sir Broderick now believed me that this was the man who caused the fire that led to his crippling accident.

"Now all we need is for Count Farkas to return to London," I said. "I want to see him brought to trial."

"Now all you need," Blackford said as he stepped forward into the room, "is to find out where he is and lure him back to London."

Sir Broderick and I had been so focused on our hushed conversation that we hadn't noticed Blackford slip back into the parlor.

"Do you know?" I asked. I wouldn't be surprised if Blackford had learned something about Count Farkas the rest of us couldn't discover. I hoped he'd give me the information I needed to continue the search.

Blackford glowered away my hope. "No. And right now, we need to concentrate on these Russians."

I SPENT THE next day at the bookshop dividing my time between waiting on customers and studying our books on painting.

By the end of the day, I thought I could tell the difference between a Renoir and a Rembrandt. Maybe.

Painting had never been an interest of mine. I needed to make up for lost time. Or practice making noncommittal remarks. In French.

On the following morning, I arrived at Hereford House at precisely ten o'clock. I was let in by the butler and directed down the hall to the back of the house. The weather was pleasant enough that I hadn't worn a cloak, so I only needed to unpin my hat and leave it with my gloves on the table. Another hat and darned gloves had already been placed there by the daughter's governess. What time did that woman begin work?

Not my business. I hurried to the morning room and sat down with the typewriter and a piece of what appeared to be scrap paper. The typewriter was much newer and nicer than mine, but filthy. I set to work at once cleaning it after putting on an apron and accountant's sleeves over my own to protect my shirt.

A half hour later, the duchess knocked and walked into the room. She glanced at my work and nodded. "I'm afraid I left you with an unplanned chore. I fired my last secretary and haven't looked at the machine since."

Curiosity made me ask, "Why was she fired, Your Grace?"

"The state of the typewriter should tell you about her work habits. I'm glad to see you take pride in your tools."

I did, and I was glad the duchess noticed.

"I came down to tell you we've had a message from the Duke of Sussex. He and the princess are traveling by train and should arrive in about an hour. The whole household will turn out in the front hallway to greet them. We'll use the dressing gong to signal everyone to assemble. You'll stand after my daughter and her governess."

Never before had I been part of a line of household help, put on parade, ranked by their status in the house. Just thinking about it annoyed my middle-class soul.

"We'll have luncheon as soon as the princess and her chaperone are settled into their rooms. I'll try sometime in the afternoon to bring her down to introduce you and to tell her you'll be her secretary as well as mine. I'll also suggest you'd make an excellent English tutor."

"Why can't we just tell her I'm to be her English tutor as well as your secretary?" I asked.

She held my gaze. "I suppose that would be for the best. I'll make it sound as if this was already decided by our government."

She was a duchess, unused to middle-class independence. "Thank you. I'm going to have to rely on you to back up what I say if we're to keep the princess safe."

"I'll do my best." The duchess walked to the door. With her hand on the knob, she faced me and said, "Ranleigh told me to trust you. That you are the very best person for this job."

My chest swelled at the praise from Blackford. "I hope I am. We don't yet know the source of the danger or the intended target."

"I'll pray that Ranleigh's right about you. Otherwise, I've put my family and staff in danger." She sailed out of the room on a cloud of lavender scent and self-assurance.

CHAPTER THREE

AFTER the duchess left, I returned to my task. Sometime later, an otherworldly echo rang through the house. Deciding this must be the gong, I pulled off my apron and extra sleeves and walked to the front hallway.

Various members of the household dashed past me to fill in lines on either side of the hall. From her mother's painting, I recognized the young girl as the duchess's daughter and stepped next to the young woman I guessed was her governess.

"Are you the new secretary?" she asked in a murmur.

"Yes," I replied and looked down into her dark eyes. "Governess?"

"For the time being." She smiled up at me, displaying a rosebud mouth and even, white teeth.

I sensed another person in the household who didn't belong, and that made her someone I wanted to get to know better.

The butler called for our attention as the duchess arrived down the stairs. As soon as she was in place, we heard the sound of door chimes. The butler opened the door and the young, blond princess strolled in followed by a scowling, middle-aged dragon. There was so much bowing and curtsying going on I didn't notice the portly man with the thinning fair hair walk in until I saw who was standing behind him.

The Duke of Blackford.

My heartbeat rapped harder in my chest when I saw him. His dark hair was ruler straight; his ever-vigilant eyes as black as his perfectly cut suit. His regal bearing and stern expression grabbed all of my attention.

The governess's as well. I heard her purr like a cat when she saw him. I wanted to tell her he was spoken for, that he was mine, but that would be an obvious lie.

I would never be able to say he was mine. My heartbeat slowed and my stomach sank.

The aristocrats greeted each other while the household stood silently by in case someone was needed. The princess's Russian lady's maid stood just inside the door, holding several small packages and staring at the floor.

Finally, after several tedious minutes, they marched upstairs to the sitting room or boudoir and we were free to go back to our usual duties. I heard the princess speak in Russian to her maid and the young, dark-haired woman followed her up the stairs.

They had nearly reached the landing when one of the maids turned and ran into another. "Watch out," the injured maid said.

Both the princess and her Russian lady's maid swiveled around to look. I watched them, wondering if their attention was captured by the maid's startled tone or the words she spoke. In English.

A commanding voice called me away from my thoughts. "I'm Amelia Whitten, the governess. And this is Lady Daisy."

"Milady," I said and gave an appropriately deep curtsy to a

little girl who was studying the artwork on the ceiling. "I'm Georgia Peabody, Her Grace's new secretary."

"Milady, give Miss Peabody a curtsy."

"Miss Peabody." Reminded of her manners, the little girl spoke gravely as she curtsied. I guessed her age at six years, her blond hair flowing down her back in ringlets.

Amelia nodded to me and led Lady Daisy up the stairs. I walked down the hall and finished my work on the typewriter before eating my solitary luncheon and reorganizing the writing supplies.

At a loss for any other chores, I stood looking out the window at the greenery along the edge of the back garden, when I heard a tap at the door. I spun around as the duchess walked in, followed by the lovely young woman and the fierce middle-aged one. The princess and the chaperone avoided looking at each other or even letting their skirts brush each other's as they walked in.

"Princess Kira, Lady Raminoff, this is my secretary, Miss Peabody," the duchess said, in a far better French accent than mine.

I gave them a deep curtsy.

"She will act as your social secretary as well as mine, and will be your English tutor."

"What?" Lady Raminoff squawked. Her French truly sounded as if an angry parrot were speaking. "Has this been approved by my government?"

"The tsar and the queen discussed Princess Kira's need for English lessons and it was decided this was the best solution," the duchess said. I was impressed with how smoothly she lied. "Princess, when would you like your lessons to begin?"

"Not for several days," Lady Raminoff said. Every time the woman opened her mouth, I wanted to giggle.

"Now," Princess Kira said. "You may leave us for half an hour." The older woman's mouth worked but, thankfully, no sound came out. The duchess gracefully gestured for Lady Raminoff to lead her from the room.

Once they were gone and the door shut, the princess sat on one of the armless, straight-backed chairs and nodded for me to sit on another. "Thank goodness she's gone. She spies on me every hour of every day."

Her French was rapid and precise. I took a moment to translate her words in my head before I answered, "Isn't that the job of a chaperone?"

"She is extra vigilant. So, please, teach me some English. I want to carry on conversations the dragon doesn't understand." The princess sounded desperate, making me think her reaction to the maid's words in the entrance hall was due only to the tone of voice.

"What do you want to discuss that Lady Raminoff mustn't know about?" Did the princess have a Russian lover she needed to keep secret from the duke? She was certainly pretty enough and wore enough jewelry to interest any number of men.

She started at my words. "Nothing. I simply want a little privacy."

I could understand that. I valued my solitude, too—and I hadn't grown up in a palace where it might be in short supply.

Giving her a smile, I said in French, "The time is after luncheon and before dinner, so you would say"—here I switched to English—"Good afternoon."

"Good afternoon," she repeated.

She had an accent, but her smile would make up for any lack in her pronunciation.

"Teach me more," she commanded.

I could tell she was smart. And from the considering glances she gave me, I suspected she was judging whether she could trust me. She was learning English for more than a little privacy. I'd just have to wait and see what else she wanted to know.

When the dragon returned in exactly one-half hour, the princess had learned greetings and her numbers and a few basic nouns. I had no idea how many of these new words she'd remember by the next day.

"Lady Raminoff," she said in French as she stood, "I've made good progress for today. I shall meet again tomorrow afternoon with Miss Peabody for another lesson."

The chaperone said something in Russian that began a heated discussion. The older woman still sounded like a parrot; the younger one acted like no one had ever dared disagree with her before. This went on for a few minutes and all the time I cursed my lack of Russian. I heard the name "Lidijik" once. Were they giving clues to the murder of the imperial guard in front of me while I stood by in ignorance? I wanted to stomp my foot in frustration.

Finally, Princess Kira turned to me and said in French, "We will continue my lessons tomorrow afternoon. Alone."

THE NEXT MORNING, I heard a tap on the morning room door and watched Princess Kira slip in, shutting the door behind her. "Miss Peabody, could we do our lesson in the National Gallery today? So I could learn the English names for painting techniques?"

"I'll try. I'm afraid I'm not as versed in painting as you are," I replied in French as I dipped a quick curtsy.

She either didn't notice or didn't care that my curtsy was not the deep reverential one she should expect from employees. "That is fine. The duke will come with us, and he'll be able to help."

"What about your chaperone?"

"We won't tell her."

"How will you leave the house without her knowing?"

"Leave that to me. Just don't ask questions. Be ready to go as soon as we finish luncheon." The eagerness in her voice told me how much she wanted to escape her chaperone. Then she looked me over. Her lower lip curled in scorn. "That is what you wore today?"

I was dressed in a peach blouse with a gray skirt. No ruffles, no silk, no jewels. I liked the outfit; the shirtwaist didn't war with my auburn hair color. I held her gaze as I said, "Yes."

There was a small sigh. "No matter."

I was going to have a hard time putting up with the princess. "What time will you finish luncheon?" I asked in French.

A smile crossed her face. "Two," she said in clear English.

After she left, I waited with mild impatience for my meal to arrive. I ate faster than usual, concentrating not on my food but on what Princess Kira had planned once she left the house. Did she have a flair for espionage and a dislike for her chaperone, or was something deeper going on? A Russian political feud? A plot to sabotage the princess's wedding?

And where did the murder of her imperial guard, the only other member of her entourage besides her chaperone and her lady's maid, fit into her plan?

I paced the room. Ideas bounced through my mind and were quickly discarded for lack of evidence. When the clock showed it was nearly time, I went into the back hall. I had my hat pinned firmly in place when Princess Kira appeared, her hat and gloves already on.

She waved frantically to me and hurried into the garden. I grabbed my gloves and followed.

Leading the way along a path past a fountain and then next to the kitchen garden, Princess Kira arrived at the coach house. She entered without knocking and walked along the far side of the Hereford coach. I could hear the grooms working in the stables but no one cried out an alarm.

The princess didn't speak English, but she'd learned the secrets of the house in a day. "How did you know how to get off the Hereford property and into this back alley?" I asked as I exited the coach house.

She gave me a smile and walked over to the coach with the Sussex crest waiting in the alleyway. The footman lowered the steps and helped the princess in. I climbed in after her to find not only the Duke of Sussex waiting for us, but the Duke of Blackford.

Sussex tapped on the ceiling with his cane and we drove off. Just an everyday outing, with two dukes, a princess, and a middle-class shop owner. I was underdressed and under-titled for our excursion.

I wanted to question Blackford on what he knew about this trip, but the presence of the princess and Sussex stopped me. Blackford met my stare across the carriage with a tiny shake of his head before he glanced away. Apparently, we were not to act like we knew each other.

"Today I wish to go to the National Gallery," Princess Kira said in French to Sussex. "I will improve my English by learning painting terms."

"I'd be delighted to escort you, milady," Sussex said, an infatuated grin on his pudgy face.

The princess continued, "You and Blackford will follow us. If Miss Peabody doesn't know the English word, you may step in."

"I'd be glad to." He really did sound glad. For two social equals, the princess was leading the royal duke by his cravat.

"There are a lot of paintings there," I said. "Where would you like to start?"

"Are there any French paintings of this century?"

"Several," I guessed with feigned confidence. "Am I not right, gentlemen?"

"I hope you'll be pleased with them," Sussex said.

Blackford turned to look out the window, pursing his lips together.

The princess gave a regal nod. "When we arrive, please escort us there."

"With pleasure." Sussex reminded me of a loyal hound.

Sussex's coach was well sprung in comparison to Blackford's ancient vehicle. I looked out the window and enjoyed the rest of the ride.

When we arrived, the dukes handed us down and started toward the beautiful classical front of the gallery. Princess Kira stopped, transfixed by the sight. "What a perfect building."

She studied it for so long, slowly turning from left to right, that Sussex finally said, "It's even prettier inside."

The princess finished her perusal and nodded to him. "We shall go inside." She gave Sussex her arm and he escorted her up the steps and through the massive front doors.

Blackford held out his arm to me. "Miss?" he said in English.

"Thank you."

"Are you her chaperone this afternoon?"

"I suppose I must be, since her chaperone doesn't know she's out of Hereford House."

Blackford raised his eyebrows. "Whose idea was that?"

"Hers."

He murmured so quietly I barely heard him say, "What is she up to?"

Once inside, blinking in the dark after the bright sunshine outdoors, we wandered a bit before we stumbled across recent French paintings. Apparently, that was Princess Kira's cue to begin her lesson. She said words in French; I gave the English translations. When a painting term was too obscure for me, one of the dukes supplied the English equivalent.

She obviously loved the paintings. She'd gaze at them and sigh, pointing out the mix of colors and brushstrokes. While she stared at the canvases with admiration, Sussex gazed at her with adoration.

This continued for a half hour, until the men wandered at a distance out of boredom. The princess suddenly said the French word for bus.

"Bus, or omnibus," I replied.

"Horse."

I translated. "Why?"

"I must have a general knowledge of English."

"When does a duchess need to know the word for bus?"

Her answer was "Bread."

We went through several more common words until the men rejoined us. Then she switched to painting terms again.

Walking into the next room, the princess froze. Then she started talking about the painting to our left in rapid French. To me it was an ordinary painting in the impressionist style, but the princess and Sussex were not the only ones studying it carefully.

A blond woman in her early twenties was also looking wistfully at the canvas. Her mauve-colored dress, with dried mud imperfectly brushed from the hem, was out of style, at odds with her stylish hat with two large feathers and her pristine gloves. She was the same height as the princess and at a distance could pass for her. Up close, however, the two women wouldn't be mistaken for each other for an instant.

I wondered if there was a plan to swap this woman for the princess. It would only work if the impersonator kept at a distance from all who knew her. I found myself looking over my shoulder for thugs to drag off Princess Kira and replace her with this woman.

Was this the reason her bodyguard needed to be killed?

"I need to get back before they miss me. Will you gentlemen please summon the carriage? We'll meet you in front of the building," the princess said in French.

"Of course." Sussex bowed over her hand and then he and Blackford left to do her bidding.

I started looking for the threat I suspected was coming, my pulse rushing in my head and my muscles poised to spring. Then I heard a rapid exchange of what I'd begun to recognize as Russian.

I swung back to see the princess and the other blonde standing close together without touching, leaning toward each other, talking in their indecipherable tongue. The princess was getting teary eyed, and the young woman's tone was soothing.

After a scant minute of talk, a well-dressed couple began to approach our alcove. Instinctively, I cleared my throat before I'd made a conscious decision to keep the princess's secret.

With a few parting words, Princess Kira whipped around and marched over to me. "Shall we go?" she said, reverting to French.

I nodded and walked through the gallery toward the front entrance with her. "Who is she?"

"Who?"

"The woman you were talking to."

"I wasn't talking to anyone."

"Nonsense."

"If you say I was talking to anyone, I shall deny it. No one will believe you." Her tone and her expression were haughty.

"This isn't Russia. I will be believed. However, I'll keep your secret if you'll tell me what is going on."

"She, uh, was a maid in my parents' house. She packed up and left without a word. I was surprised to see her here. There was a man involved, of course. They came here, but life hasn't been as easy as they expected." She looked straight ahead as she spoke, moving rapidly through the gallery's rooms without glancing at the paintings.

That was too easy. I didn't believe her. Not because she didn't look at me—I wasn't of her class, after all—but because she couldn't look at her beloved paintings while she lied.

I was going to have to keep a very close watch on her.

We walked back into the sunny afternoon, blinking at the change in light. As we descended the wide stairs, the Sussex carriage came into view circling Nelson's Column. The princess was handed up into the carriage, I was next, and we rode back to Hereford House.

"Do you want me to go in and smooth things over with the duchess?" Sussex asked.

"No. We'll go in the way we left. Perhaps tomorrow we can go to a park and Miss Peabody can teach me the English names for birds and flowers. Will you escort us, Arthur?" The princess favored him with a smile.

He took her hand and said, "I'd be delighted, Kira." I thought for a moment he was going to go down on his knees to her in the carriage, but the lack of room, or perhaps the audience, dissuaded him.

"Shall we go out the front door tomorrow?" Blackford asked. I recognized the dry tone. He was finding the princess's dramatic entrance and exit amusing.

"If Miss Peabody can help me persuade my chaperone and the duchess that she is adequate security for my honor. We'll discuss this at luncheon tomorrow." She patted Sussex's hand with her free one.

"I'll do my best." I couldn't look at Blackford, afraid my expression would give away our mutual interest in Princess Kira's excursions.

The princess had Sussex stop the carriage before we reached the Hereford coach house. The footman gave me his hand to help me descend, and I waited in the dust while the engaged couple said their good-byes. Then the princess was helped down and we hurried through the side door into the carriage house.

A gardener stood before us, as surprised to see us as we were to see him. Finally, he gave us a nod and said, "Is everything all right?"

"The Russians don't believe in wholesome afternoon outings, even with chaperones, for young ladies. Being English, we think an engaged couple can enjoy a walk around an art gallery or a park. Properly escorted, of course. We're not so feudal here in England. Agreed?" I handed him a shilling.

"Agreed, ma'am," he said, nodding his thanks. "You might want to slip in quiet-like. The Russian witch has been shouting the house down."

I smiled at him. "Thanks." Then in French, "Lady Raminoff knows you're missing."

"Well, then, we'll need to be very persuasive."

We had almost reached the door to the morning room when Lady Raminoff came squawking down the main staircase at full volume in the same strange tongue the princess had spoken in the art gallery. Princess Kira kept her voice lower when she responded, but her tone was no less forceful.

The Duchess of Hereford appeared from upstairs, a dab of paint on one hand and a lock of hair falling loose. "Miss Peabody, what has happened? Where were you?"

"Princess Kira arranged for the dukes of Sussex and Blackford to pick us up by the coach house and take us to the National Gallery. We conducted our language lesson there and then returned. She has been properly chaperoned and escorted every step of the way."

The duchess raised an eyebrow. "Nothing untoward has happened to either of you?"

"No, ma'am." At least nothing I'd share with her until I had to.

"Good. This hysteria has to stop." Switching to French, the duchess said, "Lady Raminoff, the princess is unharmed and unsullied. Please calm yourself."

"If anything had happened to her, I would have held you and this English tutor responsible. The tsar will not be pleased when I report this to him."

"Go ahead. He won't care. Nicholas is very reasonable," the princess snapped at her chaperone. At least they were now speaking French and no longer yelling.

"And your father?" Lady Raminoff's voice was still grating on my ears.

"My father wants this marriage. He will not object as long as we follow the rules of British society. He knows things are not the same as in Russia."

Lady Raminoff replied in what I assumed was Russian. I suspected what she said was not flattering to England.

"That is your opinion. I like Britain," the princess said in regal tones.

"That is fortunate, because your future is here," the duchess said, staring at Lady Raminoff. "So, how did your English lesson go?"

"Well. I plan to go to the park tomorrow for new words," the princess said.

I wondered if she'd arranged to meet the Russian girl there. Hiding my unease, I said in English, "She's trying very hard. So far, we've worked mainly on nouns. Perhaps in the park we'll try a few verbs as well. I believe the Duke of Sussex will come over tomorrow to see if he can escort us to the park for our lesson. If that's all right with Your Grace?"

"Of course, Miss Peabody. You seem to have the situation well in hand."

I wished.

"What are you saying?" Lady Raminoff demanded in French.

The duchess gave her a smooth reply, one that sounded frosty to my ears.

"I must, of course, accompany them to the park," the chaperone said.

"There's no 'of course' about it," Princess Kira snapped at her.

Why was she so against her chaperone coming with us? Was it some personal dislike, which I could understand, or was there a deeper motive?

"I will not interfere with your lesson," Lady Raminoff huffed out in haughty French.

"There is much to see and do in Hyde Park this time of year. Lady Raminoff could sit on a bench and enjoy our lovely weather while Princess Kira and Miss Peabody take a stroll and practice speaking English," the Duchess of Hereford said. She spoke with such reasonableness that I might have been the only one who heard the undertone of annoyance at her quarreling houseguests.

"That sounds like an excellent compromise," I said and earned a quick glance of thanks from the duchess.

"No." Princess Kira tapped her foot.

"Don't be difficult," Lady Raminoff said before barking some Russian.

The princess paled and said, "Very well. I will tell the duke our plans at luncheon tomorrow." She flounced up the stairs.

The duchess gave a small sigh and followed her at a dignified pace.

Lady Raminoff pointed at me and said, "Your office. Now."

Just what I needed. An argument in French.

CHAPTER FOUR

I turned around and walked to the morning room. Opening the door, I gestured for Lady Raminoff to precede me. I shut the door behind me, sat by my typewriter, and waved toward another chair. "Please sit."

She remained standing, leaned into my face, and snarled, "What were you and the princess up to today?"

I looked up at her, keeping my gaze steely. "Please sit," I repeated.

"I asked you a question, peasant."

Once I comprehended what she'd said in French, my temper rose at the insult and I allowed a hard edge to show in my voice. "If you want an answer, you will sit down and ask me like a sane person."

"Pig."

"That's no way to get an answer."

"You are disrespectful. I will get you thrown out."

"You misjudge your position and your power."

She opened her mouth, considered my words, and shut it again without speaking. Then she stalked over and lowered herself into the chair. "Well?"

"We rode to the National Gallery. We looked at paintings and went through various English nouns. The Duke of Sussex helpfully supplied painting terms I was unfamiliar with. Then we rode back here."

"You smuggled her out of this house."

"Actually, she smuggled me out of the house."

"Nonsense."

"No. It's the truth."

"How would she know how to do that? She has only been here a day."

"That's a good question for which she didn't give me an answer."

Her gaze sharpened and her voice dropped. "You asked her?"

"Of course."

"I want you to act as my eyes and ears. If she does anything out of the ordinary, meets anyone you don't know, you tell me."

"Why would I?"

"I will pay you." She named a healthy sum.

Her chaperone didn't trust Princess Kira. Smart woman. I decided to at least pretend to consider her offer. "Why don't you trust her? The princess is a sensible girl. She seems to want this marriage. She wouldn't do anything to jeopardize her future."

"She is headstrong and flighty. Her parents indulged her. The tsar's mother assigned me this role to make sure she doesn't do anything to upset this marriage or relations between our countries."

"What could she do?"

"Find another suitor. Wrap herself in scandal. Become com-

promised. Insult the royal family, which would be an affront to
the tsar's mother. There are infinite ways someone who is both
as innocent and as devious as Princess Kira can ruin herself."

Lady Raminoff was right. The princess was naive and sneaky
in equal measure, and that could be a lethal combination. "I
imagine any scandal would upset both royal families. They were
both involved in arranging this match, weren't they?"

"Yes. The tsar's mother worked with her sister to push for this
marriage in both countries."

Her sister? It took me a moment before I made the connection.
"The tsar's mother is the sister of the Princess of Wales."

"Precisely. A wrong move by Princess Kira will reflect badly
on both these royal ladies." When calm and away from the princess, Lady Raminoff no longer sounded like a parrot. Or perhaps
I'd just grown used to her painfully screechy voice. "And what
we fear the most. Princess Kira's thoughtless behavior will get
her killed by anarchists."

"Can you possibly believe any of these fears is a real possi-
bility?"

"Yes."

Oh, dear. She spoke with such assurance she shook my certainty that the princess couldn't be in danger in England. "Are
you worried because Princess Kira's bodyguard was killed?"

"Wouldn't you be? Lidijik got on well with her. He could handle
her, having known her since she was a child. And he spoke English.
Where they'll find another guard to take his place, I don't know."

So the dead guard spoke English. Was that why he had to be
removed from his post? I shook my head. "I'm sure the police
are capable of looking out for her safety. They guard the royal
family, and nothing has happened to them."

"But Kira is Russian. Your police know nothing of the anarchists in our midst. We know them. We can smell them nearby."

"This guard, Lidijik. Were you well acquainted with him?"

"He had traveled with the princess and her family before when Kira studied painting in Paris for a few months. I met him and the princess for the first time at the beginning of this trip, before we sailed to visit your queen and then to travel to London. Kira's father knew Lidijik since he grew up in their village and may have asked for him specifically, but I don't know how they made that decision."

"You weren't her chaperone on the trip to Paris?"

"No, thank goodness."

Switching topics, I asked, "Tell me about Lidijik."

"What is there to tell?"

"Someone managed to kill him in a crowded railway station without anyone noticing. He never sounded an alarm. How did someone get so close to him they could silently kill him and escape without anyone being the wiser? And why was he in the luggage carriage?"

Lady Raminoff pursed her lips as if something tasted bad. "He was in the luggage carriage because the princess asked him to get a small case for her. She'd meant to carry it in our compartment with her. It contained a sketch pad and pencils. When he didn't return, the princess sent a steward after the guard. And so he was found before the train had begun to move."

"You think Lidijik knew his killer?"

"He had to have. He wouldn't have let a stranger come up and kill him."

"Perhaps he was approached by someone who didn't 'smell' like an anarchist."

Lady Raminoff studied me for a moment. "An Englishman. An

official Englishman. That is the person Lidijik wouldn't have suspected. And the station platform was crowded with them that day."

Logical, but it moved us no further ahead. "Where did Lidijik learn English?"

"At court. He has served as personal bodyguard to the tsar. The tsar and his wife speak English to each other." She made one squeaking laugh. "They are more like an English gentleman and lady than most of the people you meet at Balmoral."

Suspicion niggled at a spot inside my brain. Had Lidijik begun Princess Kira's English lessons? How much did she already know? And if she'd learned English, why was she pretending otherwise?

I glanced at Lady Raminoff and realized the same might be said about her.

I spoke to her in English. "Are you family to Princess Kira?"

She looked at me blankly. "In French, please?"

So she hadn't learned English from the Russian court or the imperial guard, Lidijik. Or I'd have to be cleverer to trip her up. I repeated my question in French.

"No. I'm the widow of a minister who served the tsar's father for many years. Having no place in society and no money of my own, I serve the tsar's mother in whatever position she sees fit to employ me."

Lady Monthalf, whom I thought of as Aunt Phyllida, had told me of childhood friends of hers who had ended up in the same position as Lady Raminoff. Homeless and penniless once their husbands died, discarded by the new heir, these women became companions to elderly relatives and chaperones to their young in exchange for a place in society and their daily bread.

Instead of distrusting her, I found myself pitying her. And I found I had more questions for her charge. "Where would I find Princess Kira now?"

"Come. I will take you to her."

Lady Raminoff led me upstairs and down hallways until we came to a door leading to what I thought was the back of the house. She knocked and opened the door to a light-filled wonder.

The large room possessed a skylight and windows across the back overlooking the garden. The space was full of light and air. Beyond the view of the wide expanse of greenery in the garden and the dark-roofed carriage house, Mayfair stretched out under a brilliant blue sky.

A huge table and shelves to my left held paints and brushes; to my right a stack of canvases leaned against the wall. A window was opened near a bottle marked turpentine, but I could still smell the pungent liquid. Two easels were set up with works in progress on both, the princess standing in front of one, and the duchess in front of the other. The duchess looked over her shoulder at us and turned back to her work. The princess didn't turn around at all.

"I would never have guessed this room was here," I said in English.

"It's over the conservatory," the duchess replied in an aggravated tone.

"I need to ask the princess some questions."

At those words in English, the princess did swivel around to look at me, her mouth set in a tight line.

I would have bet she understood me, but it could have been only the word "princess." She must have heard that word directed at her any number of times since arriving in Britain.

"What is it?" she asked in French of both me and her chaperone standing next to me.

"I need to ask you some questions about Lidijik, the guard who was killed."

"I'm painting," she snapped. "We will talk tomorrow before luncheon." Then she swung back around and considered her work.

With both works unfinished, the two painters seemed equal in talent but their techniques and palettes were different. The duchess used paler shades and the objects in her still life were realistically portrayed. The princess employed brighter shades and more impressionistic strokes to convey the rooflines of Mayfair spread out before her.

"It's good the duke is pleased with your talent," I said in my terrible French.

"I'd have nothing to do with him otherwise," the princess replied, studying the skyline.

AFTER DINNER THAT night, Aunt Phyllida, Emma, and I were in the parlor when we heard a knock on the door. Exchanging surprised glances with my housemates, I rose to answer it and found Blackford on our doorstep.

For a moment I stared, lost between joy and disbelief. When the duke began to smile at my frozen gaze, I hurriedly said, "Your Grace, please come in."

He set down his top hat, gloves, and cane on the side table and followed me into the parlor. Emma and Phyllida both rose and curtsied. He bowed in return and I asked him to sit while Phyllida, her knitting forgotten, hurried off to make tea.

"You've come to learn what Georgia's discovered," Emma said. "I'm dying to know myself. And what have you found out, Your Grace?"

"Well, I—," the duke began.

Phyllida appeared in the doorway. "Emma, come give me a hand with the tea, please."

Emma raised her elegant, pale eyebrows and rose to join Phyllida in the kitchen.

I felt my cheeks heat. Phyllida knew how much I enjoyed Blackford's company and was giving us a chance to be alone for a moment. I wish she'd been a little more subtle.

The duke kept a sober expression. "Your bookshop is doing well in your absence?"

"Yes. Emma and Frances have everything in hand, although it's only been a matter of two days." An uncomfortable silence dropped between us, something that didn't often happen. "The Duke of Sussex is all right with you accompanying him to visit his fiancée?" I asked a little too quickly.

"I suspect Sussex is a little afraid of the princess. He's not very experienced with women and she is young and beautiful. For the first time in his life, he wants something and he's not certain he'll get it."

"You think the princess will call off the wedding?"

He looked at me as if he thought I were mad. "No. Both monarchs would make her life miserable if she tried to get out of the marriage at this point, and I don't think she wants to. Arthur, Duke of Sussex, realizes how marvelous Princess Kira is and can't believe his luck. And the lady knows how to keep him on pins and needles."

"Why would she feel the need?"

"Perhaps she's not certain of him, either, and he represents the best deal for marriage she can get. Perhaps this was how she was taught to deal with suitors. Perhaps it's just the pride and arrogance of a young woman certain of her worth."

"Once they're married, the power will all be on his side." Perhaps Kira wanted to start married life on a more equal footing than most women managed.

"No. She'll have the reins in that marriage. I know Sussex. He'll always be her tame pet." Blackford sounded disgusted.

"I don't know what your wife will be like, but I hope she doesn't think you'll be anyone's tame anything," I responded without thinking and then wanted to kick myself. We always tried to sidestep any mention of the duke's need to marry and produce an heir. His fiancée had died under suspicious circumstances, and I didn't want to think of the day when he'd settle down with another woman. Until then, I could have my daydreams.

"Whoever she may be, she won't be anything like Princess Kira. I like a woman with brains and fire and maturity. Kira may have the fire, but she lacks the rest. Ah," he said, opening the door wider for Emma as she entered with the tea tray. Phyllida followed with some biscuits on a platter.

Once we were settled with our tea, I told them all I'd learned or suspected.

After a moment of thought, Blackford said, "I think we may want to catch the young lady if Kira meets her again in the park."

"No. Don't catch her. Follow her. Learn who she is. Emma, in the morning will you ask Jacob to follow this girl from the park? We don't want him to speak to her, only to learn who she is and where she lives." I scrunched up my face and shook my head. Something about this didn't feel right.

"You think this girl is a side issue?" Emma asked.

"I can't see the princess having a hand in the guard's death or in any plot against herself or the royal family. Can you?" I asked Blackford.

His dark eyes kept me pinned to my seat while his expression gave no clue to his thoughts. "No. But I still believe the girl is at the center of whatever Princess Kira is up to. Everything else about the princess's life is regulated and expected."

"Did Jacob learn anything at the Russian embassy?"

"Nothing we didn't know before. A clerk told him everyone was shocked that Lidijik was murdered. They said he was very ordinary. Competent, but not one for gambling or taking risks. He didn't raise strong feelings in anyone he met."

I kept my eyes on Blackford's face. "Then we should proceed under the assumption that Lidijik was killed because he was Princess Kira's guard, not for anything he'd done."

Blackford nodded. "That seems like the best way to proceed. Given the desires of two governments to wrap this up quickly, we'd better work on the most likely scenario first."

Then he added, "Emma, since you're working on the burglary case, there's something you need to know. The burglars of the Marquis of Shepherdston's house have struck again. Lord Walker's residence was attacked today and the safe in his bedroom was blown up."

"Two investigations and both sets of villains are getting away with anything they want. Your Grace, this isn't working well, dealing with two cases at once," I told him.

The duke said, "Georgia, you concentrate on the princess. Other members of the Archivist Society will take care of the burglars. Whoever these villains are, they learned from their past mistakes. They did a better job of blowing the door to the safe. This time they left the rest of the house intact."

"Was there any report of who was involved?"

"It sounds like the same two masked men, one very tall, the other average height and wiry. They were both reported to be carrying pistols and wearing half masks as if going to a ball. They worked faster this time and they got away without anyone having time to raise the alarm."

"Was it another daylight robbery?"

"Yes. At a time when the streets were particularly busy due to an accident on the nearby main road. Traffic was using any route it could find to maneuver through the side streets."

"The accident was either due to good luck for the thieves or great cleverness on their part." I raised my eyebrows at Blackford.

"My thoughts exactly. Also, they timed the raid for when everyone was supposed to be on the lower floors of the house, giving the thieves access to the bedroom without being seen."

"Supposed to be?" Emma asked.

"Two of the maids had snuck up to their room. They came down when they heard and felt the explosion in time to see the burglars escape."

"And these two were smart enough not to stand between the thieves and the door?"

"Yes. That footman of Shepherdston's was foolish as well as brave." Blackford shook his head. "Poor man."

"But to know how to move through the household almost undetected tells me these thieves have a good knowledge of Lord Walker's routine as well as the layout of the house." I set down my teacup. "What did they take?"

"They were seen carrying two Queen Anne chairs and two silver lanterns. Lord Walker discovered that all the cash and jewels in his safe had vanished as well."

"Seen carrying chairs?" I burst out laughing at their audacity. "They just walked down the street with the furniture?"

"No. The two maids watched from an upstairs window and saw the cart they left in. They were able to give a vague description of their confederates. It appears there were five burglars in all, including the driver of the cart."

"This is wonderful news, Your Grace. Does Sir Broderick know of this latest burglary?" Emma leaned forward, her eyes shiny with excitement.

"Yes. He's having the Archivist Society investigate this as well as the Shepherdston robbery in the hopes that something will lead them to the burglars."

Blast. They'd be doing something useful while I would be teaching English to a pampered princess who I suspected of using me. Why couldn't I be helpful?

WHEN I ARRIVED the next morning, I discovered Lady Daisy's governess, Amelia Whitten, hadn't left her hat and gloves on the table. Until now she had always arrived before me. Had there been an upset in the household?

I had no more than entered the morning room and removed the cover from the typewriter when the duchess entered. I gave her a low curtsy. "Your Grace."

"Miss Whitten, Lady Daisy's tutor, won't be in today. Illness. I'll have to see to more of Daisy's care, so you'll be on your own with Princess Kira and Lady Raminoff in the park today." She seemed distracted, pacing the little room and rearranging small objects on tables and the mantel.

I didn't know what Princess Kira had in mind, but I decided to try to upset her plans. "Why don't you and Lady Daisy come with us? I'm sure your daughter could liven up our English lessons."

"I know she'd like that. She's fascinated with the princess, from her title to her frocks. And I think I'm due a little diversion, after trying to keep the household on an even keel. A princess and her staff as houseguests, plus luncheon guests and afternoon visitors for the princess, plus the worry about her safety." The duchess gave me a small smile.

I smiled back. "Good. It'll take two carriages, but it will be great fun. And Lady Raminoff won't have anything to complain about."

"Thank goodness." She shook her head without wiggling the stylish curls carefully framing her face. "She nearly screamed the house down when she realized the princess had slipped out yesterday afternoon. And when she realized you were with her, she demanded I fire you."

"I'm sorry. If I'd known what she planned, I would have warned you somehow." The duchess was being a good sport about the disruptions to her home. I wouldn't like to put my house at the mercy of Whitehall's paranoia or the whims of anarchists. I didn't want to make things more difficult for her.

"Well, today we'll make sure things go better." The duchess managed a weary smile and left the room.

After I had my solitary luncheon, I waited nearly an hour before a maid entered and told me I was expected immediately in the front hall.

I hurried to put on my hat and gloves and nearly ran until I would be in sight of anyone in the entrance foyer. Then I slowed to a respectable gait and stepped into the front hall.

The duchess was there with a nursery maid keeping close guard on Lady Daisy, Lady Raminoff watching Princess Kira with distrust on her face, and the two dukes, Sussex and Blackford, eyeing the whole party uneasily.

I gave the group a deep curtsy and said, "I hope I haven't kept Your Graces waiting."

"Not at all," Sussex said. "The coaches are pulling up now."

We all walked outside and divided into two groups. Sussex and Blackford took the princess and Lady Raminoff in Sussex's coach. The rest of us climbed into Hereford's coach with the help of a footman, and we started off.

Hyde Park was only a stone's throw away. But by the time the carriages reached the fashionable road entering the gardens, I could have arrived at the park faster on foot. London traffic was its usual tangle of wagons, carriages, omnibuses, and hansom cabs, blocking and then spitting out vehicles at every crossroad.

Lady Daisy spent the ride bouncing from one seat to the other, commenting on every sight. The duchess smiled at her daughter's antics without trying to restrain her. The nursery maid would have her hands full once the child was let loose in the open space.

The two carriages pulled up together inside the park near the bandstand and we all climbed down into the sunlight of a perfect fall day. Lady Daisy skipped around us, chattering constantly. I walked over to the princess, curtsied deeply, and said, "Shall we begin our lesson?"

"*Oui.*" She pointed at the carriages and asked what they were called in English. I answered and then she asked about horses, saddles, bridles, and reins.

A man pedaled past on a bicycle to the joyous shrieks of Lady Daisy. "What is that?" the princess asked.

I told her as Lady Daisy ran after him, her maid chasing after her as the tail of their parade.

Turning away from the fashionable traffic, the princess walked along a narrow path, asking the names of trees and flowers. The farther we walked, the princess leading us at a quick pace, the more Lady Raminoff struggled to keep up. Her breathing became labored.

We reached a bench and the older woman dropped onto it

gratefully. "Continue your lesson. I'll meet you back at the carriage," she said in French as her chest heaved.

"As you wish," the princess responded in a haughty tone and
continued without a backward look.

I glanced over to ask if I could do anything for Lady Raminoff
and caught a fleeting expression on her face. She was staring at
the princess's back, and the look she gave her was pure malice.

CHAPTER FIVE

B OTH dukes stopped and murmured something to Lady Raminoff, standing over her in such a way that they didn't see her expression. "Go on," she said through gasps, "I've just overexerted myself. I am fine."

"Arthur," the princess called out in French, "look at this."

The Duke of Sussex bowed to the older woman and then sprinted to Princess Kira's side. "What is it, my love?"

"The green of the grass in sunshine and in shadow. Look at the shades. Look at the texture. Beautiful." She continued walking along the path, her view of Lady Raminoff cut off by some large bushes.

I glanced back at the older woman and saw her frown at me as she made a waving gesture, telling me to catch up to the princess. Since she wouldn't be chaperoning the princess on this walk, I suspected she wanted me to do her job.

When I caught up to Princess Kira, I asked in French, "You're not happy with Lady Raminoff, are you?"

"What is the English word for busybody?" she asked.

I told her.

"And the word for interfering . . . and tattletale . . . and grim," she continued as I translated each word in turn.

"I take your point, but isn't she acting on your parents' instructions?" I asked.

"She's acting on the orders of the tsar's mother. Lady Raminoff sees anarchists under every bed and behind every tree. That is prudent in Russia, but not in England." She gave the duke her arm and continued on her stroll deeper among the trees.

I followed behind, translating articles of clothing, the sky, clouds, shade, and sunshine. The Duke of Blackford caught up to us and walked alongside me in silence.

"Isn't she the most clever lady?" Sussex finally asked.

"I'm sure," Blackford replied without a trace of irony in his voice. As the other two were ahead of us, they didn't see Blackford scowl thoughtfully.

The trail swung around and led us to a more public part of the park with a five-arched bridge over the Serpentine. On the far bank stood a small restaurant. After asking the English words for bridge and lake, the princess said, "I'd like an ice."

"Of course," Sussex said and started toward the refreshment area with the princess.

"No. You go on and take your friend with you. I wish to continue my lesson with Miss Peabody here," the princess told him.

"Come on, then, Blackford. You can help carry the ices," Sussex said and strode off down the path.

Blackford gave us a deep bow and ambled off on his longer legs to overtake Sussex.

I eyed the princess. "Well?"

"I am meeting the cook from our household in Russia. Don't tell anyone. Especially not Lady Raminoff."

"Won't the men notice when they come back?"

"That is where you need to help me."

That sounded backward to me. "Don't you mean you need me to help you?"

She made a breathy sound like a "pahf," then said, "If you say so." She turned on her heel and marched behind the closest tree. I followed her and found the same woman we'd seen the previous day in the art gallery.

Except that yesterday, she'd been a maid.

They hugged quickly and spoke in low-voiced Russian. The other woman's dress was dark green, making her hard to see among the trees and bushes.

I glanced around, pretending to be on guard when in truth I was looking for Jacob, Sir Broderick's assistant. I hoped he would follow the Russian to wherever she lived and find out her name. Twice Princess Kira had gotten rid of all her minders except me to speak to this young woman.

Jacob walked toward us carrying a newspaper-wrapped packet of fish and chips and sat down on a bench where he could see me, but not the princess or the girl. We exchanged nods as he began to eat in neat, efficient bites.

I waited until the dukes were fairly close before I whispered in French, "They're coming." Jacob had already seen Blackford and had appeared to leisurely wrap up the rest of his dinner before he melted into the trees beyond the princess and the other woman. More murmured words and a handclasp between the two women. Then the unknown blonde hurried away, past where Jacob, half-hidden by a bush, tied his shoe.

Princess Kira stepped next to me and said, "What is that smell?" as she delicately sniffed.

"Fried fish. Didn't you see the old man on the bench eating

his lunch?" Jacob had by now disappeared as he followed his quarry.

She shook her head. "Fish," she said in French as the men arrived. I answered and she said, "Ices."

We continued with the lesson as we retraced our steps, Sussex next to the princess and Blackford and I following behind. Just before we were in sight of the bench where we'd left Lady Raminoff, the princess managed to switch partners without seeming to do so. I walked next to her again as we came into view around the thick bushes, now working on phrases like "How are you?" and "Thank you for a lovely time."

Lady Raminoff, staring in our direction, hopped up from the bench when she saw us. With frantic gestures, she spoke in rapid Russian.

What now? I wished once again that I understood Russian.

Princess Kira replied in French, "And we shall return there soon." She glanced at me. "The duchess and her household have already returned to Hereford House."

"Then I suppose I am walking back," I said in wistful French, relieved that nothing worse had happened.

"Nonsense. We won't leave a young woman to see to her own safety. There is room in the coach," Blackford said in English.

Lady Raminoff continued to lecture the princess in Russian as we returned to the dirt and gravel lane for the carriage. There was nothing wrong with her breathing now.

I interrupted her in French with, "Are you feeling better, milady?"

She brushed an invisible speck off her dress. "Yes. Thank you. London air doesn't seem to agree with me."

"You had the same problem in St. Petersburg, but you hid it from my father," Princess Kira countered.

"Nonsense," Lady Raminoff said, but she bit her lower lip.

"You missed a lovely bit of woodlands," I said. The sounds of carriage wheels crunching stones and horses whinnying cut off any replies.

I was squeezed into the carriage on the return ride between Lady Raminoff and the hard wooden and metal side by the door. From my position, I could see that Sussex never took his eyes off his intended, while Princess Kira alternated between smiling at him and looking out the window on the far side. I'd have given anything to see her expression as she gazed out.

I stared at Blackford, hoping he'd get my mental message. I wanted him to tell me tonight if Jacob had been successful in following the girl.

Finally, after we traveled through knots of traffic amid surly drivers and tired horses, we arrived back at Hereford House. The footman handed me down last, as befitted my lowly position in this group. As I reached the ground, I heard Sussex say in French, "I could visit for a while if you'd like. If it would help."

Princess Kira gave him a wan smile and said, "No. Thank you, but I'm feeling a bit tired. I'll see you tomorrow?" Her last words sounded eager, not fatigued.

Either she really liked his company, or she had planned something with the girl for tomorrow.

"Yes. Yes, my love," Sussex replied.

I began to follow them into the house. Blackford was standing to the side of the doorway and as I passed, he muttered, "Tonight."

Good. He had read my mind.

The butler let me pass, and as the two dukes turned away, he shut the door. I could hear voices in the front parlor from where I stood in the hall. Three female, one male. The Duke of Hereford must have returned from his estate to see how his household was faring with the Russian "invasion."

I followed the sound to the parlor and found that the door, surprisingly, stood open. I peeked in and saw not the duke but a bearded Russian soldier in full uniform holding his cap in his hand. At his feet was a large rolled bundle wrapped in canvas.

His hair and beard seemed greasy and his uniform looked worn, as if the wool fabric had previously been used for something else. His boots were scuffed, more the sort workmen wore than the polished boots favored by British officers. I took a step back, uneasy in his presence.

Russia must be a very poor country to send its soldiers abroad looking like this.

The soldier, the princess, and Lady Raminoff were all speaking in Russian. The women were talking over each other and waving their hands. The soldier wasn't getting a chance to say much, or perhaps it was his military training that kept him from answering sharply.

"Come in, Miss Peabody," the duchess said from where she stood apart from the others. Her drawn face made her look ready to collapse.

I took a few steps in. "What is going on?"

"Apparently, we now have a Russian guard added to our household." She eyed the tall, heavy-boned man distastefully. "I suppose he can stay in the coach house with the grooms."

The man turned a fierce face on the duchess. "No," he said in heavily accented English, "I have orders to sleep under the same roof. I can sleep in the kitchen with the servants there. Is all right?"

"You speak English," I said, barely keeping my jaw from dropping.

"Is required of all guards for princess."

Belatedly, I remembered Lidijik spoke English, too.

"Sleep in the kitchen?" the duchess said, frowning. "The servants don't sleep there. I don't believe my husband would approve."

"Ask him. Is important I sleep in same building, where I can hear any attacks and protect the princess."

The princess interrupted in French. "What is he saying?"

I translated.

"Does he think he's going on my afternoon outings? During my English lessons? No. He will stay with the carriage."

"What?" the guard asked, staring with cold, black eyes at the princess. He looked angry, but I guessed it was because his orders were being countermanded by women.

I translated.

"No. On all outings I stay at her side. I am to protect princess, not carriage."

I told her what he said. I hadn't bargained on translating an argument. My French wasn't that strong. I could feel a headache starting behind my eyes. No wonder the duchess appeared close to crumpling.

"Tell him to go back to Russia. I don't need him here."

With a groan, I repeated her words.

"The tsar and her family sent me. Only they can recall me."

My headache grew as I translated, surprised at his good command of English.

"Then we need to send telegrams immediately," the princess said.

I continued in French, not wanting to translate another argument for the soldier. "Why not send a message to the embassy? Talk to them, see if they can have his orders changed." We both turned to the duchess.

"Fine. I will send a message to the embassy immediately. Then perhaps we can straighten this out and get back to normal. Or what passes for normal," I heard her add in English.

She beckoned to me as her supposed secretary and we both left the room.

We entered the morning room and she shut the door with some force. "I don't like him. I don't want him in my house."

"Let's send that note to the embassy. And I'll see Blackford tonight. Perhaps he can do something through Whitehall to get him out of here."

She rubbed her hands up and down her arms as if she were cold. "Quickly, I hope."

"What's wrong?"

"The way he looked at me with his cold eyes. As if he'd like to kill me in my bed. I know I'm being fanciful, but he scares me."

I'd learned intuition was a powerful indicator. And I agreed with her. I wouldn't want him sleeping in my house, either. "Tell him to sleep in the coach house. That's where your male servants sleep, isn't it?"

She nodded.

"I'll send Blackford over to enforce your decision as soon as I can."

Pacing the room, she said, "I hate to involve him in such a silly domestic matter."

The duchess was definitely uncomfortable with the Russian guard in her house. He didn't seem totally clean, for one thing, and her house was spotless. "It's not silly if the man frightens you. I'll send the duke over this evening."

"Thank you. If I'd known I was putting Daisy at risk, I would never have agreed to host Princess Kira. I'll ask Blackford how soon we can be rid of her and the rest of these Russians."

* * *

ONCE AGAIN, WE heard a rap on our door after dinner. I jumped up to answer, earning me smiles from both Emma and Phyllida.

Throwing the door open, I found Blackford and Sumner, Blackford's bodyguard, on our doorstep. "Come in. Did Jacob find out who the mysterious girl is?"

They put their hats and gloves on the table by the door, and the duke set his weighted cane across it. The duke looked pristine as usual in his evening wear, but it was Sumner who caught my eye. He wore a smart suit, obviously new, as were his collar and tie. I'd never seen him look less like the former soldier and current hired muscle he was.

Despite the hideous scars on one side of his face, he'd found the one woman who loved him completely in Emma. The result was Sumner would walk through fire for her. The clothes were no doubt meant to impress her, but he needn't have bothered. Emma saw past his face and his disguises, and the beauty had tender feelings for the beast.

The delight on her face when he walked into the parlor said it all.

I went to help Phyllida bring in the tea things, certain Emma hadn't seen Sumner in months. But when I returned carrying the tray, trailing Phyllida with the biscuits, Emma was saying, "If you stop by tomorrow morning, you can finish unpacking the rest of the boxes."

Setting the tray down with a thump, I said, "Sumner, have you been by the shop lately?"

"As soon as he heard you were on an investigation, he offered his services around the shop. He's very handy," Emma said and then blushed.

"Have some tea, dear," Phyllida said to Emma. "You're looking overheated."

I was going to have to ask Frances what was going on in the shop in my absence.

Blackford took the teacup Phyllida offered him, balancing it in one hand as he stared at me. "Jacob followed the girl to the East End, but once there, he lost her. She ducked into a turning off Commercial Street by Whitechapel Road."

Phyllida shivered. "Jack the Ripper's part of London. I hope you warned him to be careful."

We all nodded. Several years after Jack's last murder, the area was still dangerous.

"Princess Kira told me the girl was a maid in her parents' house, and the next day said she was a cook. Either way, if she were working as a domestic, she'd be living in her employer's home. No one in the East End can afford servants. They can barely afford to feed themselves." I drummed my fingers on the padded chair arm. "And we have another problem."

I had everyone's attention as four heads turned to look at me.

"This afternoon, a new Russian guard came to Hereford House to replace the one who was killed. I don't know what he was arguing about with Lady Raminoff and Princess Kira in Russian, but the duchess is afraid of him, and he insists on sleeping in the house instead of the coach house with the other male servants."

"How did he get his point across about sleeping in the house?" Emma asked.

"He speaks English. He says it's required of guards serving here."

"What does the Duke of Hereford say?" Phyllida asked.

"He's out in the country at their estate. He couldn't see staying in the house with three more women, or, as he calls them, the Russian invasion."

"The guard's presence is going to make it difficult for the princess to visit with the other girl," Blackford said.

"She'll do something to speak to the girl. And I expect this something will put her in danger." Or more likely, put me or other Hereford servants in peril.

"Then finding out who this unknown woman really is just became more important," Blackford said. "Sumner, I want you ready to follow her tomorrow."

"I'll do it," Emma said, setting down her teacup. "I spoke to Jacob today. He lost her in Whitechapel. He knows the area as well as I do, but he doesn't know girls as well."

"You're not going alone," Sumner said.

Emma gave him one quick nod.

"No. I'm going with you." When Sumner was determined, his looks were frightening.

From her serene expression, I knew Emma was equally resolved. "No. I have a plan for once we reach the East End. You can follow me. But watch your back."

He gave her his lopsided smile that pulled at his scars. "I always do."

She gave him a hard stare. "Sumner, don't be cocky. There are cutthroats in the East End every bit as dangerous as the assassins you met in North Africa."

"I know. And my job is to get us both out alive."

Silence filled the room like the fog that would descend on our streets this winter. I glanced over to find Phyllida wringing her hands. My insides felt the same way. Emma and Sumner would both be in danger from sources we couldn't imagine. And we didn't yet know the kind of trouble the Russian woman brought with her.

"Georgia," Blackford said, "we're going to have to learn from you what the princess plans. I'll be sure to accompany Sussex tomorrow and you can get me word then."

"I'll tell you what she tells me. Remember, it may not be the truth. The princess doesn't trust me."

"Make her trust you," the duke ordered.

I held his gaze. "She trusts no one. But you might make this easier. The duchess of Hereford wants you to stop by tonight and convince the guard to sleep with the male servants in the coach house."

He gave one guffaw. "If the duke isn't around, call on a ducal neighbor. Very well. I'll take a couple of my brawnier footmen with me and see if I can't persuade the guard to act as if he were a guest in another country." He shook his head. "Which he certainly is. Has the duchess contacted the Russian embassy?"

"Yes, but I don't know if she's received a reply."

"I'll find out." He rose and gave us a bow. Sumner immediately leaped to his feet with his gaze still on Emma.

I ARRIVED AT Hereford House at the usual time the next morning, leaving Emma to make arrangements for a member of the Archivist Society to fill in for her in the bookshop. She also had instructions to call Sir Broderick on the shop phone to tell him he'd have to put Jacob to use as his assistant in my antiquarian book business. Sir Broderick knew the business as well as I did, but Jacob would be needed to run books between my shop and Sir Broderick's study, where my father's onetime partner spent his days in his wheeled chair.

I left my hat and gloves next to Miss Whitten's, noting it must have been a short illness that kept her away the day before. I uncovered the typewriter, pulled out ink and paper from a drawer, and then left the room.

Where would be the best place to find the princess? I couldn't picture her sleeping late when there hadn't been a ball on the previous evening. I walked upstairs past the housemaids as if I belonged there and followed the corridor to the painting studio.

When I tapped and then opened the door, I saw Princess Kira sitting in front of an easel, dabbing at an impressionist canvas.

The door smashed back into my face. I fell back into the hall against the far wall, knocked into a painting the duchess had made. I heard Russian and then the door reopened.

"Miss Peabody, are you all right?" Princess Kira asked in French as she hurried toward me. The Russian guard stood glowering at me with his hand on the doorknob.

"It's a good thing I wasn't the duchess, or you'd be out on your ear," I said in English, rubbing my forehead. I hoped I wouldn't get a bruise.

"I guard princess, not duchess," the guard replied.

"What is your name?"

"Sergei Brencisovich Ivanov," he replied, snapping to attention.

"Well, get out of my way, Ivanov," I replied, shoving him as I entered the doorway. The princess stepped back to let me in; he didn't budge an inch.

"Do you speak French?" I asked in French without facing him. He remained silent.

"He doesn't. I've tested him a couple of times," Princess Kira said.

"Good. Where's Lady Raminoff?"

"Resting."

I gave the princess a conspiratorial smile. She nodded and went back to her canvas. I stood next to her, both of our backs to the guard. I heard him move about to a spot next to the door and then settle in one place.

"How will you see your friend again?" I asked, lowering my voice in the hope that the guard couldn't hear my words even if he could speak French.

"Why would I?"

"If you don't want my help, fine." I turned to leave.

"Wait."

I moved back to my original position looking over her painting. She was going to tell me something. I hoped it was the truth. And I hoped it was also true that the odious Russian soldier couldn't understand French.

CHAPTER SIX

"I'VE convinced Sussex to take me shopping today. You're to come along as my tutor while Lady Raminoff will be my chaperone. The guard will ride on the back as footman." She made a few quick touches of blue paint with her brush.

"And?"

"I plan to walk between shops, and then stop at an artists' supply shop. I will send the guard back to the carriage with several bulky packages. When his back is turned, I'll slip through a shop to the back alley. I want you to misdirect him, slow him down, whatever is necessary."

"Which shop?"

"You don't need to know that." Now a little white went on the canvas.

"I do if I'm going to misdirect him."

She sighed. "Hatchards bookshop."

A shop likely to have the back door open for frequent and

erratic deliveries. And a shop I couldn't enter without blowing my cover. As a fellow bookshop owner, the employees knew me as Georgia Fenchurch.

Now all I had to do was get word to Blackford. Out of curiosity, I asked, "Are you enjoying London, Princess?"

She stopped painting. "Yes. The color. The activity. I want to paint it all."

"Your parents' manor must be very quiet compared to cities. Here or St. Petersburg."

"Quiet, yes, but very pretty. Not unlike the countryside I saw from the railway window. Or the estate I visited with the duke on my way here. All the bustle of the harvest. Autumn flowers. The colors of the leaves changing. Thatched roofs."

"There's not a lot of snow yet?"

"Snow?" She laughed. "Not yet. I'm to return before the snow starts. By late November, we will have snow. By Christmas, everything will be white and beautiful. Do you have snow for Christmas in London?"

"Sometimes. Not often. In the north, there's usually snow."

"That's a pity. I shall have to ask Sussex to take me north next Christmas."

She continued painting and I watched in a companionable silence for a few moments. Then I asked, "What time are we going shopping?"

"Directly after luncheon." She looked over my dress. "I suppose you're wearing that."

I wore a crisp gray gown with white collar and cuffs, a lace inset on the bodice, and puffy sleeves. "Yes. I try to dress in a businesslike manner."

"Oh." Her tone contained a world of disdain.

I matched her in attitude. I didn't like her overdressing for every occasion, but at least I was polite enough not to say anything. "I'll be ready to go along as your tutor."

The princess nodded and turned her full attention to her painting. Obviously, I had been dismissed. I walked over and pulled open the door to the hall as hard as I could. All I hit was the Russian's boot.

I went back downstairs to the morning room to write a note to Blackford. Unfortunately, the duchess was sitting in the room waiting for me.

"Where were you?" she asked, her arms folded over her waist.

"Investigating. Did Blackford solve your problem last night?"

"Yes." She rose and began to pace. "That soldier gives me gooseflesh. I feel like he's measuring me for a coffin. Where is he now?"

"Guarding the princess in your studio."

"I'll have to have it scrubbed down when he leaves."

"What does Lady Raminoff think of him?"

She turned her face and hands heavenward. "Who knows? I'm sorry I invited these Russians to stay. Hereford said I was a fool. I'll have to tell him he was right—if we're not all murdered in our beds first."

She was a duchess, but I suddenly felt sorry for her. "Have you written to tell him of your fears?"

"No. I'm afraid he'll return and order the embassy to remove our guests." She leveled her gaze at me. "And am I correct in thinking the government needs to find out what the threat is and where it's coming from?"

"Yes."

"Then I'll just have to be vigilant and keep my fears to myself."

"You're very brave. I hope the duke appreciates you."

She smiled at my words. "He does."

"Did you hear from the Russian embassy about replacing Ivanov?"

"They have to confer with St. Petersburg, and someone there will ask the tsar. Blackford has promised to take this up with the ambassador. He's spending a lot of time on this problem, isn't he?"

I nodded. If he weren't, the Archivist Society and I wouldn't need to, either.

I heard a muffled cry. I glanced out the window and blinked at what I saw. Lady Daisy was being held aloft by Ivanov and crying as she squirmed to get away. As I ran out of the room, the duchess said, "What is it?"

"Lady Daisy," I cried and heard her footsteps dashing after mine.

When I sprinted out the back door, Ivanov was setting Lady Daisy down and picking up Miss Whitten. The governess's shoes dangled two feet above the ground. She smacked him with her open hand and shouted, "Put me down," in a loud voice.

He loosed a booming laugh.

I ran up to him and shouted, "Do you want to be sent back to Russia?"

He immediately released Miss Whitten and turned toward me, a gleam in his eyes. Seeing the duchess behind me, he said, "Only playing game for little one. No one hurt."

The duchess put every drop of ducal outrage in her voice as she said, "The next time you put a hand on my daughter or any of my staff, it will be the last thing you do in England before I see you thrown on a ship heading to Russia. And believe me when I say the ambassador will back me up."

"No one hurt," he said and walked toward the back door. Once past us, I heard him say clearly, "Silly women."

Following behind as the duchess returned to the house with a shaken Miss Whitten and a sobbing Lady Daisy, I went in and wrote a hurried note to Blackford. I set it on the silver tray in the front hall where the household's letters were left to be posted.

I waited a while after I finished my luncheon in the morning room before venturing out to the front hall. The tray was empty.

The flutter in my chest came when I realized this didn't necessarily mean Blackford had received my message. If he hadn't, I needed him to trust me enough to follow my lead.

"What you need, Miss Peabody?" the guard's growling voice said behind me.

I jumped and turned toward Ivanov, trying to wipe the guilty expression off my face. Why should I feel guilty, my mind lectured. The guard was the one who was untrustworthy. "What *do* you need," I corrected him. "Is the princess ready for her English lesson?"

"No English lesson today." Ivanov moved near, lowering his face toward mine. I could smell his stinking breath as he tried to force me to back up.

I planted my feet and glared at the man. But being of modest stature and with him so close, I had to crane my neck to look him in the eye. "That's not your decision."

"I am soldier to tsar. It is my decision."

"You are in England, a guest in an English house. The tsar has no official standing in this country. Therefore, you do not make decisions for the princess. Now, when will the princess be ready for her English lesson?"

He replied with a string of muttered Russian that I suspected were curses. A door off the hallway opened behind him. At the sound of Princess Kira's voice, he marched off.

The princess came up to me and said in French, "We are going shopping today for our English lesson. Get ready to leave in ten minutes."

I gave her a deep curtsy and walked back to the morning room. I saw the Duke of Sussex with her, but Blackford was nowhere in sight. How was he going to help me with the Russian guard if he wasn't around?

Returning to the front hall five minutes later, I found Blackford chatting with the Duchess of Hereford. Every hair was in place, his clothes were as immaculate as ever, his posture was rigidly straight. He appeared at ease only because the softening of his lips into a smile changed his face to a gentle mask. But the rest of his body was as coiled for action as an iron bedspring.

I wondered if anyone else could see the duke was ready for battle.

I walked up to them, curtsied, and whispered, "Did you get my message?"

Arguing voices in Russian made all three of us turn our heads. The princess, Lady Raminoff, and Ivanov were all talking on top of one another. No one was listening. Sussex stood with them, asking what they were saying and getting no reply.

Blackford turned back to me. "No, I hadn't heard that. Interesting."

An innocuous comment, but I understood what he was telling me. He hadn't received my message. He had no idea what to expect, and I didn't know how much help he'd be.

The princess waved her arms in the air and snapped a single word at Lady Raminoff and the soldier. Ivanov got out a single word before Princess Kira shook a hand in front of his face. Then she turned to Sussex and gave him her arm to escort her out to the carriage.

The rest of us followed in a ragtag parade. Fortunately, Ivanov climbed on the back of the carriage on the ledge for the footman. Five of us crowded inside and we took off.

No one spoke. Sussex stared at Princess Kira, smiling every

time she looked his way. Blackford looked out the window, glancing at me from time to time. I was smashed against one side of the carriage, from where I could see Lady Raminoff in profile glaring at Sussex.

We hit a bump and my shoulder banged against the metal frame of the carriage. I reached up to rub the sore spot, earning a huff from Lady Raminoff. "If you don't have enough room, perhaps you should ride with the driver. Or stay behind."

"That would make it difficult to teach the princess English," I said. We exchanged glares.

The silence continued.

"Princess, what would you like to study today? Perhaps we could try a few verbs," I suggested. Like running, hiding, and causing trouble.

"What does a horse do?" she asked in French.

"Horses walk. They trot. They canter. They gallop." With each verb, I moved my hand faster to get across the quicker speeds. My hand flew past Lady Raminoff's nose when I reached "gallop."

The lady gave me an angry stare. "Pardon."

"So sorry," I replied.

The princess ignored the building tension. "And people? What do they do?"

"The same, except for gallop and canter. People walk, stroll, trot, run, hurry, climb." I moved both hands as if ascending a ladder.

"We shall try these things while we're shopping," the princess replied in French. "It will help me remember. I want my English to be good for His Grace."

"I'm certain you will be brilliant," Sussex said, a smitten smile plastered on his face.

I caught Blackford staring at me with a frown. There was no

way I could tell him about the princess's planned disappearance. I hoped he kept a good watch.

Princess Kira had the carriage stop in front of a fabric shop two doors down from Hatchards. We all climbed down and went inside, the Russian soldier standing guard at the door. He alternated between peering in the shop window and carefully watching every movement in the street.

I noticed a familiar-looking coachman drive past in an ordinary-looking carriage. The well-matched, sleek black horses told me I was not mistaken. Blackford's coachman. He pulled over and let two passengers out in front of Hatchards. Emma and Sumner, dressed in working-class attire fancied up with middle-class hats and gloves. Sumner had added a cane and Emma a nice scarf that could be easily hidden once they reached the East End.

Good. They were in position to confront the Russian girl Princess Kira was meeting. Then my relief quickly died, trampled under horse hooves and carriage wheels. Who had Emma found to watch my shop?

The princess asked Sussex his opinion of different fabrics for sofas, chairs, and draperies. She finally learned he was partial to greens and blues and hated large flowers. We left after Sussex assured the proprietor that they'd be back after the wedding the following spring.

We then walked past Hatchards two doors in the opposite direction to an art supply store. The princess went mad buying canvases, frames, oil paints, cleaning chemicals, and brushes. It was more than even a large-handed man like Ivanov could manage and react to anything else. When the princess told him to carry her packages to the carriage, he let loose with a string of Russian.

"Tell him he is acting as my footman and, therefore, must

carry my purchases to the carriage and store them safely inside," the princess told me in French.

I turned to him and translated her words to English.

He growled at me. "I am guard. I am not servant."

"If you don't do as she instructs, you will be replaced," I said without conferring with the princess first.

"You are servant. Do not speak to me like that."

"Princess Kira is right," Blackford said. "You're acting as her footman. Carry her packages to the carriage, and be sure everything is stored so nothing is damaged. Otherwise, I'll personally speak to the ambassador and get you replaced. Today."

With ill grace, the soldier shoved past us and picked up the awkward packages. He led the way along the sidewalk, struggling with the bulky parcels that threatened to slip to the pavement with every step he took toward the carriage. Princess Kira lagged farther and farther behind.

Before Ivanov reached the carriage, the princess held up one gloved finger to Sussex and disappeared into the bookshop. Sussex turned to Blackford and shrugged. I'd positioned myself in front of Lady Raminoff so I could block her way.

Sussex wandered into the bookshop. I knew Princess Kira had headed straight to the back door and freedom. Hatchards clerks were used to eccentric behavior by their clients and would hardly notice one more well-dressed customer strolling out the back. Sussex would be too late to find her. But how had she learned the layout of a shop she'd never visited before?

Ivanov reached the carriage and shoved some of the packages through the window so he had a hand free to open the door. Then he looked back, didn't see the princess, and roared fearsome Russian curses as canvases and frames flew in all directions.

The carriage horses shied at the soldier's war cry. Bystanders ducked as they were pelted with flying frames or parcels of art supplies while Ivanov stormed toward us. Behind me, Lady Raminoff shoved me forward to get to the door ahead of the guard.

She made it inside, but I collided with the guard. He shoved me back, knocking me off my feet. I would have fallen if Blackford hadn't grabbed me. Before I could run into the store, he said, "What's going on?"

I righted myself, hanging on to Blackford's arm longer than strictly necessary. Opportunities like this didn't happen every day. "She's meeting that mystery girl in the alley behind the shops."

"Come on." He grabbed my arm and hurried me down the sidewalk past the carriage and the puzzled-looking driver, ignoring irate passersby who'd been struck by flying parcels. He hauled me down an alley next to a music shop. I tripped over uneven bricks and stubbed my toes more than once.

I cried out, but Blackford dragged me along at a pace that left me panting. My corset dug into my ribs. We reached the back alley and Blackford stopped. I collapsed against a grimy brick wall and closed my eyes, gasping for breath. My feet throbbed. I wished I'd dressed for active pursuits.

"This way," Blackford said.

I opened my eyes to see him gesture to the princess and the other young woman to enter the music shop. They murmured a few words between them. Then the princess came toward us and the unknown young woman ran the other way down the alley.

Several shops down, I saw Emma and Sumner lingering by the back of a milliner's.

Hurrying past us, the princess rushed down the alley, Blackford and I following. "Who was that?" I managed to gasp out in French.

"Who was who?" came her reply.

"Don't play that game," Blackford said. "You have to trust someone."

"I trust no one. It is the only way to survive," she snapped back. Then, looking slightly breathless, the princess stepped onto the sidewalk and slowed her pace as she reached the carriage.

She only had time to adjust her hat before Sussex came out of Hatchards bookshop and saw her. With a smile, he called back into the shop and then walked toward her. I doubt he even noticed Blackford and me. That was good. Blackford didn't have a mark on him or a hair out of place, but I was brushing dirt off my skirt and tucking stray curls into my hairdo.

Princess Kira turned to look at me and clucked her tongue. "You look like a slut," she said in French before she straightened my hat.

I beat my gloves together to shake off the slime from the alley wall as Sussex and then Lady Raminoff joined us. The princess looked at them and then at her art supplies. "*Mon Dieu*. Why did he make such a mess of my paints? Please help me."

The two dukes began picking up her purchases while Lady Raminoff let off a blast of Russian. Princess Kira responded in kind.

I looked around. "Where is Ivanov?"

"He went into the alley looking for the princess. He should return soon," Sussex said.

Blackford and I glanced at each other. Had he captured the young Russian woman?

A moment later, the guard marched out of Hatchards. He immediately barked at both Princess Kira and Lady Raminoff in Russian. He didn't appear out of breath or any sweatier than usual; it must be all that marching soldiers do. Lady Raminoff cringed, but the princess stared at him, completely unmoved.

At least the Russian guard was alone. I hoped Emma and Sumner had better luck following the girl after she escaped.

The princess pointed at the art supplies the two dukes were collecting and snapped out a Russian command.

Ivanov curled his upper lip and snatched up the few remaining packages. Then he held the door open while we climbed inside. We were still trying to organize the princess's purchases in the tight space when Ivanov slammed the door, climbed up on the back of the carriage, and told the driver to return home.

Sussex and I were both standing as the carriage jerked into motion. He flew onto Lady Raminoff as frames cascaded down her legs. I hung on to the packages of paints and brushes as I sat down hard in Blackford's lap.

Lady Raminoff berated Sussex in French for his rudeness, smacking him on the shoulder with her parasol. Blackford lifted me off of him as I begged his forgiveness for my clumsiness. It happened so fast I didn't have time to enjoy my scandalous position.

Princess Kira held one hand over her mouth, trying to keep her giggles contained.

"Emma and Sumner were in position," Blackford murmured, followed a little louder by, "I hope you weren't hurt."

"Only my dignity. Are you uninjured, Your Grace?" Then I whispered, "Tonight."

"Yes."

WHEN I HEARD a knock at the front door that evening, I ran to answer it, hoping it was Emma. When I saw it was Blackford, I sighed and said, "Have you heard anything?"

"Not yet. It may take them a while. They'll be back when they can." He walked past me and left his hat, gloves, and cane on the entry table. Then he strolled into the parlor.

I called Phyllida and followed the duke. "But it's the East End. There are cutthroats and thieves and murderers lurking there. What if they can't return?"

"It's London, not Calcutta."

Phyllida walked in and he bowed to her.

She curtsied and sat, twisting her fingers. "I'm worried."

"I would be, too, if it were only Emma," Blackford said. "But Sumner is with her. The two of them together could withstand an army of thieves and cutthroats. No one in the East End stands a chance against them."

"If that were true, why haven't they returned?" I snapped.

"They haven't found the girl yet, or she's still on the move. Don't worry." He looked at each of us in turn. "Emma is going to laugh at you for worrying so."

"Let her. I'm worried." I held Blackford's gaze with an angry stare. "I think we should send in some people to look for them."

"And ruin all their good work by calling attention to them? They wouldn't appreciate it. I'll check hospitals, jails, and morgues, if it will make you rest easier."

"It would, Your Grace." And I'd go to the bookshop early in the morning to check on deliveries, orders, and stocking the shelves so my business didn't flounder while both Emma and I were away. This mysterious Russian woman wasn't really our concern, but we were both heavily involved. And now Emma was missing.

Again, the thought hit me in the face like a blast of winter wind. Emma was missing.

CHAPTER SEVEN

AFTER a night of twisting the bedsheets as I turned from side to side, I arose early. Phyllida was already up when I reached the kitchen and found she'd baked sweet rolls. She had the same purple marks below her eyes that I'd seen in the looking glass. When she offered me a roll, I took a few nibbles, neither tasting it nor hungry for it.

I walked quickly to the shop in the cool of the early morning. I wasn't surprised to see the sun had deserted us, leaving a gloomy sky. It suited my mood perfectly.

Once I let myself into the shop, I turned on all the electric lights to ward away the darkness. Too bad the lights wouldn't frighten off my despair. I was certain something bad had happened to Emma and Sumner.

Nervous concern fueled my frantic work to reshelve books and check on my orders. We were out of two of the most popular magazines and the newest issues were due that day. A thump on the back door told me someone wanted in from the alley. It had to be the deliveryman with the magazines.

Unless it was Emma and she had to stay out of sight for some reason.

I ran to the back door and threw it open without looking outside first. The deliveryman said, "Sure are eager to see me today," as he carried in a large box.

"I thought you were someone else." I looked up and down the alley. No one.

He followed the box with two bundles, which he carried in clutched in two massive, ink-stained paws. As he walked out, straightening his cap, he said, "It's just Bertha and me." He patted the horse's rump and then climbed into the wagon to take the reins and nudge Bertha into motion.

I locked the door behind him and quickly checked the shipping papers against what the man had delivered. Finding all in order, I began to shelve the illustrated magazines dealing with Her Majesty's record-breaking reign.

That day was only September 21, 1896. Victoria would have to wait two more days before she'd have ruled longer than any other British monarch. The only one left standing in the way of her record was her grandfather George III. There would be church services on the twenty-third, but the parades and pomp would wait until next June.

I looked out at the rain beginning to fall on the street. They were wisely waiting for good weather to celebrate.

And I was waiting for the safe return of Emma and Sumner from the treacherous East End.

A knock on the front door made me jerk out of my daydream. I could see Grace Yates and Frances Atterby through the glass front door, umbrellas unfurled against the raindrops. I hurried over and unlocked the door.

"It looks to be a miserable day," Frances said, unwrapping herself from her water-splattered outerwear. "Hopefully, we'll be busy."

"Grace. What are you doing here?" I asked. Silly question. She must have gotten a message from someone to help us in the store.

"Good morning to you, too," she said and smiled. "Emma contacted me yesterday morning and said I'd be needed indefinitely."

"What did you tell Lord Barnwood?" Grace worked as his secretary and librarian for his large book collection.

She removed her soggy felt hat, showing off a mass of light brown curls. "He's on his way to Italy and Greece. He'll be gone for a month or more. I just need to check at the house once a day for correspondence. This investigation came at a good time for me."

Something wet wrapped itself around my ankle. I shrieked and jumped, earning me a scratch and a hiss. Then Charles Dickens, who'd adopted our street for his mousing, jumped up in our front window and began washing a front paw with his pink tongue.

"Poor Dickens. You're all wet." Grace went into the back and returned with a clean dust cloth. She began to wipe the cat off, saying, "Oh, poor baby. He has a new cut on his ear."

"I can imagine what the other animal looks like," I said and watched Dickens cautiously. He looked at me through narrowed eyes and then rubbed against Grace's arm.

"So what does Emma report?" Frances asked.

I rubbed my hands over my sleeves, suddenly chilled by my thoughts. "Nothing. She and Sumner didn't return last night."

"Hmm."

"What, Frances?" She didn't seem too worried.

"I'm sure they're fine. I've never seen two people more able to care for themselves. And each other."

"But we're talking about the East End. Cutthroats, thieves, anarchists. Disease runs rampant there. There are more threats than even they could handle."

Frances and Grace shared a look. "You're letting your imagination run away with you, Georgia. Gain the princess's trust and find out what's going on. We have the bookshop covered," Frances said.

"What aren't you telling me?"

"Perhaps they didn't return last night for another reason."

"What?"

Grace rolled her eyes at me and handed me my cloak. "Did you ever think they might want to be alone together?"

"Emma would never behave scandalously." I covered up, grabbed my umbrella, and stomped outside on my way to Hereford House. I knew Emma and Sumner were fond of each other, but I didn't think they were *that* fond. Emma was sensible. She wouldn't disappear, leaving us to worry for the sake of some time alone with Sumner.

I'd been young and in love once, and I'd spent nights away from Phyllida and Emma. They'd never made mention of it, but we were publicly engaged and he had his own shop, able to support a family. And we probably would have had a family by now if he hadn't died shortly before our wedding day.

I didn't want Emma as hurt as I'd been when he died. And I didn't think Sumner could support a family on whatever pittance Blackford paid him.

The only good I could think of that morning was that the princess wouldn't want to go out in this rain. Our seasonably nice weather had come to an end.

I walked into Hereford House, closed my umbrella, and put it in the stand as the butler raced up to me. "The duchess is waiting for you in the parlor." His head was wet with rain—or sweat—and his jacket was misbuttoned.

I handed him my cloak and gloves and hurried to the parlor. A footman opened the door. As soon as I walked in, Blackford said, "Do you have any idea where Princess Kira has gone?"

"If I slept in kitchen, this wouldn't happen," the Russian soldier announced to the room at large.

"Yes, you told us," the Duchess of Hereford replied, rubbing her hands together.

I turned to Blackford as the calmest person in the room. "I have no idea where she is. Have you heard from Sumner?"

"No. Have you?"

I shook my head. "When did the princess leave?"

"Sometime late last night or early this morning. Lady Raminoff slept through her disappearance."

"She is kidnapped by anarchists. I shall report this to the tsar and your queen. Tell Lady Raminoff not to leave her room until I question her further." Ivanov marched out of the room.

"Thank God he's gone," the duchess said as soon as the door slammed behind him.

"Is Lady Raminoff usually a heavy sleeper?" I asked.

"No," Blackford replied. "She said her cocoa had an odd taste."

"You think someone put a sleeping draught in her hot drink?" He nodded.

"Who could have drugged her? And was there any sign that Princess Kira was abducted?" The cold in the room soaked into my bones, chilling my hands.

"No." Blackford paced the parlor. "I suspect she engineered this with that girl she's been meeting. What we don't want is for the tsar or Sussex or our government to find out about her disappearance. We need to get her back before anyone knows she's gone."

"She's a little fool," the duchess said. "If word of her disappearance gets out, she'll be ruined and the wedding will be off. All sorts of rumors will circulate, and Hereford's name will be smeared by the gossip." She looked near tears.

"Where is the tsar?"

"Still with the queen. I can handle Sussex easily enough, and I have footmen downstairs who will keep Ivanov from sending any ill-timed messages." Blackford came to a stop in front of me and stared with his dark eyes glowing from a tightly restrained need to jump into action. "But we have to find Princess Kira, and quickly."

I placed a hand on his vest. "Before we do anything, have you checked the hospitals and the jails for word of Emma or Sumner?"

"No report of them anywhere, and I checked with every facility in the area." Blackford brushed my cheek with his fingertips. "They're all right, Georgia. Let's deal with the princess."

"I'm going to talk to Lady Raminoff. She knows the family. If this started in Russia, she should know." I hurried out of the parlor toward the room the princess shared with Lady Raminoff.

I knocked and entered. The older woman lay fully clothed on her bed, a bag of ice on her forehead. "Go away," she called weakly in French.

"Who is the girl Princess Kira keeps running away to meet?" I asked in the only language we had in common. With luck, I'd understand everything she said.

"What?" The woman sat bolt upright, catching the ice bag with one hand. "Nadia? Is she here in London?"

"Who is Nadia?"

She lay back down on the bed and put the ice over her forehead and eyes. "No one."

"Do you believe Princess Kira has run off to meet *no one*?" I studied her for a moment. "No, you don't. You know who Nadia is. She's the reason the princess has gone out every afternoon supposedly to study English—she has been meeting a girl of about twenty-one. Who is she?"

Lady Raminoff lay still on the bed.

I grabbed up the ice and said with all the cold fury I could muster, "If you don't want to go back to Russia in disgrace, with the princess's engagement called off, then I suggest you tell us who we're dealing with."

The woman slowly sat up and swung her feet over the side of the bed. With remorse in her voice, she said, "Very well. I'm sure the princess has been meeting with her half sister, Nadia Andropov. Her illegitimate half sister. They were inseparable until last year when someone tried to kill Nadia. She escaped, but her mother was murdered."

"Was the murderer caught?"

She shrugged. "An anarchist was hung. It is doubtful he planned the killing. He may not have even been the killer."

"Then why—?" Because it was Russia. They saw anarchists under their beds at night. I knew it was a stupid question.

Lady Raminoff gave me a thin-lipped look that told me she thought it was a stupid question, too. "I don't know how Princess Kira received word that her, uh, half sister was in London or how they arranged to meet. I'm not surprised they found each other. They've always been very close."

"Would Nadia lead the princess into danger?"

"I should hope not." Lady Raminoff's certainty quickly gave way to a worried look that matched my concern for Emma. "Well, probably not. In truth, I'm not sure. Her father warned me to watch out for Nadia. When they were children, Kira would trail Nadia around like a servant. He said he often suspected Nadia of leading Kira into risky situations. He said he tried to separate them to no avail."

"By murder?"

"Possibly, but I doubt it."

"Nadia was followed to the East End." At least, that was where the woman had led Jacob, and where I believed Sumner and Emma now were.

"What is this East End?"

"A dangerous section of London, full of thieves and anarchists."

"Blessed saints, she's been taken prisoner by anarchists. Nadia might be behind this. Kira's father, Prince Pyotr Romanov, started this by murdering his lover Marina Andropov, and now his bastard daughter is out to avenge her mother. I knew coming here would be the death of me. I'm ruined." The woman flopped back on the bed and turned toward the wall, sobbing.

I couldn't get any more out of the chaperone, so I raced back to tell Blackford what I'd learned. He wasn't in the parlor, so I followed the sounds of murmuring male voices.

The front hall looked like a battleground. Ivanov lay unconscious on the black and white tiles bleeding from a head wound and his nose. A footman sat on the tiles, holding his arm and moaning. Blackford was tapping his cane on his hand. The silver head had a reddish smear that I suspected was Ivanov's blood.

I hoped the guard wasn't dead, if only because I didn't want Blackford in trouble for killing a lowlife like Ivanov.

The duke appeared uncreased and undamaged as he commanded, "Dodson. Hughes. Tie the Russian up and remove him to a storeroom in the duchess's cellar."

"Gladly," one of them said as they began to bind the soldier in ropes.

I released a sigh. At least Ivanov wasn't dead.

The Duchess of Hereford stood by a wall looking pale. "This is a nightmare."

I watched for a moment before I said, "Your Graces. What happened?"

"Ivanov tried to slip away. I ordered him to stay in the house. He disagreed rather forcefully. This is the result." Blackford looked around him. Then he glanced in my direction and asked, "What did you learn from the chaperone?"

I reported my conversation with Lady Raminoff.

Blackford said, "Any chance they hung the killer?"

"I'd guess at least the person who paid the killer is still free. Possibly the killer, too. Do you have a telephone, Your Grace?"

The duchess looked at me and blinked. "A telephone?"

"Come next door and use mine. Calling out the Archivist Society?" Blackford asked.

"Yes. I want to send some eyes into the East End to report back today." Hopefully, they'd find Emma and Sumner. With even better luck, they'd find the princess.

The footmen finished tying up Ivanov and began bouncing him along the floor as they dragged him to the back stairs. I winced when I heard his head crack on the tiles. "That's enough, Hughes," Blackford said.

"Just getting back a little of my own, Your Grace," one of the footmen replied. I could see a welt along his forehead and an eye blackening.

"You have now," Blackford replied. Ivanov's limp body stopped thudding along the hall.

"I'd better see to my storerooms," the duchess said and followed them, calling to her butler.

"Hughes, stay here and aid the duchess's men with guarding

this man." Blackford bent down to the footman moaning on the floor. "Smith, can you walk?"

"Aye, Your Grace. Can you give me a hand up?"

The three of us made slow progress to the duke's imposing residence next door. Leaving his butler to organize care for the wounded footman, Blackford showed me into the study where we'd first met. On a table by the door now stood a telephone.

I picked it up and asked for Sir Broderick's line. He answered almost immediately.

"Any word from Emma?" I asked first.

"No. Where are you, Georgia?"

"The Duke of Blackford's residence. We need to send eyes into the East End to look for Sumner and Emma. I don't know what they're up to, so tell our scouts not to approach or act like they know them. Only see if they can find Emma and Sumner, and then report back their location by this afternoon."

"What has happened, Georgia?" I could hear his concern over the wires.

"The princess has run away. I think she may have run to the woman Emma and Sumner were following yesterday. The woman is Princess Kira's half sister, Nadia Andropov. Hopefully, they're all together and safe."

After I finished my conversation, I hung up and faced Blackford. "What do we do now?"

"Now? We do nothing."

Perhaps the duke intended to do nothing, but I was joining the search. I turned on my heel and hurried out of the library.

"Georgia," Blackford snapped and marched out of his library on my heels.

Unfortunately, I had come to an abrupt stop when I dashed out of the room to discover the Duke of Sussex standing before me. Stevens, Blackford's butler, stood a little behind him in the hall. When Blackford came out, he had to step to my side to avoid colliding with my back.

"I say, is there a problem?" Arthur, Duke of Sussex, asked as he stood in the hallway, looking from one to the other of us. One pale eyebrow was eloquently raised, and it would have taken a dunce to miss the thought spelled out on his face. *He thinks Blackford is having his way with the neighbor's servants.*

I tried to remember which commandment forbade that as I dropped into a curtsy and said, "No, Your Grace. At least nothing that would concern you."

"Perhaps you can help, Sussex," Blackford said. I whipped around to signal him to keep the Duke of Sussex out of this when he continued, "Miss Peabody's sister is missing. Since Hereford is absent, she came to me for guidance. Her sister has threatened to meet an unsuitable young man in the East End, and Miss Peabody wants to stop her. I'm taking the carriage out. Would you care to join us?"

"I'd be glad to help. Shall I get Princess Kira?"

No! Please do not let Sussex see Princess Kira in our search for Emma and Sumner. "When I spoke to her, she said she was going to spend the day painting and didn't want to be disturbed. I would consider it an honor if you would join us, Your Grace."

I should have been shocked at how easily the lie slipped from my lips. I was embarrassed by how easily Blackford and I interwove our lies. Which one of us had become a bad influence on the other?

Blackford sent for his coachman to bring the plain carriage around front and the three of us, plus a muscular footman sitting with the driver, set off. We quickly left the duke's upper-class neighborhood for alternating streets of commercial properties, middle-class residences, and working-class homes. We worked our way through the confusion of traffic in the City and entered the East End.

The driver stuck to the main roads, the others being too narrow and dangerous for a carriage. Even then, we moved at an ant's pace. We had to slowly weave our way around insurmountable objects such as parked drays loading their wares. We were forced to avoid broken carts and a loud dispute between apple sellers and flower sellers that looked to turn violent.

Riding with my face pressed against the windowpane, I looked for Emma and Sumner in vain. We passed a few blocks where the buildings seemed to stand only by leaning against each other and I could smell the decay through the glass. Other blocks looked sturdy. The institutional buildings, hospitals, schools, and police stations looked like brick fortresses that the Second Coming wouldn't bring down.

Warehouses and factories were mixed with shops, homes, and common lodging houses where the poor slept on bunks in dormitories for fourpence a night. And in between these warehouses and common lodging houses, between the sweatshops and houses sublet into rented rooms, were tiny alleys, twisting lanes, and broken fences. Shortcuts that protected criminals.

I hoped Emma hadn't ended up in a common lodging house.

At least I didn't see Princess Kira walking along Commercial Street. But then, I couldn't imagine Princess Kira in this neighborhood.

With the rain holding off for the present time, I could make out faces under hats or caps. If it were raining, people would have taken refuge under umbrellas or pulled down hat brims or used scarves to keep their faces dry.

"What does your sister look like?" Sussex asked.

"Blond. Pretty. Ten years my junior."

"Like Princess Kira." He smiled. From the empty look in his eyes, it seemed he had faded into a daydream.

I glanced at Blackford and rolled my eyes. He glared at me, and I returned to looking out the window. And then I spotted Nadia Andropov just before we reached Whitechapel Road. Sussex was looking out the other window. I tapped Blackford on the knee and gestured with my head.

Nadia appeared to be alone, walking along the street at a comfortable pace. No one was chasing her. Yet.

Blackford banged on the ceiling and the driver quickly reined in the horses, blocking a wagon whose driver shouted something I didn't want to dwell on. I opened the door and, since we weren't in the Wellington coach, climbed down safely without help.

I started to follow Nadia on foot. Behind me, I heard Blackford's voice and the carriage door slam. He must have had to stop Sussex from joining me on the pavement. The coach drew a little ahead of Nadia, looking too clean and new to belong in this neighborhood. She didn't change her speed or look around, apparently unaware of us.

Then she dodged into an alley and I was sure she knew we were there. With a sigh and against my better judgment, I went in after her. I hoped the men in the carriage noted where I had gone.

The end of the alley opened out into a wider space between the buildings on Commercial Street and the dirty backs of some two-story dwellings on the next block. Suddenly I was shoved into a doorway, a knife pressed against my throat. The sharp edge burned my skin as if she held a lit match to my neck. "Why are you following me?"

CHAPTER EIGHT

I found myself inches from the face of Nadia Andropov, the blue in her eyes as cold as a Russian snowdrift. I hadn't expected to die protecting a Russian princess. Forcing enough air out of my lungs to speak without rubbing against the blade was a trick. I whispered, "Nadia, I'm trying to find Kira."

"Why?" She pressed the blade just a little harder into my flesh. There was no room for error.

I could feel blood oozing on my white shirtfront from the cut on my throat. Somebody was going to pay. If I lived. Sweat poured off my scalp and down my back. "The British government is using me to try to keep her safe. She's gone missing, and so have two of my friends."

"Emma and Sumner?" The knife left my throat.

"You've seen them?" I nearly went limp with relief, for myself and for Emma.

She eyed me, the blade still in her hand. "Kira's with them."

"Thank heavens. Where?"

"They said home. Wherever that is."

Our flat. Phyllida would love the company. "I think I know. Do you want to come with me?"

"No. I have enemies, even in England. I have to stay in hiding."

She was no older than Emma, but she seemed to have the menace and an indifference to life of someone more hardened and crueler. "I know about the attempt on your life in Russia. Do you need anything?"

"No. I have friends here who are protecting me."

"Not anarchists." Please, not anarchists.

She shook her head. "No. They want to change the government in Russia, but they want to do it peacefully."

"How can I get in touch with you?"

Her smile reached her eyes, now the blue of a summer lake. "I'll get in touch with you. Go on. Rejoin your friends before they call out the peelers."

"Thanks for the information, Nadia. And next time, please keep that knife put away."

She winced. "Sorry. Your collar is ruined." Slipping the fabric down slightly, she added, "It's only a scratch. I hope it does not pain you too much."

It was my turn to smile. "Not anymore." I was getting out of here.

I walked back down the narrow alley and out into the street. The carriage sat waiting for me. When I walked up to it, the footman jumped down and Blackford threw open the door.

As soon as I was inside, he said, "You're hurt. What happened?"

"I received word that Emma is at home. It took a lot of persuasion to get them to tell me." I couldn't say a word about the princess or Nadia in front of Sussex. I was certain Blackford was keeping him in the dark. I hoped Blackford understood the message I tried to convey.

"Should we do battle with these ruffians?" Sussex asked.

I wished he didn't always sound like a character in an operetta. "No. They've slipped back into their hiding places by now. And truly, I'm not hurt. This was an accident."

"An accident that could have killed you," Blackford said, scowling.

I couldn't wait any longer to check if Emma and Princess Kira were at our home. "Could I ask Your Grace to take me home? I live near Leicester Square."

"Of course, Miss Peabody. After your unfortunate encounter, you must be exhausted." Blackford gave me such a look of innocence that I glared in reply. Nevertheless, he gave the order and we were again in motion.

"I feel responsible for your injury, Miss Peabody. I wanted to follow you into that alley to protect you, but Blackford said you'd learn more on your own about your sister's whereabouts."

Sussex looked so mortified that I reached out and touched his puppy-soft gloved hand. "He was right. Those ruffians would have wanted to fight with you rather than give up any information about my sister. They would have instantly recognized your superiority. I, on the other hand, was no threat. Eventually, they gave in to my pleading."

Sussex looked placated and patted my hand.

The corners of Blackford's mouth edged upward for a moment. Then he looked serious again as he said, "I'm glad you were successful. What should I tell the Duchess of Hereford?"

"Nothing. I'll go back and explain my absence once I take care of my neck and change my shirt."

The driver, having brought Blackford to my flat before, rolled down my street on his way to Leicester Square and when I gave the word, Blackford signaled the coach to stop. With words of gratitude to Their Graces, I climbed down and headed indoors.

When I knocked, Emma opened the door, took one look at my neck, and shrieked as she gave me a strong hug. I embraced her just as tightly, relieved to see her alive and in one piece after her twenty-four-hour disappearance.

I opened my teary eyes to see Sumner, Phyllida, and Princess Kira crowding around us in the small entry hall. "Thank goodness you're all right."

Emma replied, "You're not. Who cut you? Nadia?"

What had Emma's experience with Nadia been like? "Nadia told me where you were. And Princess Kira, we need to get you back to Hereford House before any more trouble starts. Let me change my shirt and I'll take you back."

I didn't realize I'd forgotten to speak to her in French until she replied in English. "Thank you."

I gave her a sharp look, and she blushed. "I hoped to find out what is occurring by pretending not to know English. May we keep pretending?"

"Yes. It gives me a reason to keep giving you English lessons and to keep watch in the household."

Sumner took hold of my head and turned it one way and the other. "A tot of brandy, Lady Phyllida, please."

"I'm fine, Sumner."

"It's for the outside of you, not the inside. Keep this cut from festering."

Phyllida returned with a small measure of brandy in a glass and Emma led me toward the bathing room.

"Just as I showed you," Sumner called out.

"Sumner's been teaching you how to care for injuries?" I asked as she shoved me into the room ahead of her.

"Yes. Let's get this blouse off of you."

My shirt was ruined. The brandy stung. The bandage was uncomfortable. Emma was being unusually silent. I broke the silence between us with, "What happened?"

"We spent the day following the woman, Nadia, until she finally came to roost after dark in a three-story building. We kept watch, waiting to see who else would join her. Just as we were deciding whether to break into the building and risk the woman escaping again, she left. We followed her to Hereford House. She went inside and came back out with Princess Kira. We followed them to the same building in the East End. It was hours after midnight before we saw them go inside. They didn't come back out again."

This didn't explain where Emma had been during the night. My fears that Emma had given herself to a man who couldn't support a family were growing.

We didn't have time to discuss this. Our first priority should be to get the princess back to Hereford House before her reputation, and her wedding, were ruined. "How did you make contact with the princess?"

"Nadia and the princess came out in the morning and we stopped them half a block away. Nadia encouraged the princess to come back with us." Emma touched my neck one final time. "There. That should do it."

I was in a foul mood by the time I put on a fresh blouse and was ready to leave with the princess. As I reached the front door, I turned around to Emma and said, "You might want to let Sir

Broderick know you're safe and sound. Half the Archivist Society is running around the East End looking for you."

"Wonderful," Emma grumbled. Sumner looked uncomfortable.

The princess put me in a better mood by finding our travel by omnibus an adventure. She looked out the window, remarking on everything she saw. She asked about routes passing the National Gallery. She studied the colors in women's clothing. She marveled at the greenery in all the parks and squares we passed.

Then she ruined it all by saying, "Who designs your dresses?"

"What do you mean?"

"Your dresses are plain. Dowdy. You need more frills and brighter colors."

I liked my dresses the way they were. I gave her a cold stare and said, "What about your frock, Princess?" It was a deep blue without frills or ornamentation except for a light blue collar and cuffs. This was the first dress I'd seen her in that I would wear.

"Nadia told me to wear something plain and not to put on any jewels. That way I could fit in better in her neighborhood."

"What did you think of where she lives?"

"The neighborhood is very poor, but Nadia's room is nice. I felt at home there."

I couldn't picture this spoiled girl being at home anywhere in the East End. "How did you reach Nadia?"

"She came to the house and led me back to her place. She's living in a building with a family who came from Kiev. They had to escape the tsar's men."

"Does Nadia think her mother was murdered by the tsar's men?"

The princess shook her head, studying the traffic passing us. Her attention was captured by a shiny maroon-colored carriage.

"What time did you and Nadia get to her house?"

"Not late. Perhaps eleven. Nadia hailed a hansom cab for us not far from Hereford House that took us most of the way. Nadia said she stopped him before we arrived at her home so the driver couldn't report where we went." She looked at me then. "What shall I tell Sussex?"

"I told him you wanted to paint today without being disturbed. If we can get in without him seeing you, you'll be in the clear."

"Then we'll go in from the mews."

The princess had been too distracted by the sights to have lied to me about the time she arrived at Nadia's house. So why did Emma lie? I suspected I knew the answer.

We slipped in from the mews without being seen and entered by the back door of Hereford House. I could hear raised voices nearby and sobbing from below stairs. I led the way to the morning room, where we shed our hats and gloves. Then, certain we looked like we'd been in the house, we followed the noise to the front hall.

Blackford was questioning one of his footmen while the Duchess of Hereford rubbed her arms and one of the Hereford footmen tried to explain something. I stepped forward and said, "Your Graces, is anything amiss?"

The duchess's jaw dropped, but she quickly recovered. "Miss Peabody. Princess. We've had a domestic accident. Nothing to concern you."

Blackford turned from his footman, one of those who'd bounced Ivanov down the hall. The footman held a cloth to his head that was smeared with the dark red of dried blood. "It appears Ivanov has abandoned his post. He has vanished, along with all of his gear. And he attacked my footman."

"I'm glad Ivanov's gone. I didn't like him," Princess Kira said with a pout.

When I'd last seen Ivanov, he'd been unconscious and trussed up like a Christmas goose. I needed a meeting of the Archivist Society that night. But first, I wanted to learn from Blackford how Ivanov had escaped.

A childish voice floated down the stairs, and then Lady Daisy hopped partway down, one hand held by her tutor, Amelia Whitten. "We thought we'd go for a walk in the garden," the governess said and widened her eyes as she looked at the group below her. "Is that all right?"

"Perhaps not this afternoon," the duchess said. "How about if we take the carriage out and go to a park? Just the three of us."

"Yes," Daisy exclaimed and clapped her hands together.

The duchess was looking wan, as if she needed to get out of the house more than her daughter did.

"I'm going upstairs to paint," the princess said.

Since I was no longer needed, I headed to the back stairs to find the source of the sobbing. I reached the servants' hall to find a cluster of maids, the housekeeper, and the cook surrounding an hysterical maid with an ice bag on her face. I tapped the housekeeper on the shoulder to get her attention. "What happened?"

"Sally was in the way of that brute when he escaped from the game larder. She leaned back into the wall to get out of his way, but he punched her anyway," the housekeeper said.

"Sally said he smiled before he hit her," one of the maids added. "And he said, 'Give that to your mistress.'"

Sally vigorously nodded her head while still holding the cold to her face.

"I'm sure she imagined it," the housekeeper said. "Don't make him more of a monster than he is."

"It would be difficult to make him sound worse than he is," I told them. "Did Sally see anyone who didn't belong in the house?

Someone had to free Ivanov from his bonds. He was well tied up and guarded."

"Sally," the housekeeper said, "did you see anyone besides Ivanov?"

She shook her head, still sobbing.

I'D ONLY BEEN using the telephone for a little over a year at this point, but I don't know how I lived before Blackford put one in my bookshop and Sir Broderick put one in his study. When I left Hereford House that afternoon, I went directly to the bookshop and called Sir Broderick. We needed to have a meeting of the Archivist Society that night. I requested him to telephone Blackford's residence to invite him as well.

I suspected Blackford now knew more than I did, and so far, he hadn't shared it with me. In fairness, he hadn't been able to, since we were never alone. With Emma keeping secrets and this investigation going in circles, I was having trouble being fair.

When I hung up the telephone, I found Frances counting the day's receipts and Grace straightening our racks of periodicals. "Is she as pretty in person as she looks in the magazine?" Grace asked.

"Who?" I knew she couldn't mean the old queen.

"Princess Kira. She'll make a lovely bride."

"She's going to lead Sussex on a merry chase after they're wed," I told her.

"Nasty?"

I shook my head. "She knows her own mind and doesn't mind getting her own way."

"Good for her," Frances said, joining us. Then she added, "The back is locked up."

"Thank you. I'll see you at Sir Broderick's later?"

They both nodded.

I decided to try to find out if they knew what Emma was keeping secret. "What's up with Emma?"

"She'll tell us when she's ready," Frances said, "and not a second sooner." She gave me a contented smile, showing me she wasn't worried. Of course she wasn't. She wasn't the one who'd raised Emma for the past several years.

Grace put on her cloak and took up her umbrella. "I'll see you later," she called out. Then she looked at me and added, "Don't worry about Emma. We'll find out in due course."

The bell over the door jingled as she left.

After I locked up and walked home, I found Emma helping Phyllida put dinner on the table. "Sumner having dinner with us?" I asked.

"Why would he do that?" Emma asked and walked into the kitchen.

"I don't know. I just thought—," I called out.

Emma came back out with the serving spoons. "Don't."

Dropping the subject I wanted to discuss, I told them both about the upcoming meeting and what I'd learned that day. Emma was subdued, but she paid attention to what I was saying. Sumner's name didn't come up again. I wondered if they'd gotten into an argument during their long time together.

The weather was windy on our walk to Sir Broderick's, but at least the rain hadn't returned. The meeting, held in the parlor again, featured a roaring fire in the fireplace, steaming hot tea, and Dominique's wonderful scones. From the crumbs on Frances's ample bosom, I suspected she was on her third one. Mrs. Hardwick served tea and then disappeared.

Jacob entered carrying a doorknob and some pieces of thin

metal. I watched him sit down and fiddle with the knob for a minute before I asked, "Are you trying to fix it?"

He grinned. "No. I'm taking a course on lock picking from one of Sir Broderick's acquaintances. I'm practicing today's lesson."

"I thought you were studying accountancy."

"I am. This is sort of a hobby. Sir Broderick says I should widen my horizons." Jacob gave me a wink and returned to his work.

I shook my head, but I couldn't hide my smile. "You're training him to be a thief, sir."

Sir Broderick gave me a dry look before he asked Emma what she and Sumner had discovered. She gave the same brief report she'd given me. Then I reported speaking to Nadia and returning the princess to Hereford House.

"She speaks English?" Frances asked.

"Yes. Quite well. Apparently she was taught at home and her tutor was Scottish. Lady Raminoff was ordered by the tsar's mother to chaperone the princess. Not trusting her, the princess began to hide her ability to speak English."

"A lie that's proven useful for us," Blackford said, studying his glass of whiskey. Why was he looking so morose?

"We intend to keep her knowledge secret," I told him.

"Good, because someone in Hereford House released Ivanov from his bonds and helped him escape," the duke told us.

Everyone leaned forward at this surprising news.

"Are you certain someone freed Ivanov?" I asked. "He didn't escape on his own?"

"Yes. The cut ropes were left behind. The door was unlocked, not broken in. His guard, one of my footmen, was knocked unconscious. He didn't see the person who hit him, but the length of wood he was attacked with could have been wielded by anyone."

I watched Blackford closely. "When did this happen?"

"Not long before I arrived home after dropping you off."

"So it couldn't have been the princess, and it is very unlikely to have been Nadia. Were some of the staff eliminated from suspicion?" I asked.

"Very few. They all seemed to have been working separately. And none of them saw anyone suspicious loitering nearby."

I shook my head. "Is there any way out of this puzzle, Blackford? The more we learn, the less we know. We have no idea why the Russian guard was killed or by whom, we don't know who the person is in the Hereford household who was working with Ivanov—"

Blackford interrupted me. "Who wasn't a Russian soldier."

CHAPTER NINE

"WHAT?" Sir Broderick gripped the wheels of his chair. "If Ivanov wasn't a Russian soldier, then who was he?"

"We don't know. I checked with the Russian embassy after he escaped. They'd just heard back from St. Petersburg. Someone there checked with the tsar. No one was sent to replace the guard who was killed. Ivanov was an impostor."

"Why? Why go to such an elaborate disguise when there must be easier ways to get into Hereford House?" I asked.

"Into Hereford House, yes. To be there at every step the princess takes, no." The duke steepled his fingers. "And we have another problem. The tsar wants to send one of his household guards now. Whitehall is fighting his request."

"The princess told me she didn't like Ivanov. She won't trust anyone else who comes in and says he's a Russian soldier."

Actually, she'd said she would be terrified by another guard after the bullying, deceitful Ivanov.

The duke smiled faintly. "The duchess said if they send another soldier, she'll ask the princess and her party to leave."

"She was frightened of Ivanov. I'd believe her threat," I told him.

"Won't that hurt relations between the two countries? Especially in light of our feud in the Balkans," Sir Broderick said.

Blackford nodded. "I passed on her message."

"What did Whitehall say?" I asked.

"Besides saying the duchess and I weren't being helpful? I was told to pass on a statement to all of you from Whitehall. Find out who Ivanov is working for, who in the household is aiding him, and what the threat is to Princess Kira. As quickly as possible."

"They don't want much," Grace said.

"Could we convince the duchess to let Nadia stay at her home? That way the princess is less likely to wander off," I suggested.

"Give me the name and address of the people she's staying with, and I'll check them out with my friends on the force," Adam said.

Emma hadn't appeared to have listened to our discussion. Now she looked around the room and said, "Sumner and I will go back into the East End and follow the family. We'll find out if they or Nadia are involved."

"Will you be staying away overnight, frightening Georgia again?" Frances asked, her eyebrows raised.

"If need be, I'll stay down there several nights. You don't need to worry, Georgia. I grew up there. I can take care of myself." Her expression was angry.

What had I done? "I'm sure you can. I care about you, and I worry."

"Well, don't."

The room grew quiet.

Finally, Frances said, "Grace and I will mind the bookshop."

"I'll ask the duchess and then let you know whether to bring Nadia to stay at Hereford House," Blackford said to Emma. Looking around, he added, "Does anyone have any other ideas?"

We shook our heads.

"On the Shepherdston matter, another house had the safe blown up and furniture stolen two days ago. The owners, the Underhills, were away in Scotland shooting, and the servants sent a telegram to them telling them about the attack," Blackford told us. "The servants hadn't informed the police—they were waiting for instructions from the Underhills—and were of little use when the owners had a Scotland Yard inspector sent around.

"This time it was a nosy neighbor across the street who was most helpful. She wrote down the name on the removals company van before they covered the load with a tarp, concealing the name. She said they employed a crew of five. Two men went inside. Two outside loaded the van. The fifth drove the cart. The man in charge was medium height and wiry. And he spoke with a foreign accent. When they left, the driver drove away and the others walked off in different directions."

"Could it be the same people involved in blowing up Shepherdston's safe? Supposedly they spoke to each other in a foreign language," Grace said.

"And the maids at Lord Walker's said the burglars had an accent," Adam Fogarty said. "I'll speak to the neighbor and then talk to the maids again. If you'll give me the name of the removals company, Your Grace, I'll get on to them, too."

Blackford gave him the information and then said as everyone rose to leave, "Sir Broderick, Georgia, I have something for you on a different matter."

Emma was chatting with Jacob as they left the room. She didn't say she'd wait for me like she usually did.

I drew a breath and walked nearer the cloud of heat rolling out of the fireplace. Blackford glanced at the now closed parlor door and said, "Count Farkas has again been in touch with the man who owns the farm where your parents were killed, Georgia. He's somewhere in London."

"I want to see Count Farkas. I want to speak to him. Now." I'd waited over a decade to catch the man who killed my parents. Now that Blackford had learned the killer was back in London, I wanted to meet him that night.

"All right," Blackford said. "After we find Ivanov and stop whatever threat might be following the princess."

"No. I agreed to wait the last time we worked together and he escaped before I could confront him. This time, I want to meet him before he has a chance to leave the country."

The two of us stood in front of Sir Broderick, staring into each other's eyes with gazes that wouldn't give way. I could see the gray flecks in his black eyes darken. I nibbled on my lower lip and watched his mouth form a flat line. He inched toward me and I felt myself sway into him.

"I have a better idea," Blackford finally said.

My eyes narrowed. I didn't trust his "better idea."

"Do you still have the ball gowns you ordered for your Georgina Monthalf disguise?"

"Of course." They must have cost the earth. Blackford paid for them, ensuring they never quite felt like mine. Knowing he'd admired my appearance in them, I would never part with them.

"There's a ball at the Austrian embassy tomorrow night. I'd like you to go as my guest. I will invite Count Farkas to make our acquaintance during the dancing."

Finally, a face-to-face meeting with my parents' killer. "I would love to accompany you, Your Grace."

"Remember," Sir Broderick said, "the Austrian embassy is Austrian soil. You can't arrest him there."

Blast. Would I never get him into police custody? Would I never see him hang?

I let loose a deep breath. "All right. We'll do it your way. But I want a private meeting with him, even if it has to be within the embassy."

"I'll have to introduce you under your given name. No aliases this time."

I smiled at Blackford's words. As if I'd want Count Farkas to think I was anyone but the daughter of the couple he'd killed a dozen years before. I wanted to see his face when I accused him of his sins.

I stomped out of the parlor to find Frances and Jacob waiting by the door. No Emma.

Oh, dear. She was truly angry with me, and I hadn't any idea why. "Where's Emma?"

"Sumner came by a few minutes ago, and the two of them left for the East End. Apparently, Sumner has made contact with a Russian anarchist group and they're going to find out what this group knows about Ivanov and the murder of the Russian soldier."

I opened my mouth to protest, and Frances grabbed my arm. "You'll have to let go sooner or later. Emma is an adult, capable of making her own decisions. Sumner has made inroads with the anarchists, and this may be the break we need."

"Can't he do this alone? This is dangerous." The panic in my voice was unmistakable.

"Georgia, no one is more capable of taking care of herself than

Emma." Blackford gave me his arm and said, "Let me give you a ride home, and you can continue to yell at me about Sumner taking a young lady into the East End for an investigation."

He hustled me outside and led me over to his infernal Wellington carriage. I was so angry I jumped right in without needing assistance. He climbed in after me and signaled his driver to proceed.

I complained, berated, and threatened for five minutes before I noticed we weren't headed toward my home. "Where are we going, Blackford?"

"Just taking a nice evening jaunt around town while you blow off steam like a railway engine." He smiled.

I glared at him, furious that he wasn't upset by Sumner's actions. "I am not blowing off steam, as you so sweetly put it. I'm concerned. I'm worried. I'm distressed."

Blackford leaned forward, and in the light coming in from outside the carriage, I could see his dark eyes staring into my brain. "What is truly bothering you, Georgia? Are you afraid Sumner will ruin Emma and abandon her like you were by your onetime lover?"

I almost struck him in my blind fury. "I was not ruined and abandoned. We were due to get married and the banns were being read when he died. I was devastated. Emma was there for me then. And I want to be here for her now. I truly don't want to see her hurt."

He reached across and surrounded my hand with his. The heat from his body rose up my arm, calming me slightly, although I was still jittery with fear. "What are you most afraid of," he asked me gently, "seeing Emma hurt, or seeing her leave your home and your life?"

"Both." My eyes began to leak the tears I'd held back for days. I groped in my bag for a handkerchief.

Blackford handed me a pristine square of monogrammed white linen and I pulled my hand away to cover my face with the cloth and both hands.

"She's a grown woman, Georgia."

I sniffed loudly. "I wish everyone would stop saying that."

"They would if you didn't keep carrying on like a fool."

"A fool?" Now I was really angry. How dare his high and mighty grace judge me? "I seem to remember you forgetting to report your sister's death for two years."

"That was different."

"How exactly? Because you're a duke and I'm in trade?" I waved his handkerchief like a warning signal.

"No. Because Margaret may have been mad and may have been a killer and could never be allowed to have a family. Emma deserves every happiness she can find." His voice was pitched low, but I could hear the underlying sorrow.

"I'm sorry. I shouldn't have brought up that unfortunate—" Now it was my turn to reach out and pat his hand.

He snatched my hand and held it. "Leave them alone to find their own way."

"How will he ever be able to support a family? He works for you, Your Grace."

I could see his rueful smile in the weak light filtering into the carriage. "I don't pay as badly as all that."

"Still, to raise a family on servant's wages? I'll have to find him work at the bookshop so they can make ends meet."

"They'll be in better shape than you think."

"Emma and Sumner?" Neither had a penny beyond their salaries. I'd bet on it.

"You find that strange?"

I thought of all the times I'd seen them together. They made a fine couple. But. "Neither comes from money. I don't see how Sumner can afford a household and a family. And if he hurts her, Your Grace, I'm coming after both of you."

His smile reached his eyes. "I'd expect nothing less."

THE FOLLOWING DAY at Hereford House was uneventful. The princess began to demonstrate her knowledge of English, giving me all the credit for her quick mastery of the language. The duchess's eyebrows rose skyward, but she said only, "I'm glad you're making such rapid progress." After the princess gave a particularly long statement in English, Lady Raminoff's eyes narrowed and she said, in French, "Perhaps, Miss Peabody, you could teach me to speak English so fluently in only a few days' time."

I had no answer that wouldn't have compounded the lie.

I had little to do in the morning and wandered out into the back garden, where I found Lady Daisy with her governess, Amelia Whitten. They were counting petals on the late-blooming flowers and studying the breeze by watching the clouds. Being around them, listening to Lady Daisy's bright laughter, smelling the dirt carefully turned by the gardener, watching the colors of the leaves soften to red and gold, I found it hard to believe there was any worry or danger in the world.

"What a beautiful day," I said as I joined them.

"Yes, it is," Miss Whitten replied, rising from the stone bench.

"Oh, no. Please sit down," I said to her. "Good morning, Lady Daisy," I added with a curtsy to the little girl.

"Good morning. I can count up to one hundred," she told

me, her chin in the air. She'd be beautiful and leading everyone by the reins in a dozen years.

"You're an accomplished young lady," I said, hoping that was the proper reply.

Daisy skipped off, and I sat on the bench next to Miss Whitten. I turned my face to the sun and said, "How long have you been in the Hereford household?"

"I've been Lady Daisy's governess for a year. I'm not really part of the household."

"How is the duchess to work for?"

"All right. The duchess doesn't need a secretary this time of year. Why are you here?" I could hear the suspicion in her voice.

I turned to look at her and raised my eyebrows. "I've been teaching the princess English. Once she's left London, the duchess plans to work on a book on the history of English painting. I've been hired to help her with writing the book." I put a hand on her arm. "Please don't tell anyone. The duchess doesn't want word of this to leak out."

"Now, who would I know to tell? And why would I do such a thing? I'm not interested in other people's business." She frowned as she turned away, and left my hand hanging in midair. "Please come back, Lady Daisy. We have more of your lesson to do."

She rose then and said, "If you'll excuse me?" and walked off. When Daisy reached her, the governess led the girl by a grip on her arm into the house.

I followed, the beauty of the day dimmed. If the governess knew I was a fraud, who else had already seen through my disguise?

I found Princess Kira in the duchess's studio with the duchess, both of them hard at work on large canvases as they worked in companionable silence. Lady Raminoff sat knitting in a corner.

I stood where I could see both paintings. The duchess worked on a study of one of the servants doing mending, her gray gown and white apron at odds with the bright flowers on the table next to her and the open window in the background. Princess Kira worked on a bowl of fruit in the impressionist style. Around the bowl, she had painted a white cat curled up and licking one paw. She painted the cat from memory.

"Don't lurk," the duchess said without looking at me.

"I need to have a word with you when you're available," I told her and walked over to sit near Lady Raminoff.

"Have they found that dreadful Ivanov?" Lady Raminoff whispered in French.

"Not so far, but we now know he wasn't a guard sent by the tsar or his government."

"Then who—oh, Lord, not an anarchist. It's a wonder we weren't all murdered in our beds!" Her voice rose into a squawk.

"I didn't tell you to alarm you. Only to let you know so if you spot him again, you can escape before he sees you. And tell the duchess where you saw him." I hoped she'd have enough sense to report back and not get a case of the vapors at a critical moment.

She nodded. "I hope he's gone back to Russia and is never seen again."

"But you're going back to Russia soon. Aren't you afraid if he goes back there, he'll be a danger at a later date?"

"We know how to deal with his type at home." Her grim tone told me how Ivanov would be treated if he were caught in St. Petersburg. "The Okhrana will know what to do with him."

"Okhrana?"

"The Russian secret police. The people who keep us safe from anarchists and revolutionaries. And terrible people like Ivanov."

If the two sides kept attacking each other, sooner or later they'd tear their country apart. I was glad British tradition allowed everyone to voice their opinions. Then I remembered the suffragettes and lost my feelings of superiority. But at least the suffragettes hadn't thrown any bombs yet.

"What are Kira and Nadia up to?" Lady Raminoff asked, giving me a sharp look.

"Visiting."

"Kira must have been the one to drug my chocolate. Then Nadia came in and the two of them ran off in the middle of the night. That is hardly a social call."

"What do you think they are doing?"

"Kira is a stupid girl, and Nadia is trying to disgrace the royal family. I asked you to find out what Kira is up to. Tell me."

I gave her a dark look. "There's nothing to tell."

Lady Raminoff glared at me before she turned to indicate Princess Kira and whispered, "She already knew English, didn't she?"

"You'd better ask her," I replied.

"She knew. And you're here because you work for the British secret police. What do you call your Okhrana?"

My eyes widened at the thought of secret police in my country. We were better than that, weren't we? "We don't have secret police. We do have private citizens who assist the regular police and our government when there is a, uh, an unusual situation such as we have here."

"What good would a mere girl be as protection against anarchists?"

I reached out and patted her arm. "Don't worry. There are a lot of people working very hard to keep you and Princess Kira safe."

"But who," Lady Raminoff asked, looking down at her knitting, "is going to save Kira from herself?"

The duchess put away her brush and paints. She rose from her chair and walked over while Lady Raminoff drew a little away from me to focus on her yarn. "Miss Peabody, you wanted a word?"

I rose. "Yes, Your Grace."

"Come with me." I followed her downstairs to the morning room and we settled ourselves on facing chairs. She looked at me through narrowed eyes and said, "Now, what do you need?"

"You make it sound like I'm not the first person to ask for something this morning."

She sighed and her whole body seemed to sag, although she still appeared as rigidly upright as you'd expect a duchess to be. "Princess Kira wants her sister to stay for a visit. Lady Raminoff wants protection provided by the police to keep her safe from Ivanov, who's going to murder her at his first opportunity. My husband does not want to return until this mess is cleared up. My daughter doesn't want a governess. My—"

"How long have you employed Miss Whitten as Lady Daisy's governess?"

The duchess appeared surprised at my question, but she considered a moment before answering. "She arrived a little after we came here for Easter. No, it must have been June. It was about the time Whitehall asked us to welcome Princess Kira into our home. Why?"

"Did she have good references?"

"Of course."

"Did you check them?"

"Her most recent reference left for Australia. The father is first secretary to the governor there, and the whole family left. I haven't been able to reach them yet. And I know her other reference. They moved to Scotland and the wife died. I never followed up. Why?" She peered into my eyes. "You're frightening me."

"I suppose I'm being overly cautious about anyone new to your household. Nothing more specific than that." I didn't think I should tell the duchess that her daughter's governess had lied to me. At least, not yet.

CHAPTER TEN

"A RE you going to have Nadia stay here?" I asked the duchess. "Kira's sister? I suppose so. Kira's maid will have to take care of her. My household is stretched thin enough as it is. This wretched dinner party of Kira's is turning into a state occasion."

"Dinner party?" This added a new difficulty to guarding Princess Kira.

"She's invited the Russian ambassador, his wife, and her cousin, Grand Duke Vassily Alexandrovich, to dinner, along with Sussex and some British diplomats."

"It will make it easier to keep the princess safe with her sister under the same roof." I hated broaching this other subject. "You know Ivanov wasn't sent by the Russians?"

She shuddered. "I never trusted that man."

"I think he was sent to be the inside man in your household."

"Then I'm glad I made him sleep in the carriage house."

"But someone let him loose. Someone in your household?"

"I don't think so. With all this uproar, my household has been thrown off schedule. Anyone could have slipped in through the back garden and released him."

"How easy would it have been to find him?"

"The only place we had to keep him was the game larder. It didn't take much effort to empty it of the little that's left from last fall. Unfortunately, it's close to the back entrance. In fact, it's just below this room."

She drummed her fingers on a side table. "Anyone coming in expecting to find Ivanov in the kitchen or the servants' hall would have come first to that doorway and his guard. If we'd known someone was planning to meet him, we could have taken precautions. As it was, it was easy for him to be freed and escape without anyone being the wiser. Except Sally. Poor Sally."

"And she doesn't remember seeing anyone from outside the household before she ran into Ivanov?"

"No, but she was just coming into the hall from the kitchen when she ran into him."

My theory that an anarchist was hiding in the Duchess of Hereford's household was weak. "Since it's becoming widely known that the princess speaks English, I'm putting it around that I'm to help you with a book you're writing on the history of painting in England."

The duchess made a sour face. "All right, as long as we can drop that as soon as the princess leaves."

"Gladly. What is she doing about telling Sussex she speaks English?"

"She plans to learn from you very quickly and let him be amazed at how intelligent she is."

I laughed. "She doesn't think her fiancé is very bright and she plans to use it to her advantage. Poor Sussex. He doesn't stand a chance."

The duchess bit back a smile. "But he'll make her happy, and that is its own kind of brilliance."

Poor Sussex, as I began to think of him, arrived for luncheon by himself as I was crossing the front hall with the duchess. I stayed in the background while the duchess walked forward to greet him and sent a maid to ask the princess to join them.

"I expected Blackford to come with you. You two seem to be inseparable," the duchess said.

"He's a good friend, helping me lose my shyness around Kira. But he couldn't make it today. Something about a meeting in Whitehall. I suppose I'll have to impress the princess on my own." Sussex smiled, looking a little uncertain.

I hoped someone would tell him he didn't have to impress Kira. She needed this marriage as much as he did.

"She's very fond of you, Arthur. I'm sure you're going to have a wonderful life ahead of you." The duchess took his arm. "Let's wait for Kira in the dining room."

They walked off, and I went back to the morning room to try to piece together what I'd learned. And to worry about Emma.

I'D LEARNED NOTHING more by the time Blackford came to take me to the Austrian embassy ball. I wore a pale green gown with a beaded design in the skirt, flounces in the sleeves, and very little bodice. Phyllida had done the best she could with my hair, but we both missed the success Emma had with controlling my curls.

The duke was politeness itself. He bowed over both my hand and Phyllida's, put my cape over my shoulders, and wished Phyllida a good evening. Then he led me outside and said, "There are those in Whitehall who don't want us confronting Count Farkas tonight."

"Why? Do they want to do it themselves?" I grumbled, knowing the response would be negative.

"The Austro-Hungarian Empire is the counterbalance to Russia, to the Ottoman Empire, and to Germany, depending on the issue. It saves Britain a lot of diplomacy and possibly bloodshed. No one wants to upset the Emperor Franz Joseph."

"And Count Farkas?"

"Is a leading supporter of Austria inside Hungary. Not to put too fine a point on it, but Franz Joseph needs Farkas, and we need the emperor." He helped me into his tall Wellington carriage and climbed up behind me.

I sat next to him, bracing myself for a jerky ride in the ancient coach, and snapped, "Murder is fine as long as the murderer is necessary to British diplomacy."

How could Blackford consider diplomatic necessity more important than justice? I thought he shared my goal. I was wrong and it hurt. I scooted over on the seat to put more distance between us.

He captured my gloved hand. "No, Georgia, it's not all right. Someday we'll be able to get Count Farkas in front of a judge, but don't expect any success tonight. With luck, we'll learn something we can use in the future."

We? "Are you including yourself in the quest to see justice for the deaths of my parents?"

He held my gaze, neither of us blinking as we jolted along. "I can't think of any cause I'd rather be part of."

Blackford was going to help me. He understood. I wanted to shout with joy. What I did instead was to shake the hand that held mine across the carriage bench. "Thank you so much, Your Grace."

"The pleasure is mine, Miss Fenchurch." He gave me a solemn nod.

Then we grinned at each other like a pair of fools. Tomorrow, we'd continue running in circles trying to figure out why a Russian soldier had been killed on British soil. Tonight, we were happy to be working toward a different goal while taking part in a glittering ball. At least that was why I was smiling. I was never sure about Blackford.

When we reached the embassy entrance, Blackford exited the coach first and then swung me down from the carriage, hands on my waist. Knowing this wasn't proper, my cheeks heated, but my heartbeat sped with the thrill. Fortunately, the torches threw their light on the grand entrance to the embassy, so no one would notice our behavior in the half-light of the street.

He took my arm and guided me inside, giving our names as the Duke of Blackford and Miss Fenchurch. This was a first, since I always seemed to be in disguise when we were in public together. We handed off our evening cloaks and walked forward to the receiving line in the great hall.

The hall seemed to be all black and white marble. Floor, walls, columns, busts in alcoves. A perfect cold, shiny backdrop for the gowns and jewels. With only Phyllida's pearls at my ears and throat, I was woefully underdressed.

Blackford didn't seem to notice. He kept a proprietary hand on my back, leading me forward to be introduced to the couple in front of us in line. My jaw dropped when I understood Blackford to say in French, "Monsieur Ambassador. How are our friends in Paris?"

I recovered before the ambassador bowed over my hand and I then stumbled over a few pleasantries in French with the man and his wife. Born diplomats, they didn't laugh at my poor accent or the way I stared at the woman's Worth gown. I'd never been envious of clothes before, but then, I'd never been this close to a gown fresh from the *maison* of the master. The shimmering fabric alone must have cost a fortune.

Suddenly I felt like my beaded, pale green gown could just as easily be worn to clean the kitchen.

At least the kitchen would have been warm. The magnificent high-ceilinged reception hall had no visible heat source, and I was not the only woman with bare upper arms of gooseflesh. I envied the men their evening coats and uniform jackets.

I gave a deep curtsy as I went through the receiving line, and received a nod in return. Blackford rated a bow. Then we entered the ballroom, a huge space with crystal chandeliers powered by electricity and a wooden floor polished until it shone like glass. Along the edges of the room were yellow satin cushioned chairs with intricately carved, curved legs and backs. The walls were covered in silk dyed to match the chair cushions. The double-headed eagle coat of arms, emblem of the Austro-Hungarian Empire, was mounted in gilt paint on the wall above the orchestra.

Blackford, elegant in pure black wool as soft as silk, acted as if I were one of the queen's granddaughters. He was all good manners, keeping up a conversation while I gazed at all around me. He translated the greetings he shared with a German minister and an Italian count whose names I didn't catch, giving me a slight opening into those exchanges.

The orchestra was playing a waltz as more and more couples joined in, swaying across the floor in a bobbing motion. It looked like a rainbow sea of glitter and smelled like a garden.

The duke steered me toward one tall, thin man with a chest full of medals and a sash on his evening coat. "Grand Duke Vassily Alexandrovich, I didn't realize you'd reached London. How are you?" Blackford asked in English.

"My dear duke, it is good to see you again. I only arrived today." They shook hands enthusiastically.

"Then I suspect we'll meet at some government negotiations in the coming days."

"The tsar sent me to head our delegation this time, and we have a great number of issues to discuss. I won't have a minute to breathe. I fear this trip will be all work."

"Surely you'll have an opportunity to meet with Princess Kira and her fiancé, the Duke of Sussex. That should count as a pleasure."

"For me, perhaps. For you young people, not so much."

They both smiled at this and then Blackford said, "May I introduce Miss Fenchurch?"

The man took my gloved hand and bowed over it. "Enchanted."

"Grand Duke, I've had the honor of meeting Princess Kira," I said to him. "Are you related to her?" As a greeting, it lacked finesse. But then, I was feeling my lack as well.

"She is a cousin as well as a countryman. And soon she will become your countryman, too."

"Yes. Apparently, her sister moved to England ahead of her."

"Her sister?" He looked startled. Then his expression cleared. "Oh, you mean Nadia. Half sister. I don't envy you having Nadia and her friends in your country."

"Really? Why?"

I stared at him, and unfortunately, he seemed to realize this wasn't a conversation to have at a diplomatic ball. He gave me a tight-lipped smile. "Everyone should have a chance to change their ways. I should not have spoken out of turn."

He turned to Blackford and bowed. "I hope to see you again soon, my friend. And it was delightful to meet you, Miss Fenchurch."

When we were on our own again, I asked, "Blackford, why is a Russian minister in town? Isn't the tsar leaving Scotland for home in a day or two?"

"I think so. But Grand Duke Vassily is here for consultations with the ambassador and Whitehall that have been scheduled for quite some time. His visit is separate from the tsar's holiday with the queen."

Something in his tone made me study the duke's face. "What's wrong with that?"

"He's just added talks with the Admiralty and Scotland Yard."

"Is something up?"

"You've been around Princess Kira long enough to know something is always up with the Russians."

"And he's her cousin? Do all the Russians speak English?"

"The royal family does. Grand Duke Vassily is the tsar's uncle, and a second cousin once removed of Princess Kira's. I think." He shook his head. "I try not to fixate on the relationships between all these Russian royals."

I looked at him closely and saw the hint of humor in his eyes.

The orchestra began to play another tune and dancers changed partners or left the dance floor. "May I have the honor of this dance?" Blackford murmured in my ear. His breath brushed my skin, warming it as a tremor of excitement ran straight to my brain.

All I could manage was to nod eagerly.

A man approached Blackford on his other side. "Duke. We need to talk. About the railways," he said in heavily accented English.

Blackford nodded to the finely dressed gentleman. "Have you spoken to Van der Lysson? He's here tonight, too."

"Yes. A couple of the other partners are here as well. We're going to have a meeting now."

Blackford turned to me. "Georgia, I'm sorry. This is business. I'll return as quickly as I can, and then we'll have our waltz."

I smiled and curtsied to him as he bowed. Inside, I was deflated, but I tried to mask my disappointment.

He walked off with the portly, middle-aged man and I was certain I was already forgotten. I wandered around the edge of the room, watching the dancers twirl across the floor and listening to the Babel of voices that filled the air around me.

The swarm of bodies had warmed the room enough that I was no longer freezing. Unfortunately, their heavy use of clashing scents made me want to sneeze. No one glanced my way. I felt very unroyal in this illustrious gathering.

Many of the men were dressed in the uniforms of their country's armies, and their costumes were more colorful than the ladies'. The rows of medals on their chests gleamed brighter than many of the ladies' jewels. There was much to see and report back to Emma and Phyllida.

No, just Phyllida. My mood sank lower.

A page in a red uniform with gold braid approached me and, bowing, handed me a note. I took it and read handwriting now familiar from the notes he'd sent to the bookshop.

Follow the page to the mezzanine and join me in the parlor.

Count Farkas

Finally, I was going to meet my parents' killer.

I could scarcely contain my satisfaction. I was going to face the evil man and Blackford wasn't there to stem my brutal remarks. And they would be brutal. He'd killed three people in London and who knew how many others around the world. I envisioned myself burning this shameless man into abject misery with my scalding tongue.

It was too bad I wasn't allowed to have him arrested in the embassy. Perhaps I could have the police waiting when he left the ball.

I rounded the floor on the page's heels and climbed the red-carpeted staircase to the mezzanine. The music was muted on this level but the sweeping sounds of the waltz were still clear. Several couples walked past me in close conversation. None of them looked my way as I was shown into the parlor.

There were people on this landing and on the floor below to hear me if I screamed. I'd be safe enough if Count Farkas were so foolish as to try to harm me.

The man I'd learned was Count Farkas rose from a gold-brocade-covered sofa and bowed. His silver hair gleamed in the light from the chandelier. He was as neatly and crisply dressed as Blackford, but his jacket held a line of medals. I was glad Blackford would never dress with such ostentation.

The door shut behind me with a solid thud, and I looked around to find the room was windowless. Red silk covered every inch of the walls, including the backs of the doors. I could no longer hear the orchestra.

"Don't worry. We won't be disturbed. The walls of this room are very thick," he said, walking toward me.

Good. My words would be freer without an audience. Still, I'd have been happy to know a rescue party could hear me if I needed to be saved from this madman.

"Won't you sit down, Miss Fenchurch?"

"I won't stay that long." And I was staying between Count Farkas and the door, just in case.

"Are you certain?" When I continued to glare at him, he said, "Very well." He remained standing several feet away from me, his icy pale eyes holding no emotion. "I am Count Farkas. If you would prefer, you may use the anglicized translation, Mr. Wolf."

I had no idea how long I had before someone broke up our meeting so I jumped directly to the question I most wanted to ask. I took two small steps toward him and glared. "Are you going to deny that you murdered my parents?"

CHAPTER ELEVEN

"DEAR me, child, is that how it appeared to you? An accident, I assure you. Please, sit down, and I'll explain." Count Farkas used the courtly diplomatic tone I'd heard all over the ballroom tonight in a dozen different languages.

"You mean lie." I remained where I was, unwilling to match his conciliatory attitude. I found I was beginning to quiver with anger.

"No. I swear to you, in an oath on my honor, that your parents' deaths were an accident. I began the fire simply to warm your parents. Your mother complained of the cold in the cottage."

"It was a warm day."

"But stone cottages seem to capture the cold in their walls, don't you think?"

Despite my best efforts, I asked, "What happened?" I don't know why I bothered to ask. I was sure to be lied to.

"The fireplace failed. A problem caused by repairs being done to the cottage." He held his hands out, palms toward me, as if saying, *None of this was my fault.*

"You escaped. They didn't."

"I thought they were right behind me."

"They were tied to their chairs," I shouted at him. How could anyone be so dense?

He scowled. "Why do you say that?"

"I saw them."

"Then why didn't you untie them?"

A question I'd fought with every day since then. "The fire was too far advanced. Sir Broderick was leading the way through the flames. A beam collapsed, landing on Sir Broderick right in front of me. By the time I pulled him out, it was too late. The whole building collapsed."

"You pulled a grown man out of there? You were little more than a child. That was very resourceful of you." His smile was as cold as his eyes.

"I had no choice. He was pinned to the floor by the beam."

"So you made a choice. You saved Sir Broderick and left your parents to die. You were the one who didn't save your parents. Not me."

Now I was shaking. "You tied them up. You started the fire. You took us there at gunpoint." I yelled the words at him. His expression never changed.

"You seem to be upsetting yourself, Miss Fenchurch. Tell me, how is your romance with the duke progressing?"

I blinked at him. "Romance? With Blackford?"

"I see how you look at each other. How you work in harmony. None of this would have happened if your parents hadn't died. You should thank me, Miss Fenchurch."

"Thank you for murdering my parents? Are you mad?" I'd gone back to shouting.

"If your father had simply told me where the Gutenberg Bible was, none of this unpleasantness would have happened. And you would never have met Blackford." He never raised his voice. His tone remained reasonable.

"My father didn't know where the Bible was. He couldn't tell you. And you murdered him for it."

"His death, and your mother's, dear lady, was an accident. If I'd known how weakened the structure was, I never would have taken them there."

"Why did you? Why not talk in our bookshop?"

"With all the traffic in the street? I couldn't trust your father not to lie to me. I needed to convince him to tell me the truth."

"And Denis Lupton? Did he need persuading?"

"Your father and Lupton worked together to defraud me."

When I opened my mouth to protest, he held up a hand to silence me.

"Yes. They were involved in taking my Gutenberg Bible and hiding my possession away from recovery. I wanted what was mine." For the first time, his voice held passion.

I could barely make a sound as I gasped out the words. "You're more concerned with a book than with human lives?" He truly was mad.

"That book is more than three hundred years old. Neither your father nor Lupton would have lasted that long."

I stalked toward him. "That doesn't give you the right to kill them."

He shrugged his shoulders. The smooth black fabric of his suit absorbed the light from the wall sconces. "They had no right to steal from me."

"That's your answer? To meet a wrong with a greater wrong?"

"The Bible says an eye for an eye."

I would never win this argument with a man who'd made up his mind years ago. "The Bible also says, Judge not, lest ye be judged. In this case, good advice, since my father had nothing to do with Lupton or your Gutenberg."

"Your father knew what Lupton did with my Bible. If he'd trusted me with the information instead of foolishly protecting Lupton, he and your mother would have been immediately released."

He sighed and paced a few steps. "I now know your father wasn't in possession of my Gutenberg, since you moved your residence and your bookshop. You didn't take my Bible with you, nor did you leave it behind hidden in a wall or under the floorboards. I was sorely disappointed that your move didn't uncover my Gutenberg."

Then he turned to me and in his most understanding, malicious tone, he added, "You've done much better with the bookshop than your father did. Better location, nicer store, more stock. You have a natural flair for bookselling, unlike your father."

"How dare you speak of my father like that? He was a good man. A good father." My fists and my stomach muscles clenched in a half-conscious desire to fight.

"No doubt he was a good father, but not a good salesman. He couldn't even convince me of the truth. That he had no idea where my Gutenberg Bible was."

"You killed my parents for nothing." I tried to keep a sob out of my voice as I leaned on the back of a chair to help me stay upright.

"An unfortunate circumstance."

"An unfortunate—!" I stepped around the chair as fury strengthened my limbs. I would have hit him if the door hadn't opened at that moment. Blackford walked in, accompanied by the man who'd greeted me coolly in the receiving line. Apparently, ambassadors don't like to welcome nobodies.

Count Farkas bowed and said, "Your Excellency."

"I am ready for our meeting now, Count."

I gave the ambassador the deep curtsy his title demanded. The count bowed to me and I gave him a cold stare. Then the two foreigners strolled out of the room. I shook with unrelieved anger. Blackford walked over to me and said, "Georgia. I'm sorry."

"For what? Because the count killed my parents over a misunderstanding? Because he now calls it an unfortunate circumstance? Because he values books more than human life?"

"Yes."

I tipped my head up, trying to keep the tears brimming in my eyes from rolling down my cheeks.

Feeling something shoved into my hand, I looked down and found another of Blackford's monogrammed handkerchiefs. As I mopped my eyes, I said, "How many of these do you carry with you?"

"As many as I think may be needed in the course of an evening. Knowing you'd meet Farkas tonight, I thought to be prepared."

Laughing and crying at once, I threw my arms around Blackford's shoulders. He embraced me as I sobbed on his smooth jacket. He murmured in my ear and rubbed my back, assuring me this wouldn't be the end of our dealings with Count Farkas. The man wouldn't always be protected.

"I think I'm upset because he was right. My parents' deaths were my fault. I chose to pull Sir Broderick out of the fire first. If I'd left and run around to the back of the structure, I could have pulled them out. At least one of them. Instead I chose Sir Broderick, and my parents died."

"No, Georgia, none of that was your fault."

"I feel like I made the wrong choice."

Blackford held me at arm's length. "No. You did the best you could. You started with the problem in front of you and then went on to the next one. If you had decided to run around the outside of the house and then broken in, giving the fire more time and oxygen, they might all have died, and you with them." He pulled me close again and ran his gloved hand up and down my back. "You should be proud of what you succeeded in doing. Don't feel guilty. You made the best choice you could. A choice no seventeen-year-old girl should have to make."

Slowly, his words and his touch took effect and I regained control over my emotions. Two words penetrated my whirling mind. *Our dealings.* I looked up at Blackford and wiped my face on his handkerchief. "Did you mean what you said? That we would try to bring Count Farkas to justice together?"

"Yes. As long as you are looking for justice and not revenge."

"I hope I'm looking for justice in the deaths of my parents. In moments of grief, I fear I want revenge. Is that wrong?"

"No."

With that one word, my heart soared.

"As long as when you act, it is to bring Count Farkas to justice."

I nodded, and then I glanced at his sodden jacket. "Oh, Your Grace. I am so sorry."

He lifted my chin with one forefinger. "Don't worry about it. I have a very good valet. But I think we should leave now, and from the looks of your face, I think it should be by the side entrance. Otherwise, I might get a reputation as a cad."

"You could never be that, Blackford."

"I'm glad you think so."

Smiling, he escorted me out another door and along an empty

corridor. Then we walked down a dark stairwell and a narrow hall to the front entrance, where we picked up our cloaks and Blackford retrieved his top hat. I could hear a beehive full of voices, but none of the revelers were in sight. They must all have been in the ballroom. Dancing the waltz I'd wanted and now wouldn't have with the duke.

I was glad we didn't meet any of the other guests. My face must have looked as devastated as I felt.

The duke's carriage appeared after a minute's delay and Blackford lifted me inside. My limbs were as limp as day-old lettuce. Then he climbed in, sat down beside me, and held my hand.

"Count Farkas took three lives here and who knows how many elsewhere and he feels no remorse. He called murdering my parents, who had nothing to do with his stupid Bible, an unfortunate circumstance. He thinks of their deaths as an accident. A misunderstanding. Oh, Blackford, I feel dirty just from being in the same room with him."

"He didn't hurt you, did he?"

"He never touched me. I did, however, want to hurt him."

In the light spilling into the carriage from the lamps outside, I saw him smile. "I bet you did."

We sat in silence for a little while, listening to the clop of the horse hooves on the pavement. Slowly, I gained mastery of my nerves.

"The business I was called away on—"

"That prevented us from waltzing," I said, my waspishness a sign I wasn't completely in control of my tongue yet.

"I am sorry about that. I'm also sorry that the meeting left me with the feeling that our American partners are trying to cheat us. I'll have to sail to New York soon."

That grabbed my full attention. "No. Blackford, we have an investigation to complete."

"I promise I'll not leave until it's finished, but then I'll be gone for some time. I have a series of investments in Canada and the United States and it's been quite a while since I visited them."

"And you're being cheated on one of them?"

"I fear so. It makes me wonder what is happening with the rest of them." He put his arm around me and pulled me close. "But right now, you have all my attention. You and our investigation."

I could have done without his words telling me he'd soon sail to America to check on his investments. First I felt abandoned by Emma. Now Blackford. What was next? My stomach churned with sorrow and frustration.

"Emma. Sumner. What are they doing? Do you know?" I asked him.

"I know he loves her. I know he'd die before he'd let anyone harm her. They're all right. Don't worry."

"But I do."

"I'd worry about your bookshop if I were you."

I shifted to stare into his eyes. "What has happened to my bookshop?"

"Nothing. How can you not see it?"

I settled with my head against his shoulder. "I feel like Emma has been sneaking around with Sumner lately. I know she's fond of him. But I know nothing with certainty."

"Neither do they. When they make up their minds, they'll tell us. So we must be patient and wait."

Tears sprang up again unexpectedly and I swiped at them with Blackford's soggy handkerchief. I was going to lose Emma. I was sure of it. And I was going to miss her. Just as I would miss the duke.

"You can't hold her back."

"I'd never dream of it. But I'll miss her. She's been like the little sister I never had. She was maybe thirteen, uneducated, dirty, and undernourished, when she was captured in the course of a murder investigation by Scotland Yard. She's lived with Phyllida and me ever since."

"I didn't know that," Blackford said. "Does Sumner?"

"I suspect she's told him. Especially since they're working in the East End, where she lived before her arrest and subsequent placement in my home."

"How did she end up living with you?"

"Emma and the gang of thieves she worked with were inside a house when a murder occurred. They were caught and charged with the crime. The Archivist Society was hired by the son of the victim, who suspected a business associate of his father was the true murderer. The son turned out to be right. Sir Broderick went to school with one of London's top barristers and convinced him to take Emma's case. The barrister convinced the judge to let her live with Phyllida and me."

I reached up and put a finger over Blackford's lips. "Please don't mention it to anyone. I don't want Emma embarrassed by her past. But you've become so much a part of our work—"

"I'm honored that you trust me. Ah, here we are." He banged on the roof of the carriage with his cane and the driver immediately pulled over. He opened the door and climbed down, then reached up and lifted me to the ground.

Instead of stopping in front of our building, the carriage, I found, had placed us along the Victoria Embankment on a stretch of pavement overlooking the Thames. "Why are we stopping here?"

Blackford bowed to me. "May I have this waltz?"

I laughed with joy as I gave him my hand, and we began to dance along the sidewalk as he hummed "The Blue Danube Waltz."

It was a very staid waltz. He performed none of his sweeping movements from the ballroom. We swayed in time to his tune, our clothes brushing as we moved, our shoes bumping against each other's. Still, it felt heavenly to be held in his arms. My dancing slippers barely touched the concrete.

Reflections from the streetlamps on the bridges flickered on the waters of the Thames. Horse hooves from passing coaches clicked their accompaniment to the duke's humming. Trees made a live canopy above us. No ballroom had ever been as magical.

The duke turned his head so he could reach my lips with his.

Our faces hovered inches apart. Our gazes were locked on each other's eyes. Blackford stopped humming. His eyes appeared to grow darker as my eyelids fluttered closed. The longing became unbearable and we shifted closer until our lips touched.

I felt warm and breathless, and I was conscious only of Blackford. Marveling at how such a stern face could hold such a gentle mouth. Breathing in his scents of brandy, smoke, and fresh linens dried in cold air. Reveling in his constant assault on my emotions.

I don't know how long the kiss lasted. I finally realized we'd stopped dancing when the duke pulled away and murmured, "I'm going to miss you during my travels."

"I'll miss you, too, Your Grace."

"Then I'll have to make my journey as short as possible."

CHAPTER TWELVE

EMMA didn't return that night. Few words were exchanged between Phyllida and me at the breakfast table. She gazed glumly at her porridge, stirring it constantly, and she didn't carry the extra burden of knowing she'd soon miss Blackford as well.

I decided to bring up the person whose absence worried us both into silence. "She's fine, Aunt Phyllida," I said, using her honorary title. "Blackford assures me Sumner would lay down his life to protect her."

"That's what worries me. His death would crush her. Just as her death would crush us." She shoved her bowl of porridge aside uneaten.

"No one is going to hurt Emma, and no one is going to hurt Sumner. They'll both return in fine shape as soon as they learn what the anarchists are doing. Then they'll take us both to task for being silly."

Phyllida rose and gave me a shaky smile. "You're right. Now, you need to check on the bookshop before you go sleuthing for the day, and I need to make up my marketing list before the Ternbulls come for the laundry."

I had on my hat and gloves and was heading for the door when Phyllida popped her head out of the kitchen. "Georgia, I've been thinking about what you told me last night about the count. I think you should be very careful of your surroundings. He's a Hungarian, and I've heard they're all crazy."

"He's crazy enough to think his explanation is sufficient. I don't need to worry about him. He needs to worry about me."

"You don't think he'll attack you since he admitted he killed your parents? You're a danger to him."

"He has diplomatic immunity. Also, he thinks of me as an unimportant middle-class bookseller who doesn't have his precious Gutenberg. I'm not important enough for him to bother with."

All of Phyllida's fears and insecurities were written on her face.

I gave her a big smile. "Don't worry about me. Worry about that shopping list."

When I arrived at the bookshop, I discovered the front door unlocked. I doubted Frances had arrived before me, and Grace didn't have a key. Had they left the shop unlocked all night?

I entered quietly, looking around the unlit space. Enough sunlight came in the front windows that I could tell by a quick glance that no one lurked among the shelves. The back hall and office would be a different matter, though. I picked up the duster I kept behind the counter and moved forward cautiously. It wasn't much of a weapon. I'd have felt safer with Emma and her knife. Drat that girl for not being there.

I stopped at the entrance to the back hall and saw motion in the office. "Who's there?" I called out, lowering my voice to hide any quavering.

My heart jumped as I saw more motion. Someone was coming out of the office. Had Frances Atterby chosen today of all days to arrive early? Had I misjudged Count Farkas? Had someone used a skeleton key to break into my shop?

Clutching the feather duster with its wooden handle, I stood my ground. Blood rushed to my head, taking my breath away with it.

"I thought you'd never come in," Emma said, stepping forward. Sumner was right behind her.

"What are you doing here?" Not the brightest reply, but it was hard to think with my heart galloping around my chest.

"We can't meet at home. We suspect that we were followed. So we're here to rob you." She shrugged and added, "It's as good an excuse as any."

I stared at Emma as she made her matter-of-fact statement. "I think you'd better tell me what's going on."

"We've joined a group of anarchists. Russians mostly, but a few Poles, Hungarians, and native English East Enders. Ivanov is involved with them."

"He doesn't know who you are?" I thought back over my travels with Princess Kira to meet her sister and my meeting with Nadia in the East End.

"No. I saw him when Nadia escaped, but he didn't see us. He didn't seem interested in catching her, fortunately. Still, he doesn't trust us."

"He didn't like my boots." Sumner's rough voice cut through the air between us.

I looked down. Sumner wore the handcrafted, smooth leather boots he always wore no matter the disguise. They appeared to be his one concession to comfort. "Be careful. Ivanov is a crafty, dangerous man. If he doesn't trust you, you're in trouble."

"Sumner was brilliant. He knew how to convince Ivanov. He

started a fight about it, saying he'd stolen them from his last master when he was fired. Said they fit like a dream. Said he'd kill rather than give them up. They're all a bit frightened of him now." Emma smiled at him with pride.

"We took Nadia to Hereford House early this morning," Sumner added in his familiar rumble. "She's safely out of there until we find out what they have planned."

"So they have something planned?"

Emma nodded. "It's the reason the guard was killed. To slip Ivanov in. We learned Ivanov killed the guard and stole a button and an epaulet so they could be copied. A tailor in the group made his uniform. I made friends with the tailor and he told me. He's afraid of Ivanov."

"Is Ivanov there to learn the layout of the house?"

"No. They have someone else inside for that. He carried messages and a package. Now, we need to steal a few pounds from you in coins." Emma gave me a grin.

"You've wanted to do this since you first heard about the bookshop. And Phyllida thinks you're so respectable," I teased her. There was nothing funny about the situation, but I couldn't show how afraid I was for them. It wouldn't help. "I've got a small burlap sack in the office for coins. Use that."

"Blackford will make it up to you," Sumner said, backing up so Emma and I could fit into the crowded office. "Tell him to take it out of my wages."

I ignored his words. Sumner would need all his wages to provide a home for Emma.

"If he asks, Sumner said he was hired by the duke for muscle, and then fired after the job was done. He refused to say what the job was," Emma told me as she dropped coins into the sack.

"What's the plan? Who are the targets?"

"We don't know the plan, but the princess is the target. Plus someone else."

"Sussex?" I asked.

"No, I don't think Sussex is a target. Most of the anarchists, led by a man named Mukovski, talk a lot about revolution all over Europe but they have no plans to fight with anyone. The attack will come from Ivanov and a couple of others. And Ivanov's people don't seem to be upset about who might be hurt. Whatever it is should happen in the next few days." Emma cinched up the sack, handed it to Sumner, and added, "Wait a couple of minutes before you raise the alarm. And put on a good performance."

"I will. Good luck. And be careful." I hugged her.

"Tell Aunt Phyllida not to worry." With a nod to Sumner, Emma walked out of the bookshop by the unlocked front door. Sumner followed, shutting the door quietly behind him.

I watched them out the window, glad there was still little traffic in the lane. Then I went back into the office, leaving the safe door open. I lay down on the dirty floor and then disheveled my hair as I rose again. I counted to ten and then walked slowly to the front door.

Knowing they'd be around the corner on the main road by now, I walked out, holding my head and calling, "Help. Police," in a feeble voice. The jeweler's apprentice from next door and Grace, arriving to help out at the bookshop, appeared at the same time.

I caught Grace's eye and she urged the apprentice to find a bobby while she took care of me. She helped me inside while the lad ran off and then whispered, "What's going on?"

I murmured in return, "I heard from Emma and Sumner. The robbery was a ruse to talk to me. They were being followed. Just play along."

"Tell me later," she said as the jeweler and the wife of the greengrocer filled the doorway. A boy selling a halfpenny broad-sheet preaching revolution and equality craned his neck to see what the excitement was.

I told my story twice, once to them and then again to the bobby. I sniffed and moaned and said how two men had forced their way in when I arrived and threatened me to make me open the safe. They'd hit me on the head and knocked me out. When I revived, I found money taken from the safe and the men gone.

Frances arrived while I was telling the bobby my tale of woe and she and Grace sprang into action, ushering out the other merchants from our street and encouraging me to go home and rest. They'd take care of the shop for the day.

Since I had to hurry to get to Hereford House, I readily agreed. As soon as the bobby left, I told them what I'd learned from Emma and Sumner and walked home to change clothes.

Phyllida took one look at me and said, "It's a good thing the Ternbulls haven't arrived for the laundry yet. Quick. Get out of those clothes. What have you been rolling in?"

I told her part of what Emma had told me, focusing on how, because someone was following her and Sumner, she couldn't come home to see Phyllida. I also told her what Emma had said: that this would only be for a few more days.

I didn't tell her the anarchists planned to attack shortly.

WHEN I FINALLY arrived at Hereford House that morning, I found excitement had already arrived. After I left my gloves and hat on the table in the back hall with those of Amelia Whitten, Lady Daisy's governess, I went upstairs to see if either the princess or the duchess needed me. In truth, I wanted to see how Nadia fit into the household.

I met the duchess coming down the hall with her lips pursed together and clutching her hands in fists. "Never invite Russians into your home. Never," she told me as she walked by in the direction of her painting studio.

At least she hadn't noticed I'd arrived late.

Knocking on the door of Princess Kira's room, I found myself instantly facing Lady Raminoff. "Ungrateful wench," she said in French.

"Pardon, madame," I said, wondering what I'd done now.

"Not you," she snapped. "Nadia wants her hair dressed like Kira's, and Mila refuses to wait on a bastard dropped on her by Kira's whim. The duchess says she has no one to spare to be lady's maid to Nadia, which sounds like a poorly managed household to me. And I'm being moved to another room so Nadia can stay in here with Kira while they plan their crazy behavior. Such boldness."

"Who's Mila?" I asked the room in general in English.

"She is." Nadia pointed at a young, thin, dark-haired woman in a black dress, who unleashed a stream of loud Russian back at her. I'd not seen the maid since the day the Russians had arrived.

Kira responded in a nasty tone in Russian, interrupted by Lady Raminoff shouting something short. The room fell silent.

"Princess Kira," I said in French, hoping Nadia and Mila wouldn't understand my questions of the princess, "how long has Mila worked for you?"

"Not long. She was lady's maid to a friend in St. Petersburg. When she heard where I was going, she begged to come along as my maid. My own maid didn't want to leave Russia, so I agreed."

"How did you know about Nadia's story?" I asked Mila in French.

She looked at me blankly.

I asked again in English and she answered in a thick accent, "The story is all over St. Petersburg. Anarchists attack important people all the time. But there is no reason to attack this woman or her mother. They are unimportant. Whores. Beneath contempt."

This was where I expected her to spit on the floor. Fortunately for the duchess's expensive Turkish carpet, Mila restrained herself.

Unfortunately for all of us, Nadia unleashed a stream of vindictive English. "At least my father is somebody. A prince. Who's your father? Nothing."

"At least he married my mother. She wasn't a whore, like yours."

Then the name-calling began in earnest. In English. I discovered the Russians knew words I'd never before heard a woman utter. I was glad Lady Raminoff didn't speak English.

It was abundantly clear Mila wouldn't be serving as lady's maid to Nadia. "Princess Kira, I suggest you ask the duchess to have an agency send over a lady's maid and you will pay the woman's salary."

I forgot to switch back to French and so did Princess Kira. "I pay for nothing. Embassy pays my bills."

"Then you'd better ask the ambassador, nicely, to pay for your sister's lady's maid."

She gave a sniff. "I write him letter."

While she readied stationery and ink, I turned to Lady Raminoff and spoke in French. "I think we've found a solution, if the ambassador will go along with the idea."

She gave an unladylike snort. "He's already grumbling about her bills and her behavior. I've been ordered to keep her in line."

"At least the Duke of Sussex is happy with her."

"And he's the one who must be. I suppose we should be grateful for that." She gave me a weak smile before returning to her chair to work on her embroidery.

I joined Kira as she finished her letter. "Would you post this to the embassy, Miss Peabody?"

"Of course, Princess." I curtsied and left the room, searching for the duchess on my way downstairs.

I found her engrossed in her painting. She looked up after a moment and said, "I suppose I asked for all that has befallen me, since I agreed to have the princess stay here."

I waved the message the princess had given me for posting. "The princess has written the ambassador, asking him to pay for a lady's maid for Nadia while she stays here. The lady's maid is to come from the agency you use. Is that satisfactory, Your Grace?"

She smiled. "Very. Good for you for suggesting what I can't say within the bounds of good manners."

"The princess has been an expensive visitor?"

"It's worse than entertaining our royalty. She takes the carriage whenever she wants; orders new clothes she doesn't plan to pay for and has them sent to this address, which will hurt my reputation with tradesmen; then she plans an elaborate dinner party at my home using my servants, my food, and my silver; her maid steals food from the pantry; they disrupt—"

"Her maid, Mila, steals food?" I was certain the duchess fed her servants well, and that would include Mila.

"Yes. And so far my cook and housekeeper haven't been able to figure out what she does with it. It's too much for a little thing like her to eat."

"They can ask her. She speaks English. I learned some new words today, but nothing that can be used in polite company. Mila and Nadia could both teach me how to curse, and it's my native tongue, not theirs."

"Mila speaks English? I've been told by the servants and by

Kira that her lady's maid can't speak English. Of course, we all thought Kira couldn't speak English, either." The duchess looked pensive.

"The Russians, at least the ones I've met, are a deceptive bunch." And I couldn't wait for them to leave. I was constantly trailed by fear for Emma and Sumner's safety.

The anarchists Emma and Sumner were involved with were crazy, dangerous people. And if the whole Russian ruling class were like Princess Kira and Lady Raminoff, I could understand the anarchists wanting to be rid of them.

"My staff will be glad to know Mila speaks English. It will make questioning her easier." She picked up her paintbrush again. "Is there anything else?"

"I have an idea. The Duke of Blackford has a parlor maid, Mary Thomas, who was once a lady's maid. She's a clever young woman and could help us keep an eye on the Russian ladies."

"I don't think Blackford would mind lending her to us for a short while. Do you want to ask him, or shall I?"

"I will. I'll have to set this up with Mary." I dropped a small curtsy and left to post the princess's letter.

I walked back to the morning room to see if anything was there that I needed to do as part of my supposed job. I opened the door to find Amelia Whitten, Lady Daisy's governess, searching through the desk.

She straightened up, shut the drawer she'd been rifling through, and looked me in the eye. She didn't even blush.

"May I help you, Miss Whitten?"

"I was looking for some blank paper to use for Lady Daisy to practice her handwriting. I've run out."

I picked up several sheets from the stack by the door. "Will these do?"

"Nicely." She took them from my hand as she tried to leave. I blocked her way. "Where's Lady Daisy?"

"Having a tea party with her nursery maid."

I stared hard at her. "Next time you come to borrow something, bring her along. She livens up the house, don't you think?"

"Yes." She shoved past me and escaped at just short of a run.

I sat down and gazed into the back garden. What was Miss Whitten up to? For that matter, why was Mila stealing food? Then I leaned forward, watching as a figure slipped along the edge of the garden from the direction of the carriage house. Ivanov.

He wore worn, dark trousers and a jacket with a working-man's cap, letting him blend in on the London streets, but it was definitely Ivanov. I'd know his unkempt beard, his craggy face, and his tall bulk anywhere.

Leaping up, I raced to the back door and skidded to a stop. One of the maids watched me curiously—the maid still displaying the black eye and bruised face given to her when Ivanov escaped. "Are you expecting a visitor?" I asked.

She looked down at her damp dress and the bucket of dirty water she was using to scrub the stairwell coming up from the kitchen. Then she looked at me as if I'd grown a horn out of my forehead. "Yeah, the Prince of Wales."

"Ivanov is back. Better inform your mistress."

Her eyes widened. "Oh, Gawd." She plunked the bucket on a step, sloshing water, and ran back down the stairs. "Mrs. Green. Mrs. Green."

I stepped backward into the lavatory on the landing, hoping I wouldn't be noticed.

I left the door open a crack and held my breath as Ivanov entered. He blinked at the darkness after the bright day outside. I held still, wondering how he couldn't hear the pounding of my heartbeat. I could have reached out and touched him. And I was certain if he found me spying on him he would kill me. I was terrified my trembling would give me away.

After what felt like an eternity but must have been mere seconds, he moved past me and up the three steps to the main level.

I stayed where I was, afraid he'd notice me before he did whatever he came to do. When I peeked out, sure I'd see him partway down the hall, he was gone. I blinked. He had vanished. Where was he?

Slipping out of my hiding place, I heard the rumble of his voice and the softer murmur of a woman's voice. I couldn't make out their words, and I couldn't tell who the other voice belonged to. Tiptoeing forward, I hoped none of the boards would squeak and give me away. His voice, the louder of the two, was distinct enough that I was certain he was speaking English, but I still couldn't make out the words. He had to be close by, but the morning room and the library were both empty and I knew he couldn't have gone past me to use the back stairs.

I reached the front hall, still on my tiptoes. No sign of Ivanov, and I could no longer hear the sound of his voice. Where had he gone? I quickly peered down the other hallways and started up the steps when the duchess came down toward me.

"Where is he?" She sounded as imperious as Blackford. *A skill they both must have learned in the nursery.*

I looked around as if I expected him to suddenly appear. "I don't know. He came in the back door past me and down that hall, but then I lost him."

"Good Lord. He could be anywhere. Kendrick, look upstairs. Check the nursery, check with Princess Kira." The butler mounted the stairs at a rapid pace.

"Come with me." A young, dark-haired footman hurried to

obey the duchess's command and I trailed behind as we opened one door after another on the main floor.

Ivanov was nowhere to be found.

"Sally." The black-eyed maid hurried toward her mistress. "Run out to the carriage house and ask any of the men out there to come here quickly. We'll search the whole house from cellar to attic until we find him."

The maid turned and hurried toward the back door, when a young man half-dressed in a footman's uniform raced in. "You'll never guess who just walked out of here and into the carriage house." Then he looked past Sally and saw the duchess. "Your Grace." His bow was as sloppy as his apparel.

"Ivanov." The duchess gazed at him as he nervously tucked in his shirttails. "I'm glad you came in to tell us. We were about to start searching for him. Which way did he go?"

"Coachman stepped in to stop him, but Ivanov punched him. Knocked the wind right out of him. The Russian kept marching into the alley and then headed south."

"Was he carrying anything?" I asked.

"Not that I saw, ma'am."

"He didn't appear to carry anything in, either," I told the duchess.

"So why did he come back?" she asked, her eyes widening. "If you hadn't seen him and warned the household, what would he have done?"

A crash echoed inside the walls. I looked around in surprise, expecting the roof to cave in at any moment. The duchess scowled and the servants froze. After what felt like an eternity but was probably thirty seconds, footsteps could be heard pounding toward us. There was no one in sight.

The wall across from the morning room swung out into the hall and nearly hit me. I gasped and leaped backward. Kendrick, the butler, stepped ungracefully into the hall and said, "We have a problem, Your Grace."

Peeking around the section of wall, I could see a dark bundle of clothes. And a hand.

CHAPTER THIRTEEN

I looked past the butler's feet to see Lady Raminoff sprawled at
the bottom of a flight of steps. Her legs were up the first three
steps and her trunk and head were at the bottom. Her skirt was
up past her bony knees. My first thought was that she would hate
to be seen like this.

The duchess gasped and sank toward the floor as her eyes
rolled back in her head. The footman she had ordered to come
with us earlier was standing next to her and was able to catch
her. Then he looked at the butler with a panicked expression, the
duchess limp in his arms.

"Put her on the couch in the morning room," I told him. Then
I turned to the half-dressed footman. "Get a constable. Now."

Kendrick nodded at the men to follow my directions and then
said, "Sally, stay with Her Grace."

In an instant, the hallway was empty except for Kendrick,
Lady Raminoff, and me. I had room to bend down close to her,
feeling for a pulse and examining her neck and head.

"Her ladyship?" Kendrick asked.

"Dead."

Church bells began to peal somewhere nearby. I turned and stared at the butler in shock. Why—?

"Thanksgiving service for Her Majesty's long reign. Longer than her grandfather's." Kendrick nodded as if this was to be expected.

I loosed a sigh and began again to examine the victim.

"Could you please right her skirts?" the butler requested.

"No. We mustn't alter anything until the police arrive." I straightened. "Where did you find everyone when you went upstairs just now?"

"Lady Daisy was fine. She was with her nursery maid. The Russian maid, Mila, was the only one in the princess's room. I was heading toward the other end of the floor when I heard a loud thud in the direction of the nursery and went back. On my way I opened the door to the stairs and saw Lady Raminoff at the bottom." Kendrick glanced at the body and then looked away. "I came down to see if I could help the lady."

"So you didn't see Miss Whitten, the princess, or Nadia?"

"No."

"Did you see anyone in the hall when you heard the thud?"

"No. I was heading toward Their Graces' rooms. There was a bend in the hallway blocking my view."

I held the collar of Lady Raminoff's gown away from her skin and said, "Kendrick, would you say these bruises were made by hands as large as Ivanov's?"

He shuddered as he faced the corpse and then bent down and held one hand about six inches from her neck. "These were made by smaller hands than mine, and Ivanov had huge hands."

"I'd guess they were made by a lady's hands. I think Lady

Raminoff died from strangulation and then was thrown down the stairwell."

"Good heavens. Who would do that?" The butler sounded horrified at the idea.

The footman returned with a young constable. Both men stared at the scene, stunned into silence.

"You need to get help from your police station," I told the bobby. "This woman's been murdered."

He walked stiffly away, his eyes still wide, and a moment later I heard his whistle blast twice from the front steps. The sound mixed with the church bells.

The footman was still staring. I turned him away with a hand on his shoulder and said, "You must go out to the carriage house and make sure no one leaves that way. Find out if anyone left after Ivanov."

"He did this?" the footman asked, looking at the butler.

"We don't think so," Kendrick replied.

The footman nodded and left by the back door.

"If you'll guard the crime scene for a moment, Kendrick?" I asked and then went into the morning room to find the duchess sitting up.

"She's dead, isn't she? It was those terrible stairs. We had a maid hurry down them a year ago and twist her ankle. I'll have to tell Hereford to seal them up, once and for all."

"She was strangled, either there or elsewhere, and then dumped there."

At my brutal words, the duchess's eyes widened. "She was murdered? In my home? By Ivanov? Is that why he came back?"

"She was murdered, but it's unlikely Ivanov did it. The finger mark bruises around her neck are too small to have been made by Ivanov, or even by Kendrick. She was killed by a woman."

The duchess looked at me coldly. "You were put in my household by Blackford to prevent such things."

"I failed." What else could I say? "But I won't fail again."

"We can only hope." She sounded skeptical.

"It means I'm going to have to ask some painful questions. Starting with where you were when Sally found you."

"I was in my studio painting."

If I hadn't been looking at Sally at that moment, I wouldn't have known the duchess had lied. But after her initial shock, Sally stopped staring wide-eyed at the duchess and nodded her agreement. The duchess was a good employer. I was sure Sally didn't want to lose her post, and it must have seemed like a small lie.

Then the duchess rose and walked slowly out into the hallway. The butler and two bobbies were clustered around Lady Raminoff. "Give them whatever assistance they need, Kendrick," the duchess said as she passed.

A loud rap on the front door sent Kendrick to open it as one of the constables said, "That'll be the police photographer."

By the time the duchess and I reached the front hall, the photographer was carrying in his equipment, followed by Sussex and Blackford. Sussex looked around at all the faces staring at him and said, "It wasn't necessary for everyone to greet me, but thank you. Is Princess Kira receiving company?"

I looked up to the landing at the top of the main stairs. Princess Kira, Nadia, and two maids looked down at us and the excitement as more bobbies entered the house. Sussex could see the princess on the landing from where he stood, but good manners prevented him from admitting this.

He was allowing her to decide if she wanted to talk to him, and the silly girl probably wouldn't respond until a maid came up the steps to ask her. I thanked my lucky stars I was part of the middle class and didn't have to wait on such stupid customs to speak to anyone.

The duchess had the presence of mind to walk forward and say, "She always looks forward to seeing you, Duke," as she took his hand.

When Blackford glanced at me, I made a small gesture with my head as I made a wincing expression. He nodded, and I knew we'd speak before the end of the day.

I rushed up the stairs to Princess Kira and Nadia, knowing this would be my only chance for a while to question them. "Where were you?"

Kira glanced at Nadia, who said, "I was watching Kira paint. What is going on?"

"Lady Raminoff is dead."

"She was an old lady and a dragon who shouldn't have been a chaperone. It was too much work for her heart. I'm not surprised," Kira said with the same icy disregard she showed for her Russian guard.

"She was murdered."

Kira gave Nadia a frightened look. "It wasn't her heart? Good heavens. First Lidijik, now Lady Raminoff. They are after me."

"Sussex is here," I told her, "and he wants nothing so much as to keep you safe. Before you go down to see him, I have one other question. Were you and the duchess painting the same object?"

"The duchess wasn't in the studio, and I didn't see her until she greeted Sussex just now." Princess Kira walked gracefully down the stairs as if she were entering a ballroom. Nadia followed her with nearly as much grace but more purpose.

I walked down the hall to the nursery to find Miss Whitten overseeing Lady Daisy's penmanship.

"Where were you when Kendrick came in here looking for you?"

"When was that?" She seemed more belligerent than frightened.

"Shortly before he found Lady Raminoff's body."

My words seemed to shock the belligerence out of her. "I went to find the duchess, to ask if I could take Lady Daisy to the park. She wasn't painting, so I headed back to the nursery. When I did, I saw Kendrick ahead of me. He opened the door to the secret staircase and then disappeared."

"Did he see you?"

"I wouldn't think so."

"Was anyone in the studio?"

"Not that I saw. I thought I heard someone and called out, 'Your Grace,' but no one answered."

"Did you see Lady Raminoff at any time this morning?"

"No. I heard her arguing with someone earlier, but I don't know who."

"When was this?"

"Before I gave up trying to teach and went to look for the duchess. All this screeching and arguing is bad for lessons. That's why I decided to take Lady Daisy to the park today."

"What language were they arguing in?"

"I think Russian, but I'm not sure. Lady Raminoff screeched every time she spoke, so all languages sounded the same coming from her mouth."

"And the other person?"

"The other person spoke more softly. I couldn't tell you if it was a man or a woman."

"Could it have been Ivanov?"

She shook her head. "His voice was more like a rumble of thunder. I thought I heard his voice when I went to talk to the duchess after Lady Raminoff stopped shouting, but I can't be sure. Probably one of the footmen."

"Did you know Ivanov was in this house this morning?"

She put a protective hand on Lady Daisy's shoulder. "No. When?"

"While you were looking for Her Grace."

"Heavens. He didn't come in here, did he?"

"He was overheard speaking to an unknown woman in the secret staircase that opens just outside the nursery. The staircase where Lady Raminoff's body was found."

She wrapped her arms around herself and walked away. "It wasn't me. I want nothing to do with that brute."

Maybe now she'd tell the truth about Ivanov. "He tried to force his advances on you, didn't he?"

Miss Whitten shook her head. "No. He had no interest in me. He was trying to frighten me. That's what he seems to enjoy."

For someone who hadn't been helpful in the past, Miss Whitten was certainly providing a great deal of detail now.

AFTER DINNER, I headed alone to Sir Broderick's for our meeting. It was too dark to see the clouds that had rolled in during the afternoon, but the damp was finding its way through every seam to chill my skin. Knowing Emma was in disguise in the East End in this threatening weather was not lifting the satchel of worry on my shoulder.

Everyone was waiting when I walked in. I quickly poured myself a cup of tea and sat down next to Frances. Sir Broderick opened our meeting by saying, "Today our monarch has ruled longer than any other in Britain. None of us was alive when Queen Victoria was crowned. The next time you think things are changing quickly, remember we do have one source of stability."

I wasn't sure if this was a cause for celebration or despair. Turning to Blackford, I asked, "How was the atmosphere at luncheon today, Your Grace?"

"The duchess seems ready to wash her hands of her houseguests. Princess Kira and Nadia skirmished all through the meal. In Russian. If I spend much more time in that household, I'll learn to speak the language whether I plan to or not." His lips forced a brief smile, but none of us was in the mood for humor. "Tell us what happened from the beginning."

I did, with all the detail I saw or was told.

"Had anyone shown you the location of the secret staircase?" the duke asked.

"No. Only when Kendrick opened it to show us Lady Raminoff's body. I hope the coroner was called in." I studied Blackford's face.

"The police surgeon has seen the body. He agrees with your assessment that the killer could well be a woman because of the small hands, although she'd have to be strong."

"Tell us more about this hidden staircase," Jacob said.

"There was a time when things like servants' stairways were disguised with even the entrances hidden out of sight. Hereford House goes back to before the Georges, and in subsequent renovations, they left the secret panel passages alone." Blackford smiled. "They were great fun when we were children."

I could imagine a little, dark-haired boy sneaking down those stairs with his friends and peeking out from a slightly opened hidden panel.

"Would Ivanov know where to look for this staircase?"

"Everyone in the house knew about it. The servants used it regularly." Blackford turned to me. "Since Ivanov wasn't seen to carry anything in or out of the house, has the duchess checked her jewelry? He and his accomplice could be nothing more than thieves."

"And murderers." I stared into his eyes until I felt the familiar pull of his gaze drawing me closer. It was all I could do to keep from putting my hand on his sleeve. The fire of his determination shone in his dark eyes and made me want to help him succeed in whatever crazy plan he was creating.

"You don't really believe their main goal is theft," I added. "If they're thieving, it's only a sideline to what they mean to accomplish. But was Ivanov's aim in joining the household to get close to the princess or to Lady Raminoff? Was she the target all the time?"

"Georgia, you're the only one we have in that household to figure out what Ivanov and his accomplice have planned before something else goes terribly wrong." Sir Broderick rolled his chair around to face me directly.

"Not for long. Your Grace, could we borrow Mary Thomas to act as lady's maid to Nadia? She wants one and the duchess has no one to spare. She could act as an extra set of eyes around the Russians."

He nodded. "I'll explain what is required and send her over to meet with the duchess tomorrow."

I turned to Sir Broderick. "Do we want to proceed on the assumption the princess is the target?"

"It must be the princess. Lady Raminoff could only be a bonus for an anarchist. Perhaps their target is the ball at the Russian embassy in honor of the engagement."

"How would skulking around Hereford House help them smuggle something into the embassy?" I kicked myself mentally as soon as the words escaped my mouth.

Blackford bounced the side of his fist against the chair arm.

"It wouldn't, blast it, and Whitehall's attention has been drawn elsewhere. If you or Emma and Sumner don't find out what they have planned before they strike, diplomacy between England and Russia will suffer irreparable harm. The Russians have already signed accords with France against us, and the Ottoman Empire grows weaker and less able to hold them back by the day."

"We wouldn't go to war with Russia again, would we?"

"We were stupid enough to get into that mess in the Crimea. I wouldn't be surprised at any idiocy Whitehall and the Admiralty could dream up between them."

Shaking his head, the duke continued. "Whitehall seems to think I have the leisure to drop everything to take care of its problems, but I don't. Georgia, I'll be over by luncheon to see what you've been able to uncover."

"I'm worried about one part of this investigation, Your Grace. The duchess lied about where she was when Ivanov entered the house." I looked at Blackford, wondering if he knew anything that might clear up this problem.

"You don't believe she had anything to do with it, do you?" Sir Broderick asked.

"No, but it would make the investigation easier if I knew where she really was. Other alibis rest on it. And one of those alibis, I suspect, hides a murderer."

Blackford's only reply was to raise his eyebrows before offering me a ride home in his carriage.

Several times during our ride he seemed to be on the verge of saying something to me, but then he'd look out the window and keep silent. I immediately wondered if he'd found time to choose a wife. He needed to produce an heir, and that required a duchess. Or perhaps his American trip was to consider heiresses in the New World as well as to check on his investments. Was he planning to return home with a bride? His correct manners in the carriage and on my doorstep reinforced my fears that I'd soon have to stop my silly daydreams of becoming Blackford's wife.

Once I entered my home, I couldn't settle. Fear of failure to stop the anarchist plot and save lives mixed with worry about how the Russian government would react toward my country. I'd become fond of the duchess and Lady Daisy and didn't want any harm to come to them. Emma and Sumner were risking their lives to infiltrate the anarchists and I wanted to protect them and the rest of the Archivist Society working to uncover this plan.

In the past day, I'd found my worries about Emma being out at night alone with Sumner had changed to my worries about Emma being rejected by Sumner after their adventure was over. She hadn't said too much since she first met him, but she didn't need to. One glance at her when she looked at Sumner should have told me what was behind their travels to the East End.

I hoped to be happy for her, but I was also envious. Blackford was a duke, for pity's sake.

England was changing. In a few years it would be a new century. Someday the gregarious Prince of Wales would be king. But an English duke had never married a middle-class bookseller and Blackford was as traditional as a duke could get.

Between hopes and fears for Emma and struggling with my tattered dreams about Blackford, I spent the night angry and unsettled and pounding my pillow.

CHAPTER FOURTEEN

A S soon as I arrived at Hereford House in the morning, I
planned to look for the duchess. Instead, I found her coming out of the morning room as I put my hat and gloves on the
table in the back hall. I gave her a curtsy and said, "I wish you'd
told me about the staircase across the hall."

"You didn't know about—oh, never mind. I never want to
see those stairs again. I'm going to have Hereford seal them up."
She wrapped her arms around her middle.

"Please. I'd like to see how easily they're accessed."

She nodded. "I forget there might be someone in the house
who's never seen our hidden steps. The servants can't resist showing them off to anyone new."

I followed her along the hall, where she ran her fingers above
the wainscoting. A section of the wall, wallpapered and paneled
to blend in, swung open. I stuck my head into the opening and
took my first good look at the steps without Lady Raminoff's

body in the way. The staircase was poorly lit with a thick, dull carpet that appeared sufficient to muffle footsteps.

"Is any of your jewelry missing? We thought it might be what he was after."

I turned around to see the duchess holding her stomach and looking ill. "No. The nursery is near the top of these stairs. If I find out he was even thinking about hurting my baby, I will send the Russians packing back to St. Petersburg and the Prince of Wales can forget about any more favors from Hereford."

"The Prince of Wales asked you to take in the princess?"

"Yes. He and the men in Whitehall."

"Why?" The word slipped out before I could take it back.

"Wales, his brothers, Hereford, Blackford, they all feel sorry for Sussex. His father was Victoria's much younger cousin and was always sickly, leaving their only child to be raised by his wife, the formidable Dowager Duchess of Sussex." Her sigh told me she'd dealt with the woman before. "He'd still be squiring Mummy around if Victoria hadn't looked in the Almanach de Gotha and found Princess Kira. I feel sorry for Sussex, too, but not to the extent of endangering Daisy."

"Where is the dowager duchess now?" I needed a clear picture of these people. A clue to our present investigation might be hidden in the past.

She walked back into the morning room and sat rather heavily on the nearest chair. "Victoria made the sacrifice and asked the dowager duchess to be a lady-in-waiting. The plan is to have Sussex safely married before the dowager duchess can destroy his chance at happiness."

"He does seem to be happy with the princess." Besotted might be a better word.

The duchess looked into the middle distance and smiled. "Yes. It's sweet, isn't it?"

Before I could respond, she turned her gaze on me and said, "Life goes on, even with a murder in the house. We need to get the invitations out to the princess's dinner party. Here is the list of people to invite. Grand Duke Vassily will be the guest of honor."

I looked at the list and blinked. "How many will be at the dinner?"

"Twenty-four. And don't think I didn't have a problem convincing her to narrow the list."

"And you want me to handwrite the invitations?" I knew that was the normal procedure—I was acting as her secretary, after all—but I had an investigation to carry out.

"Of course," she snapped, and then immediately looked embarrassed. "You don't type invitations, and this isn't important enough to have them engraved. You'll find the paper for invitations is in the third drawer in the desk."

I sat down by the desk and opened the drawer. There was more than enough heavy cream card stock, but I didn't see this ending well. "My handwriting is neat but plain. Is the princess certain she doesn't want to write them out herself?"

The duchess looked heavenward as if for help. "She's far too busy painting and shopping and making demands on my servants. The cook is ready to quit over her constant menu changes and criticisms."

"What has the ambassador said about paying for a lady's maid for Nadia? Blackford is sending over the maid I told you about to talk to you this morning. And I'll need to talk to her, too, but secretly."

"The ambassador is consulting with St. Petersburg. Frankly,

I think he'd like her to leave England as soon as possible and her family doesn't care if she ever returns home. I ask when I should expect her to return to her family, and she keeps saying she doesn't know. She and Sussex need to discuss their plans for next spring first. Sussex would let her put on a carnival at their wedding if she wanted." Her voice rose with exasperation.

Then she lowered her head, took a deep breath, and slowly released it. "Please don't tell anyone about my pique. She's really a lovely girl."

"If she's that much of a strain, perhaps you ought to tell the duke. Ask a friend to invite her to a shooting party far from here."

"I tried that. She declined the invitation. She said she needed to stay here to paint and throw this dinner party for her cousin Vassily."

"Oh, dear." Declining invitations now for frivolous reasons would have serious repercussions on her life after she and Sussex were married. Polite society didn't decline invitations to shooting parties for anything less than childbirth or death. Or a previous invitation. "I hope she didn't tell Sussex to go without her."

"She did. He declined as well so he could stay here with her."

"Didn't he suggest strongly that they really ought to accept the invitation? That she'd enjoy herself there?"

"He suggested. I don't know how strongly. Of course, I feel like a fool since I wrote and asked the Duchess of Merville to extend invitations to the two of them."

"No one thinks this is your fault, Your Grace."

She sighed and nodded. The woman had been looking pale for days. The princess was wearing her out. Living with a murderer in the house wasn't helping.

And then another thought tapped me on the shoulder. "Are you expecting another child, Your Grace?"

The duchess gave a tremendous sigh and said, "Please don't say anything. I'd like to tell the duke before this makes the rounds of gossip."

I wondered if I ought to tell Blackford but her sharp look dissuaded me. "No. I won't tell." Then a possible explanation to the duchess's lie came to mind. "Was Your Grace suffering from morning sickness when Ivanov arrived here rather than painting in your studio as you said?"

She nodded. "I felt so badly I returned to my room. I was hoping my lady's maid was there to fix me a bromide. She wasn't, and I found myself being sick into the chamber pot. I was still bent over it when Sally came in and told me Ivanov had been spotted."

"You might want to let Sally know it's all right for her to tell me the truth."

"Yes. She backed me up very loyally."

"And I need her to tell me truthfully if anyone was in your studio." She might provide an alibi for one or more of the possible stranglers. The poor duchess looked so miserable I said, "Why don't you put your feet up and rest while you tell me exactly how you want these invitations to read?"

"You've never done anything like this before, have you?"

"No, and I don't want to upset the princess and make things more difficult for you."

We spent the next fifteen minutes together as the duchess sat with her feet up and her eyes shut, explaining the intricacies of formal invitations. At the end, I had produced one good copy of the invitation and a few trials had landed in the fire the duchess had ordered built to warm the room.

"Will anyone be available? This is short notice," I said. The dinner would be held in three days' time.

"All of these people are in town, and most of them are

involved in the diplomacy surrounding Grand Duke Vassily's visit. They've expected this invitation since before the man arrived in England."

"Kira isn't inviting her sister?"

"Nadia's her half sister, and it's the circumstances of her birth that would make Grand Duke Vassily and the rest of the Russians refuse to sit down with her. That's what she told me."

"How is Nadia taking it?"

"Surprisingly well. She's the one who told me, not Kira. Nadia just shrugged it off as part of life dealing with Russian nobility." The duchess rose slowly from her chair. "I suppose I've hidden long enough from my responsibilities. Let me know when you have the invitations done, and I'll have a footman deliver them rather than wait for the postman."

I gave her a nod. "Thank you, Your Grace."

By the time the duchess and her guests had finished their luncheon, I was waiting in the front hall with the addressed invitations.

"That was quick work, Miss Peabody," the duchess said.

"Let me see," Princess Kira said.

Nadia curtsied to everyone and began to climb the stairs. Her pleasant expression seemed sewn on her face and her back was rigid with anger. She might claim she didn't mind being left out of this dinner, but clearly she was unhappy.

"This is so plain. You'll have to do it over and use a fancier hand." Princess Kira smacked them back into my palm.

"If you want a fancier hand, you'll have to do it yourself."

The house and everyone in it seemed to hold their breaths. I shouldn't have been so bold. A person in the position I was pretending to occupy wouldn't have been so outspoken. Not that the princess didn't deserve some plainspoken truth.

"How dare you?" the princess said.

"I am sorry, but I can't provide a fancier hand. The work is neat and unsmudged, but if it doesn't suit, perhaps you could make the invitations fancier," I said, trying to sound contrite.

Blackford stood to one side, no expression on his marble-chiseled features.

"I don't have time. You'll just have to do a better job," the princess said, not bothering to pretend to have trouble with English.

Blackford picked the top one up from my hand. "They're neat, perfectly aligned, correctly spelled. Everything an invitation should be. Perhaps Russian standards are higher than English ones."

Princess Kira opened her mouth and then shut it as she realized the trap she nearly walked into. If she said Russian standards were higher, the people who mattered in her new life in England would think she should go home and marry a Russian. Or do the invitations herself. And by this time, she must have realized how this sounded to Sussex. He wouldn't stay enamored forever.

"What do you think, Arthur?" the princess asked Sussex, an adoring smile on her face.

"They look fine to me. You mustn't worry about it, my darling."

"Very well. Send them out," the princess said with a pout in her voice.

I kept my mouth shut as I straightened out the invitations and passed them to the footman who appeared at my side. With a bow to the duchess, he left the house.

I glanced up to the landing at the top of the stairs. Nadia stood looking down with hatred etched on her features. I tried to guess who she was looking at. Was it Princess Kira, or was she looking at the Duchess of Hereford? Or me?

Kira walked away with Sussex, and Nadia's furious gaze followed her. I wondered if the princess knew how much her sister loathed her.

Then Nadia glanced over and saw I was watching her. She walked away, her head held high.

A HALF HOUR later, I was summoned to speak to the duchess. I followed the maid to the dining room. When I entered the room, I found the duchess with Mary Thomas.

"With Russians all over the house, this seemed as private as possible at this time of day," the duchess said.

"Mary, I know you were lady's maid to Clara Gattenger—"

"Part of the day, miss."

"And we need you to be lady's maid to the princess's half sister, Nadia Andropov. We need you to listen in and report back anything they say that might be important. It could be dangerous, but it will help the Archivist Society," I told her.

"Will this help find who killed my brother?"

"No. This is the other investigation we're working on. You have every right to refuse, and it won't be held against you."

She lifted her chin. "The Archivist Society is helping to find the person who killed my brother. It's only right I help you in return."

"Thank you. You can report back to me or to the Duke of Blackford. Try to keep an eye on Nadia, the princess, and Mila, the other lady's maid. They all speak English. If they speak Russian around you, don't worry. The rest of us don't know any Russian, either."

Nodding, she said, "I'll do my best. When do I start?"

I WAS STILL rubbing my sore right hand from all the careful writing I had done when I reached the bookshop that evening. Frances was assisting a woman who'd probably be our last customer of the day. She saw me and gave a nod toward the office that made her chins wobble. I waved and walked to the back of the shop.

Emma sat on one of the chairs, looking up at me through a black eye. Her lips were cut and swollen on that side and a bruise ran along her cheek.

I jumped over stacks of books delivered that day to reach her. I bent down to give her a hug and said, "Dear Lord. What happened?"

"One of the anarchists has decided he doesn't trust me. Well, he caught me eavesdropping on the leader of a group of thugs, Griekev, who was speaking to a woman." She tried to smile and stopped with a grimace. "You should see my attacker now."

"You stabbed him?"

"And have myself and Sumner thrown out of the group just as it's paying off? Never. Sumner beat him to a pulp. Nastiest fight I've seen in ages." She started to shake her head and then clutched her jaw.

"You're hurt."

"Just sore. And will be for a few days."

I winced in sympathy. "Is Sumner all right?"

"He's pretty banged up. I've got to go back to see to him. I just came to have you get a message to Sir Broderick. I overheard the leader talking. The target is Grand Duke Vassily, who's meeting with our diplomats. Something is happening at lunchtime the day after tomorrow."

She rose and gave me a hug.

"Is there anything I can do?" I asked her. "Do you need any money?"

"I need to buy ice and brandy and some clean bandages."

I shifted back so I could look her over carefully. Her hair was dirty and messy; her skirts and half boots were worn and grimy.

She wore a shawl we'd have to burn when this was over. I had almost a pound in change in my purse and I gave her every halfpenny.

Just gazing at her bruises made me nauseous. Emma was beautiful and kind. The idea that some man was so evil that he'd beat her made me shake with anger at him and fear for her. "Who is this brute? Was it this Griekev who did this?"

Her eyes gave away her guilty conscience. "No. Ivanov."

"Dear heavens. You know the man's a killer. And since he killed the guard, he's attacked a maid at Hereford House and frightened the child's governess. He has no qualms about hurting women. Please be careful."

She slipped the money into her pocket and hugged me again. "I can't wait until this is over."

"Neither can I." Then I added, "This woman talking with Griekev. Would you recognize her again?"

"No. She always comes in the back way. I've never seen her, but she seems to be important to Griekev. He immediately goes to see her whenever she's in the building."

"This is getting too dangerous. Go back and get Sumner. Then the two of you leave that place and come home. I don't think there's anything more to be learned from the anarchists."

"We need to find out who this woman is first." She squeezed past me and stopped in the doorway to the office. "When this is over, we'll need to talk."

"What's wrong, Emma?"

But when I reached the doorway, she was already slipping out the back entrance into the alley.

I went out to the shop to find Frances closing the door behind her customer. Picking up the telephone, I asked for Sir Broderick's home. I gave him Emma's message.

"How is she?" His voice boomed out of the earpiece.

I glanced at Frances and said, "She's been struck by Ivanov, the large brute who killed the Russian guard. Sumner reportedly beat him for attacking Emma, but suffered injuries in the fight."

"Does she want us to call this off?"

"I asked her to, but she said no. But she's very happy this will be over soon."

"So are we all. I'll arrange a meeting for tonight. We need to plan now that we know when the attack will come." There was a pause, and I thought I could hear Sir Broderick smile as he added, "Will you call Blackford and invite him, or shall I?"

"I will," I responded too quickly.

Stevens, the duke's butler, answered the telephone at Blackford House. "His Grace isn't in at the moment," he said. "May I take a message?"

"Yes. This is Georgia Fenchurch. Tell him there's an emergency meeting tonight at Sir Broderick's. We need his expertise. And so do Emma and Sumner."

"She's a lovely young lady, miss. Sumner will take good care of her."

"Stevens, you've met Emma Keyes?"

"Yes, miss. She's come by the house with Sumner a number of times. Oh, His Grace is available now."

Blackford's voice came over the earpiece. "Georgia, can you come to Blackford House immediately? Grand Duke Vassily is here and he's told me an interesting story."

"Of course, Your Grace."

When I hung up, Frances was standing across the counter from me, waiting. I set both pieces of the telephone where they belonged behind the counter and said, "We have a meeting at Sir Broderick's tonight." Her dry expression made me add, "But you heard that. You heard all of it. I have to leave for Blackford

184 Kate Parker

House. The duke says one of the Russians has information that might help."

She laid her hand on mine. "Then get going. Just make sure you get to Sir Broderick's on time. This meeting may be a long one."

I caught a hansom cab to hurry me to the duke's residence. When I arrived, I was shown into the duke's study, where Blackford and Grand Duke Vassily were seated in armchairs with brandy snifters, looking over an antique book.

"What is the meaning of this?" the grand duke asked as both men set down their drinks and rose. He certainly saw me as an intruder.

"Grand Duke Vassily, you met Miss Fenchurch at the Austrian embassy ball. In truth, she is working with me to keep Princess Kira safe. She is posing as the Duchess of Hereford's secretary to keep an eye on the household."

"It is too bad you weren't also keeping Lady Raminoff safe." He bowed over my hand. "But I don't understand why I should tell this young lady what I told you in confidence, Blackford."

"I want you to tell her all you have told me about Nadia Andropov and the Romanovs. I believe it is important enough for keeping the princess safe that Miss Fenchurch should hear it, too."

"She's an unmarried lady. It would not be proper to speak of such things in front of her." The grand duke turned his back on me and strode toward the fire.

Why did men always try to protect women, I wondered, when we were the ones who had to hold society together after they made a mess of things?

CHAPTER FIFTEEN

"I N service to my queen, I have heard many worse things, I'm sure,"
I told Grand Duke Vassily, trying not to sound too annoyed at
the man who was trying to protect my tender sensibilities.

"It reflects badly on our royal family. I don't want to see such
stories spread in your newspapers."

Ah, so he wasn't really worried about my tender feelings. He
was afraid something unpalatable would appear in the London
press. "Nothing I have heard or will hear has ever appeared in
the newspapers. Nor will it."

"Please," Blackford added. "I wouldn't ask if it weren't
important."

After a moment, the grand duke shook his head. "Very well. But
there will be diplomatic repercussions if any of this leaks out."

I nodded. Blackford pulled over his desk chair and we all sat.

"The Christmas before last, Marina, Nadia's mother, burst
into a Romanov family celebration and begged the tsar on bended
knee to acknowledge her daughter as his cousin. Poor Nicholas

had no idea who the woman was, although she was dressed appropriately for the occasion, which indicated that she had some resources. The tsar's mother and some of the other ladies of the court knew, including Kira's mother, Princess Sofia.

"Before anyone could stop the young tsar, he asked, 'Who is your daughter?'

"Marina told him, including the child's paternity. Prince Pyotr Romanov. He was right there in the hall! Prince Pyotr, Kira's father, ordered Marina to leave immediately, but the tsarina stopped him and asked if the woman and her daughter had been looked after.

"She denied it. Said they'd been given castoffs. And her daughter was a blood descendant of Nicholas the First. She, Marina, wanted nothing but for her daughter to be styled a princess just like the rest of Nicholas's great-granddaughters."

"What did the tsar decide?" I interrupted to ask.

I earned a dark look in response. "He dithered, as usual. Eventually he passed it to one of his ministers, where the matter died. But the incident of Marina invading the family gathering, that didn't die.

"Gossip flew around St. Petersburg. Kira's mother, Sofia, was embarrassed at every ball, every Christmas entertainment. Marina was spotted at many of these events. No one knew how she learned of them or how she entered and left again without being stopped."

"Someone powerful was on her side," I said.

"Yes. At the time, gossip swelled but no one knew who was aiding Marina. The following summer, she was murdered in her home on Prince Pyotr's estate. Nadia was supposedly also attacked but escaped. Of that, I have no proof.

"I do know Prince Pyotr was called before the tsar to explain himself. He claimed his wife had ordered men to kill them both. When asked, Kira's mother, Princess Sofia, said only, 'What would you have done? I will not be embarrassed by her any longer.'"

"How do you know this?"

"I was instructed by the tsar to conduct the investigation."

It made sense for the tsar to ask his uncle to investigate his cousin. Especially since they were all members of the Russian royalty. I nodded.

"Nadia escaped. I didn't know where. I didn't try to find her. This past Christmas, I learned the tsar's mother, with the help of Lady Raminoff and other older women, had orchestrated Marina's appearances the year before at all the holiday festivities."

"Why?"

"They didn't approve of the way Prince Pyotr had handled the situation, and none of them likes Sofia. She's a silly, vain, self-important creature who thinks of nothing but herself. Marina had fire, spunk. And she was a beautiful but kind woman. Her only blind spot was her overpowering loyalty to her daughter."

"And it was the tsar's mother who sent Lady Raminoff along as Princess Kira's chaperone. Did she hope the princess would ruin herself in London?"

"No. She was afraid she would and wanted a stern chaperone in place. She fears Princess Kira is as silly and vain as her mother. Sofia is a thoroughly stupid woman. Her daughter's behavior worries the entire royal family. In Russia, Princess Kira is known for her willfulness and foolish disregard for propriety."

"What did she want Lady Raminoff to do if Princess Kira misbehaved?"

The grand duke looked me straight in the eye and said, "Anything necessary. In Lady Raminoff's eyes, that would be everything up to and including execution."

Were all these Russians crazy? "Did Nadia know Lady Raminoff's role in helping her mother?"

"Probably. Although the women of the former tsarina's court were acting to see a financial settlement was made to Marina and her daughter in the hopes they'd leave Russia. They weren't in favor of Nadia being honored as a princess."

The grand duke took a sip of his brandy and said, "One of the reasons I am here is to present Nadia with a financial settlement."

"Does she know this?"

"I sent her a message as soon as I came to London, asking her to meet me at the embassy. We are to meet tomorrow morning."

Blackford escorted me to the front door. When I told him about the Archivist Society meeting that night, he shook his head. "I have a previous engagement I can't turn down."

As Stevens, his butler, helped me on with my cloak, I watched Blackford walk away. Dejection weighed down all my bones and removed the air from my lungs.

I went home, vowing not to tell Phyllida any of this. That was easy. The hard part was finding a way to tell her I'd seen Emma without alarming her. As soon as she saw my face, she said, "You have news. Tell me."

"Over dinner." I sniffed the air. "Something smells delicious."

Her eyes narrowed. "Leftover roasted chicken and vegetables from last night, but you knew that. Tell me now."

"Let's sit down."

She went pale, but she walked into the parlor, head held high. We sat across from each other and I took one of her hands in mine. "The man who killed the Russian bodyguard struck Emma. One side of her face is cut and bruised. Sumner beat the man, but it must have been a terrible fight. He was injured. I don't know how badly. But they learned the attack will come the day after tomorrow at luncheon. This is almost over."

"Thank the dear Lord. Is Emma all right?"

"Her wounds are superficial. She'll be fine."

"And Sumner?"

"Emma didn't seem alarmed. We're having a meeting tonight, but they won't be there. They don't dare give away their role at this late date."

"Why can't they leave now, this very instant?"

"They can. I asked. But they won't."

Phyllida bowed her head for a moment. Then she raised her face and said, "You're going to Sir Broderick's tonight?"

"Yes. Do you want to attend?"

"No. I'm not fond of all this excitement." She took a deep breath and let it out on a long sigh. "I'll put dinner on the table."

Phyllida was unnaturally quiet during the meal, and all my attempts at conversation fell flat. "What's wrong?" I finally asked.

"What do you think?" She paused after her snappish reply and said, "I'm very fond of you, Georgia, but Emma is like the daughter I never had. She's the age of any children I might have had if I'd been allowed to marry. And now we don't know if she'll survive. If they'll both live and get married—" Her voice broke on a sob.

"Now. Now. Neither one has said a word about marriage."

"If they don't, Sumner has ruined her. And he loves her too much to ruin her. You only have to look into his eyes to see it. The only question is whether Emma has accepted him, and whether they'll both live through this." Phyllida leaped up from the table, grabbed a couple of dishes, and hurried into the kitchen.

I cleared a few more and followed her. "They'll be fine. Perhaps you need to begin to plan a wedding."

She looked up from where she leaned on the sink. "Do you think so?"

"Yes." In truth, I had no idea, but I could lie with apparent sincerity when it came to Phyllida. There was no point in both of us being worried sick.

I hurried, but it was already nearly dark by the time I knocked on Sir Broderick's door. The streetlamps had been lit and the wind had risen, making for a cozy evening indoors. Jacob opened the door and then took my cloak while I removed my hat and gloves.

"We're in the parlor," he told me.

"We're making a habit of this."

"I've had to call in the lift people for service. The contraption's getting a workout." Jacob grinned widely and my face must have reflected his joy.

Sir Broderick had slowly grown stronger over the years after nearly dying while trying to save my parents. He'd increased the size and reach of the Archivist Society over time, but he'd never before come downstairs. He wasn't walking, but it was as if his physical horizons had suddenly widened with Mrs. Hardwick in the house.

I entered the parlor to find Mrs. Hardwick pouring a cup of tea for Adam Fogarty while Frances Atterby took a scone from Dominique. For an instant, I looked around for Emma and then my shoulders drooped under the weight of my worry. Emma wouldn't be here tonight. God only knew if she'd be here for our next meeting.

Mrs. Hardwick poured me a cup and said, "You're looking very down tonight, Georgia. Worried about the investigation?"

"Yes." Among other things.

"It will be all right. You'll see."

"Perhaps." How could she be so sure?

A few other Archivist Society members showed up and we greeted each other before sitting around the parlor in a circle. Adam Fogarty paced behind our seats, occasionally settling behind one of us for a few moments. I guessed he was shaking out his bad leg. I'd seen him do it before, but I wasn't about to quiz him on his pain.

I had enough of my own that night.

Sir Broderick sat with his back to the roaring fire. "Georgia, tell us what you learned today," he said in a loud voice, which quieted the others.

I told them what Emma had told me about the fight and the attack. "The two points she found out were the attack comes the day after tomorrow at lunchtime and the target is Grand Duke Vassily. Adam, can you find out from your friends where the Russian will be then and what kind of security Scotland Yard is providing?"

He paused behind Frances's chair. "Yes. I'll have all the details by noon tomorrow."

"That'll only give us twenty-four hours," Grace Yates said. "And when we find out where the grand duke will be, we need to put a Russian speaker in there to coordinate from inside."

"And to translate any last-minute remarks by waiters, staff, anyone who speaks Russian that might give us a hint as to where the threat is coming from," I added.

"We don't have a Russian speaker," Sir Broderick said. "Does anyone know someone who can help? Georgia, what about someone at Hereford House?"

I thought of the Russian speakers staying there. The princess, Mila the maid, and Nadia. One of them could be Lady Raminoff's killer. I shook my head. "I wouldn't trust any of them with this."

"I understand. Anyone else?"

Everyone shook their heads.

"I'll make some calls, but we're going to have to count heavily on what you can find out from Scotland Yard, Adam. They must have a Russian speaker they can put into the grand duke's party for the day."

"I imagine they do. I'll ask them, but it sounds like something they'll think of right away," Fogarty replied.

Sir Broderick looked around. "I would have thought Blackford would have come tonight. You did call him, Georgia?"

"He had a previous engagement. He offered his apologies."

Sir Broderick frowned. "We can only hope he can make it tomorrow night. We'll have to meet then to learn what Adam has for us."

"Do you want me to fill everyone in on what we've recently learned about the burglars who are using dynamite?" Adam asked.

"Yes. Are you making progress?" I asked before Sir Broderick had a chance to speak. I wanted to tell Mary Thomas if possible.

"The Yard had speakers of some foreign tongues talk in front of the witnesses to the burglaries. To learn which one sounded the most like the robbers. Turns out they were speaking Russian. And the witnesses gave matching physical descriptions. One tall with a beard, large hands, and a short temper. The other medium sized and clean shaven. He appeared to be in charge. They believe he's the brains behind the explosions and the robberies."

"Has that helped Scotland Yard?" Grace asked.

"The constables on the beat in Whitechapel were instructed to keep an ear out for any mention of dynamite in the Russian community or these two men. A snitch reported a gang is being run by a Russian who uses dynamite. Some of the members are Russian, some English. All nasty characters. Their lair is somewhere off Commercial Street."

"You've had great success, Adam," I said. "Wish us the same progress tomorrow."

"I also looked into the removals company whose name was painted on the side of the cart seen at the burglaries. It's a large firm. Turns out a cart was stolen last summer during the heat wave. Two Londoners were hired a few days before they and the cart went missing. The firm would like the cart back, but so far it's vanished. The men never returned to work, nor have they been spotted."

"Good work, Fogarty. That's all for tonight," Sir Broderick said.

We all began setting down our teacups and rising, looking at each other in confusion. I wasn't the only one who'd expected a long session planning how we could stop an anarchist attack two days hence. But without Blackford, and without knowing the grand duke's schedule, we couldn't plan for the inevitable assault.

"Georgia." Sir Broderick beckoned me over to his chair. I drew as close to the fire as I could stand. "Try to get Blackford to come to tomorrow's meeting. This was originally his idea, keeping the Russians safe. We need to know what he knows about the grand duke's movements."

"I'll visit him in the morning before I go to Hereford House."

He smiled. "You're being almost as bold as Emma. Dropping in on a man, especially that early in the morning and unchaperoned."

"Emma and I drop in on you at all sorts of odd hours."

He struck the armrests of his wheeled chair. "This is your chaperone here. Blackford provides no such assurances."

"Or Sumner," I added, thinking of Emma.

"We know how that will end."

"I hope so. Emma will be ruined if he doesn't marry her." I caught myself wringing my hands and forced them down to my sides.

"Then let's hope the anarchists don't find out their part in our investigation so they both live."

I didn't need to hear that. Sickened and terrified by the thoughts running through my head, I ran from the room, neglecting to say good-bye to Sir Broderick, Jacob, or Mrs. Hartwick. I threw on my hat, cloak, and gloves and dashed out of the house.

I was so distressed as I hurried along the pavement that I didn't hear the footsteps behind me until a strong grip pinned my arm.

CHAPTER SIXTEEN

I loosed an audible gasp as someone reached out from behind me and took me prisoner. Swinging around, I kicked my attacker in the shin and then stomped on his foot.

"Georgia, stop it."

I blinked and stopped my foot from connecting with his other shin as Sumner shoved me into the alleyway between two houses. "Sumner. What's wrong?"

"They're on to us. We need to get Emma out of the robbers' hideout."

Robbers' hideout? Weren't they following anarchists? "What's she doing there?"

"They took her prisoner. Griekev and Ivanov." He looked down. "Georgia, I can't save her alone. I need help." His words came out on a sob.

"We'll help you. Come back with me to Sir Broderick's."

"It's not safe. I might have been followed."

"All the more reason for you to come with me. I have an idea."

Taking his arm, I rushed us back to Sir Broderick's doorstep, our heels clicking in unison.

Jacob opened the door looking surprised. We shoved past him and shut the door. "Where's Sir Broderick?"

"Right here." He glanced at us from a point just beyond his lift. "You'd better come into the parlor. Mrs. Hardwick, more hot tea, please, and bread and ham. Jacob, the medicine chest."

I took my first good look at Sumner and my heart sank. He was thinner, bruised, and his shirt was marred with blood. His forehead and one ear were cut. The eye on the scarred side of his face was nearly swollen shut. If he looked like that, what had happened to Emma?

We led Sumner to a chair in the parlor, and while Mrs. Hardwick saw to tea and food and Jacob had Sumner remove his shirt to deal with his injuries, I ran upstairs to the study.

Once again I got the butler when I telephoned Blackford House. "I need to speak to Blackford immediately."

"His Grace is not at home."

"Stevens, this is a matter of life or death for Sumner and Emma. Where is he?"

"Life or death?" His tone changed from stuffy to shaken.

"Yes. Emma is being held prisoner and Sumner has asked for our help. Ours and His Grace's. We have to save her."

"Oh, dear." There was silence on the line while Stevens dithered. "One moment, please."

It was the longest moment I'd ever experienced before indistinct sounds came over the line. Then I heard the words, "Where are you, Georgia?" in Blackford's stern tones.

"Sir Broderick's."

"And Sumner?"

"He's here. Emma's been taken prisoner."

"Stay there. I'll arrive with help as quickly as possible."

The line went dead, and I rushed back down the stairs to the doorway of the parlor, where I met Jacob coming out with a basin of dirty water. "How is Sumner?"

"He'll live."

"Sumner thinks he was followed here. Can you slip out the back way and bring Fogarty here without being seen?"

"Good idea, Georgia," Sir Broderick called from inside the parlor.

"I'll be back quick as I can." Jacob hurried off and I went into the room.

Sumner, bandages showing on his neck, arm, and chest, sat in a chair with a plate of cheese, ham, and buttered bread on his lap and a cup of tea by his side. A fresh shirt, obviously one of Sir Broderick's, strained over his shoulders and upper arms and didn't quite reach to button over his chest.

I took one curious glance at his muscular, hairy body before good manners made me look toward Sir Broderick. "I reached Blackford. He'll be here shortly."

"Good. As soon as he, Jacob, and Adam Fogarty arrive, we can make our plans."

Sumner set down his plate and began to rise. "We need to get down there now and rescue her. There's no time to lose."

"Sit down. Eat. By the time you finish, they'll be here and we can listen to your intelligence and make our plan. We'll have her safe before daybreak."

Sir Broderick's voice carried such command and assurance that Sumner sat down, but he still looked sulky. Then his hunger got the best of him and he began to gobble down the food.

Jacob returned with Adam Fogarty a few minutes later. Sir Broderick spoke as if we were in an Archivist Society meeting, and in a way we were. "Adam, I think when we make our plans, your job will be to contact your friends at the Metropolitan Police and bring in reinforcements to make the arrests."

Fogarty nodded. "My pleasure." Then he paced across the room and back.

Mrs. Hardwick brought more food and Jacob helped Sumner polish it off.

When Blackford arrived, he brought two footmen with him. "I'm not sure how much manpower we need."

"Plenty," Sumner said, finishing his tea. "They have lookouts on all the surrounding streets. Their gang knows every alleyway and rooftop in the area. We need to capture the lookouts on the route we take to the building so we can take 'em by surprise."

My first instinct was to dash to the East End and rescue Emma by force of will alone. Struggling with my desire to leap into action without a plan, I asked, "What happened tonight?"

"They were waiting for us. Griekev and Ivanov and some others. They knew about the Archivist Society. While Ivanov and his thugs beat me up, Griekev overpowered Emma and held a knife to her throat. Ivanov took her knife before Griekev dragged her upstairs and the rest tried to throw me in the cellar. I escaped to get help." The air seemed to leave his body. "I left Emma behind."

"We'll get her released," I assured him, although I didn't feel as confident as I tried to sound. "How long have they been on to you?"

Sumner exhaled in frustration. "I don't know. We thought we'd been careful. We pretended to be a couple suffering hard times and willing to work at anything for the highest bidder. But they knew about the Archivist Society and our meetings here. And they knew you're a member, Georgia, pretending to be Her Grace's secretary."

We had tried so hard to keep our existence secret. My first guess was that someone in Hereford House had betrayed us. From the look on Blackford's face, he had the same thought.

"How are we going to take the lookouts by surprise?" Blackford said.

"How many people are out on the street in that area at one or two in the morning?" I asked.

"Enough. Whores and their customers. People who work unusual hours. Bakers. At least the warehouses and breweries don't open until after four." Sumner looked puzzled by my question.

"So any man loitering in the streets could be a lookout? What if these men were approached by a whore? Wouldn't that distract them from their task?" I gave him a smile.

Sumner returned the smile. "Yes."

Blackford shook his head. His face had taken on an obstinate look the moment he realized my plan. "No. It's too dangerous."

"Not if you fellows grab them while they're distracted." What could be easier?

Sumner turned glum again. "Once we get inside, the building is a three-story house with a rabbit warren of rooms. A different family rents each room on the first two floors. The third floor is well guarded." He looked down, discovered he'd been stacking the plates in threes like the floors of the building, and set his hands in his lap. "It's where Griekev and Ivanov sleep and hold their meetings to organize their crimes. They have a gang of about six or eight men. Vicious street fighters."

I wanted to know more. "How many staircases in the building? Do they all go to the third floor? Are there any passages into the buildings on either side?"

"Two staircases. The one in front goes to the third floor. The one in back is in a two-story addition. The addition connects with the front building on both floors. You can reach the addition through the gate to the wagon yard on the left-hand side of the building."

"Who else uses this wagon yard?"

"The warehouse next door."

"So there are two ways into the building. The front door and the wagon yard leading to the back door." If I had to sneak in, I knew which entrance I'd choose.

Sumner nodded.

"Do you know the layout of the third floor?" Blackford demanded. He was looking and sounding more ducal by the moment.

"No, they never included me in their meetings. There's no knowing in which room they're holding Emma." Sumner picked up a fork as if to throw it, hesitated, and then set the fork down carefully on the table.

"Then I'll just have to enter while you deal with the burglars and try to find out where they have her. Mrs. Hardwick, do you have any children's slate-marking chalk?" She and I exchanged looks.

"Yes. And some items in my rag bag we can use to make you a costume that will attract those lookouts." She signaled me to follow her.

"What do you have in mind?" I asked when we entered the basement.

"How daring are you?" She raised her eyebrows.

"I'd go down there naked if it would rescue Emma."

Mrs. Hardwick searched my eyes and then nodded. With some snips, a few quick stitches, and terrific costuming sense on her part, I soon looked like a woman of the streets. When we walked back into the parlor, conversation stopped.

Perhaps because I was showing a great deal of bosom. Or possibly the amount of leg visible, well above my ankle. Whatever the reason, most of the men were looking at the ceiling or the floor. Blackford was gaping at me like a schoolboy.

The duke finally swallowed and said, "I don't think we should risk it, Georgia."

"Did you bring your ordinary, unmarked coach?" I replied.

"Of course. Oh, all right. You may lead the lookouts astray with your charms. But once we reach the building, you'll stay out of sight in the coach."

"No."

"Georgia, show some sense."

"You show some, Your Grace. I'm going in to find Emma. Once you overpower this gang, look for my chalk marks on the walls to rescue us both."

"She has a good plan, Blackford," Sir Broderick said.

Jacob and Adam Fogarty nodded.

Blackford looked at Sumner, who shrugged and said, "I don't like it, either."

Blackford mumbled something I probably didn't want to hear and reached into the inside of his jacket. He pulled out a folding knife and handed it to me. "Do you have any pockets in that— that—?"

"Yes." I put the small knife and the chalk in the pocket.

Sir Broderick tapped his fingers on the wheels of his chair. "Adam, it might not be a bad idea to fill Inspector Grantham in on what has transpired."

Fogarty nodded and wrote down Sumner's directions to the building that had become Emma's prison. He left first by the back door to avoid being seen by anyone who may have followed Sumner. It wouldn't take Adam long to reach the inspector or his police contacts.

A few minutes later, the rest of us left and piled into the coach or up with the driver. At Blackford's insistence, I had a full cloak cover my outfit.

Sumner silently brooded as we traveled toward the East End, his gaze on the floor by his feet. I couldn't have that. I needed to know every detail he and Emma had learned about the group and the building where she was prisoner. None of us could afford a mistake.

"Is there anything you haven't told us?"

He glanced at me and then back to the floor. "No."

"So the people in this building aren't anarchists? They're robbers?" I was no longer sure who we were going to meet this night.

"Most of the people on the first two floors are immigrants working in sweatshops in the area. A few of them are professional anarchists and as poor as their neighbors. Their printing press and office is in the first floor of the back addition to the building. The robbery ring has the third floor and a room of the second floor in the front."

"Anarchists aren't supposed to believe in any government. Every man should be free to do what they want. But even anarchists must learn soon enough that life doesn't work according to their ideals. The powerful rule the weak. So, who's the power behind this group of revolutionaries? Ivanov?" Blackford asked.

"No. There's one person Ivanov listens to. Maybe even follows. Andrei Griekev. An average-sized bloke with a great way of talking. He can convince anyone of anything. He makes people, even Ivanov, do what he wants by making them think it was their idea and that they want to do this thing more than anything else in the world. Griekev's the leader of the robbers." His gravelly voice was the only sound inside the coach. Outside, the clomp of horse hooves rang out in the sleeping city.

Sumner looked at me and said, "Griekev has hired thugs that

keep the neighborhood in line. And I've seen them carrying in things that have nothing to do with anarchists. A fancy chair. Some expensive-looking paintings."

I was forming a picture of the group in the building where Emma was being held. "Is Griekev the one Emma heard talking to a woman about something that will happen at lunchtime the day after tomorrow?" I realized it was after midnight. "Or, rather, tomorrow?"

"Yes. And he's the one who took Emma prisoner as a traitor. You can guess what they do to traitors."

My stomach flipped over. I felt the knife in my pocket and knew I'd be able to use the blade on Ivanov and Griekev. My only concern was that something so small could do any real damage.

Sumner continued, "I'm afraid Griekev will let Ivanov loose on Emma. Ivanov's wanted to torture her since we arrived. He started to beat her up once until I stopped him. Emma's never shown any fear of him, and he can't stand not to be feared."

I'll show him fright. "Why didn't you pull her out of there when Emma attracted Ivanov's interest?"

"Emma didn't want to leave. She thought with Ivanov focused on her, I'd have a better chance to find out what Griekev had planned." Sumner's face looked grim in the faint light inside the carriage. "When I'm done, Ivanov will be sorry he ever thought about harming Emma."

His tone sent icy water dripping into my veins. Ivanov had more to fear from Sumner than he had from me, and I was ready to rip the Russian limb from limb. Then I'd give Emma a good talking-to for not getting out of that situation in time.

I looked out the window. We were still crossing the City of London. Couldn't the horses go any faster?

In a few minutes, Sumner said, "Stop," and Blackford signaled the driver to pull over. "The first lookout will be around the corner, halfway down the block on this side."

I climbed out, confident someone would follow to help me. I sashayed around the corner and strolled down the street. It was dark. There weren't streetlamps on this narrow lane and clouds blocked any light we might have received from the quarter moon. My eyes adjusted to the gloom enough that I was able to notice movement ten paces ahead of me.

I needed to have faith someone was guarding me from behind.

Sauntering up, I put a hand on the man's rough fabric shirt and said, "Are you lonely?" in a sultry voice.

"Yeah," he grumbled and tried to paw me.

It was all I could do not to smack him silly. I slid around him, drawing my hand across his chest so he turned to face away from my rescuers. "That'll cost ya. But with some coin, you can have a lot more. What would you like tonight, handsome?"

He grabbed me and smashed his filthy lips against mine. Then he jerked backward and in the gloom I saw a pair of hands had put punishing grips on his shoulders. A moment later, he was flat on his stomach on the stones as one of the duke's footmen expertly tied him up.

"We go on foot from here," Sumner said.

I went first, following Sumner's directions, and between us we silenced a second watchman. I didn't think I'd been overheard by the men until Blackford slipped next to me and whispered, "I'm lonely."

He must have felt my startled jump, because I heard a hint of his chuckle. "This is the place, Georgia. Stay behind us where you'll be safe."

"No. You need me to go inside and find Emma while you fight

these crazy Russians." I grabbed his hand and gave it a squeeze. "Just remember to come find us if we can't get out."

"It's the building on the left. The first house past the warehouse." He embraced me for a moment. "Georgia, know I will find you if it's the last thing I do."

He sounded so serious my heart stumbled at the sudden ache. Don't let him be prophetic.

The sound of a series of blows and shouts to our right told me the robbers' guards had found us. The men fanned out while I melted into the building across the street. While grunts and thuds echoed around me, I used the buildings and the night for cover.

Just before I reached the gates to the wagon yard, a man rushed out to join the melee. I flattened myself against the sooty brick wall of the warehouse, but he didn't turn my way. As soon as he was past, I slipped in. Lamps by the doors to the warehouse gave me enough light to rush across the yard.

The back door was unlocked. From what Sumner had said, it wouldn't make sense that they'd keep Emma prisoner on the first floor. As soon as my eyes grew accustomed to the faint light coming in through the row of large bare windows, I made out the shape of machinery in the high-ceilinged area. This must be the print shop for the anarchist papers circulating throughout London.

I saw the staircase and started climbing, marking the wall with my chalk. When I reached the second floor, I stopped and listened. Not hearing any voices, I opened two doors. Inside one of the rooms were cots, piles of bedding, a few articles of clothing, a chair or two, and little else. In the other, I found a woman and two children sleeping. But no Emma.

I tiptoed away. The corridor ran along the inside of the building toward the front, lit by a single lantern. As I walked along, I

heard a baby wail and a mother shushing it. I guessed these rooms
would be occupied by families not involved in the craziness I could
hear outside. A small child stuck his head out of a door and was
roughly pulled back inside by someone threatening him with a
spanking. I heard snores from behind another door.

I reached the front of the building, marked the staircase with
chalk, and hurried to the third floor. Now I heard nothing but
the sounds of bobbies' whistles coming from outside and men's
shouts. Help had arrived for Blackford. I hoped he was all right.

The first room I entered was a large, square, richly appointed
parlor with a small oil lamp burning on the mantel. I could see
draperies pulled back from the windows. I bumped into an end
table and put my hand on it. Marble. Running my hand against
a chair, I felt the satin upholstery.

I picked up the lamp and kept going. The room next to the
parlor was a well-appointed bedroom in black and green that faced
the street. Then I walked down a long hallway until I finally
reached two more bedrooms, one in blue with oak paneling and
the other in pink and violet and ruffles. Three residents. Two male,
one female.

I could think of only two leaders of this group and they were
both male. Who used the pink bedroom?

There was no sign of Emma or her jailers. Blast it, where was she?

CHAPTER SEVENTEEN

WITH a sick feeling in my stomach, I was about to dash down the long hallway to the stairs. Emma had to be on another floor. Or in another building. I wheeled around in the center of the hall, realizing something was wrong with the layout on this floor. The hallway had no doors off the length of it, but the bedrooms facing the front and back of the floor weren't nearly long enough to meet in the middle.

What was in the space in between and how could I get in? There had to be a hidden room in the center of this floor.

Holding the lamp up, I studied the walls in the hallway between the parlor and the green room in the front and the other two bedrooms at the far end of the building. A couple of fine paintings hung on the otherwise plain walls. There was no chair railing to hide a switch. No handle or doorknob. Nothing to hide an entrance or a sliding panel.

I could hear horses below in the street. I guessed these were pulling the police wagons used to transport the prisoners. I knocked on the wall and heard it ring hollow.

I hurried into the parlor and felt around the carving of the mantelpiece. Nothing swung open. Nothing clicked.

Footsteps pounding up the stairs made me jump. I ran into the hall and saw Blackford and Sumner arrive in the light of the lamp I'd taken from the parlor. "Where is she?" the duke asked.

"I don't know, but there has to be a hidden room behind this wall."

Sumner knocked on the wall in a few places. "It sounds hollow."

Blackford disappeared into the parlor and returned in a moment with the andirons from the fireplace. Handing one to Sumner, they began to attack the wall. Sumner broke through first, and I could see light through the hole. He and Blackford went to work breaking chunks of plaster off to enlarge the hole until we could squeeze through, one at a time.

I went last, but not by choice. Emma was tied to a chair in the middle of the room. Several feet away were another chair and a table where a single candle burned. I coughed as I tried to breathe the thick, stale air now coated with plaster dust. The room smelled of dirt and candle grease and sweat and fear.

Emma's body sagged against her bindings. Her hair had fallen loose of its topknot and there was a smear of blood on her dress. I wanted her to move, to cry out, anything to show she was alive. But she remained limp.

Blackford cut Emma's bonds while Sumner held her face as he stared at her closed eyes and kept murmuring her name. It had to be enough to give me hope.

As Blackford finished with the ropes, she pitched forward and

Sumner swung her up into his arms. Blackford grabbed one wrist. "I feel a pulse, but it's weak. Is she breathing?"

Sumner turned his ear toward her mouth. "It's very shallow. We need to get her to a doctor."

I held up the lamp and saw the outlines of two openings. One toward the front of the building and one toward the back. I hurried to the door leading to the front and found the mechanism to open it attached to the dirty wall. "Come on."

I went first with the lamp, with Sumner carrying Emma right behind me, and then Blackford after he blew out the candle. The duke whistled when he saw the contents of the parlor shining in the lamplight. "We'll have to send the constables back for all of this. And find someone to open that safe."

"What safe?" I asked as I hurried to follow Sumner down the stairs.

Blackford's reply was a grumble.

When we reached the street, Blackford's carriage was waiting for us. Blackford issued orders to his footmen, who walked back to stand by the front door before he leaped into the carriage. Sumner lifted Emma's limp frame up to him.

By the time I scrambled into the carriage, Sumner was seated with Emma in his lap and across one seat. I squeezed in between Blackford and Jacob. The lamp I held showed me all three men were bruised and bloodied, but I didn't see any serious injuries. Emma didn't seem to move or breathe. She lay slack in Sumner's arms as he stroked her cheek and murmured in her ear.

"What happened?" I asked as the carriage jolted into motion.

"We were outnumbered," Jacob said, "but we kept them busy until Adam arrived with the police."

"Ivanov? And Griekev?"

"No sign of either one of them. And I suspect more than a few of their thugs got away," Blackford said. "Once we get Emma home and fetch a doctor, I need to reenter their rooms. See what I can learn about their criminal activities."

"There's a printing press and offices on the first floor in the back. If they're running a ring of thieves out of there as well as the anarchist press, I'd look there as well as the rooms on the third floor. Their furnishings are as nice as yours, Your Grace."

"I saw those paintings in the hallway. One's a Gainsborough, I think," Blackford said without a trace of irony.

"In a hallway in an East End tenement?" I found that thought amazing.

"Where better to hide stolen goods?" Jacob replied. "I'd like to go back with you, Your Grace."

"Thank you, Jacob."

Sumner looked at Emma's expressionless face and then at Blackford.

"She's going to want to see you when she wakes up, not us," I told him. "We'll leave you to get the doctor and then you and Phyllida can take care of her."

"Thank you," Sumner said in a weary voice.

"We?" Blackford said in surprise.

"You're not getting rid of me," I told him.

"At least change your clothes," he said, eyeing my scandalous attire. "And you'll have to hurry. I don't look forward to another battle with those thugs they employ, and they'll be released by the magistrate soon enough."

Phyllida looked ready to swoon when Sumner carried a still-unconscious Emma into our home, but she took a deep breath and directed him to Emma's bedroom. Then, setting her shoulders back like a soldier on parade, she marched into the kitchen and began to make strong tea with plenty of sugar. Heaven knew we all needed it after the night we'd had.

And it wasn't over yet.

I hurried into my room and removed my costume, which Phyllida mercifully hadn't noticed. Fortunately, I'd left my corset and stockings in place. I needed only to pull on a dress I wore for hauling books around the bookshop and hurried back to join the pair I found pacing in the parlor.

"We promised to wait until Sumner returns with the doctor," Blackford said. "In case we're needed."

His gaze traveled in the direction of Emma's room.

As his words sank in, I joined in the pacing. After a moment, I found it impossible to wait. I marched back to Emma's room and found her lying on the bed, her eyes shut. I helped Phyllida finish removing her clothes. Her dirtied and bloodied dress already lay on the floor. I turned her while Phyllida sponged off the worst of the dirt and blood.

Her purple bruises and cuts left by Ivanov a day earlier were evident. Now she had a new slice across her neck that had bled onto the neck of her dress and bruises on her arms in the shape of large fingerprints. I didn't see any head wounds, yet she didn't stir.

Poison.

I was livid at their cruelty. I was going to kill Ivanov. Or Griekev. Or the unknown woman. Or all three. With my bare hands around their throats.

I could hear Sir Broderick's voice in my head, saying, *No. We will turn them over to the police, and we will provide evidence of their crimes. That is our job. We are not executioners.*

How many times had he said that to me about my parents' killer after their deaths? Too many to count in those first years.

My temper had been banked over the years, but I'd never truly been able to put out the fire.

Leaning over the bed, I smelled Emma's breath and checked her head for signs of a lump. No odor of poison, no lumps. Her breathing was shallow and slow. I decided this was a sign she'd pull through and released a great sigh.

Phyllida finished bathing her, and then the two of us pulled a clean shift over her and tucked in the bedclothes. I knew she'd be in good hands with Phyllida and Sumner.

I walked from her room, ready to attack the leaders of this ring of thieves with their expensive tastes. The first person I met in the hallway was the doctor, who greeted me distractedly and moved on. Phyllida hurried him to the bedside while she began to catalog what little we knew about Emma's condition.

Sumner was in the parlor with the men, all of them on their feet. "Did anyone get some tea?"

They all shook their heads. Then Blackford looked over my gown and nodded to himself. Apparently he approved of drab gray where he didn't like light-skirt flamboyance.

"Let's go," I said to Blackford and Jacob. "Sumner, sit down and relax. You'll have a long night ahead of you. Try to rest now. And have some tea. You look peaked."

His voice grumbled from deep in his chest but indistinctly as he resumed pacing.

I shook my head at his nervous energy, but I couldn't claim to be any better. I was rushing around as if my actions alone would make Emma well. I waited for the other two men to leave my home and then brought up the tail of our strange procession. A duke, a young assistant to Sir Broderick who'd begun life in the East End, and a female middle-class bookshop owner.

"I borrowed another lantern from Lady Phyllida so we'll have two to search the place properly," Jacob told me, setting his next to the one I had grabbed from the fancy parlor in the tenement.

I picked up the lantern I'd borrowed and looked it over under the streetlights in my neighborhood. "The outside of this is made of silver."

The two faces inside the carriage stared at me and then the duke took the unlit lamp and studied it. "Definitely silver, and I've seen its mate before. When we no longer need it, I should return this to its rightful owner." He signaled and the carriage began to roll.

"Who?" I caught his gaze and held it.

"Remember the robbery at the Marquis of Shepherdston's more than a month ago?"

"How could I forget? The thieves blew up part of the house." Then I looked at the delicately sculptured lamp. "Do you mean—?"

"This is one of the pieces that was stolen."

Pieces of the two cases began to fall together. Unfortunately, I was so tired I couldn't make sense of the whole plan. "We need to tell Scotland Yard. They've been chasing all over after the thieves."

Blackford smiled. "I think we just solved the case."

That left me with even more questions. "But I thought Ivanov was an anarchist. And yes, anarchists make bombs like the one used to blow the Marquis of Shepherdston's safe. That's what killed Tsar Alexander. But I thought anarchists didn't believe in people living in luxury. Their rooms in that building are certainly opulent."

"Perhaps they only object to other people living in luxury." Blackford's tone was dry. "It's a useful way to fund their work and their newspapers. You can't think there's much money in being a rabble-rouser."

"I wonder if everything in the rooms on the third floor was stolen."

"Probably." In the glow of a streetlight as we passed, I could see Blackford's smug expression. "Especially that Gainsborough."

"Why would anarchists want to live in such luxurious conditions? Why not sell those goods as well to fund their revolution?"

"We'll have to catch them and ask them."

His solution didn't make sense to me. "What if the anarchist cause was just a smoke screen for their real intentions? Maybe they're really a gang of thieves who are hiding behind the anarchists."

"The anarchists have a history of robbing to fund their work. The only difference with this group is they're in London and we have to stop them."

He was probably correct, but it still didn't feel right. I looked out the window of the carriage and realized we had returned to the tenement. As we climbed down, I asked, "Which building did Nadia live in?"

Blackford opened his mouth and shut it again before saying, "I was going to ask Sumner. So far as I know, only he and Emma and the anarchists know."

When I looked at Jacob, he shook his head. "I never found out where Nadia lived. She gave me the slip in this neighborhood."

The residents of the area in the street at that hour gave us surreptitious glances as they shuffled by on their way to work in local sweatshops and factories.

We were joined by the duke's footmen who'd stood guard by the front door. Inside the building, I could hear sounds of children running and babies crying and muffled voices as we walked to the back of the first floor and searched the printing shop. We found broadsheets and papers pertaining to anarchy, but I was more interested in the cheap two-shilling editions of Russian literature, history, and philosophy. I picked some up and glanced through them. I didn't know if the books had been written in English or translated. Either way, the fiction was brooding and colorful. The wording sounded like that of a native English speaker.

I was lost in a story when a young man hurried into the office, pulling his suspenders over his shirt as he came in. "What are you doing?"

The duke faced him. "Who are you?"

The man straightened and looked Blackford in the eye. "Nicolai Mukovski. Who are you?"

"I'm the—"

If this man was an anarchist, there was no way Blackford's next words would get us anything but a debate. "Georgia Fenchurch, and we're here from the Archivist Society. Actually, it's what's on the third floor that concerns us. That, and the kidnapping of a young woman."

"Then you should be on the third floor. You English claim you believe in property rights, but then you storm through here like the Okhrana, the secret police, looking at everything." His heavy accent sounded like Princess Kira's. Even if I hadn't heard his name, I would have known he had to be a Russian immigrant.

"Unlike the secret police, we haven't destroyed anything." I gave him a smile. "We just wanted to make sure you weren't involved in that gang on the third floor."

He made a dismissive gesture. "They pay our rent and a stipend to our workers, but they are not believers in our cause. We keep our mouths shut, and they protect us from raids from your police."

"Have the police ever raided you?" Blackford demanded.

"No," the man admitted.

"Then why would you need protection from them?"

"It's only a matter of time. The agents of the Okhrana are everywhere. The capitalist masters don't like us to spread our message of equality." His thin face was split by a smile that didn't reach his eyes.

Before Blackford could begin a debate, I said, "Have you seen what your proletariat brothers have set up on the third floor?"

He looked at me, puzzled.

"Come with us." We all marched up to the third floor. In the light of our two lanterns, we could see the paintings had been taken off the walls and the doors stood open.

"They didn't come by us," the footmen said.

Blackford strode into the parlor and pointed to a safe standing open in the corner. "You don't keep equality in one of those."

Mukovski blinked as he looked around him at the pristine draperies and ornate furniture. "We'd see them carry crates in and out of here, but they paid us not to notice such things."

"I'll bet they did," Blackford muttered.

"All the small items have been removed," I said, walking to check the bedrooms. It was the same in all three rooms. The furniture was in place, but all the small, valuable objects were gone, along with any clothing. Still, the draperies, wallpaper, and furnishings showed these had been elegant surroundings in the midst of East End squalor.

I turned to Mukovski, who'd followed me from room to room, his eyes and mouth round. "Did the people who lived here ever invite you or your comrades to these rooms?"

"They hired one of the women to clean for them. Stories went around, but they let us know we weren't welcome up here."

I made a sweeping gesture toward the rooms. "It appears your protectors have deserted you. That'll mean no more money for food or broadsheets. They don't deserve your loyalty. When did they come back tonight to remove their things?"

He surveyed rooms that had lost their lived-in appearance and his shoulders slumped. "Half an hour after the fighting outside ended. It was only Ivanov and Griekev. They filled up a wagon and left not more than ten minutes before you arrived."

"We saw a wagon come into the yard next door and leave later on. We didn't think anything of it. They headed east," one of the footmen said.

"They had to take their valuables somewhere. Where did they go?" Blackford demanded.

"They didn't tell me." Mukovski jutted his jaw out.

"And you didn't ask," Blackford said. "That shows a great deal of equality in your dealings with them."

Mukovski gave him an angry stare and turned to leave.

Blast. If anyone knew where those thugs had taken their loot, it would be this man. And Blackford had set Mukovski against us with his regal attitude.

I grabbed the printer's arm and said, "Please. Do you have any idea where they could have gone? They poisoned their kidnap victim and we want to know if there's an antidote." When he hesitated, I pressed on. "Emma's a friend of mine. A dear friend. I want to save her life, if it's possible."

"Emma Sumner?"

Was that what she'd called herself during this investigation? "Yes. The men who lived on this floor poisoned her. I want to save her. Help us." Desperation rang in my voice.

"Emma is a good soul." He ran a hand through his longish, limp hair. "But I think her husband, Sumner, is a Russian secret policeman. A member of Okhrana. Him I do not trust."

I shook my head. "No. Sumner was a British Army officer before he was wounded. He works for the Archivist Society, the same group Emma and I work for. We are dedicated to getting justice for people when the police fail. There's nothing secret about our work." Well, not much, I admitted to myself.

He studied me for a minute. "You are sure Sumner is not Okhrana?"

"Very sure."

"But Griekev said he was Okhrana."

"Griekev's a liar. Please. Help us help Emma. Where could Griekev and Ivanov have gone?"

"I followed them once. Mistrust is bred into us. They have a warehouse about three blocks away." He gave us the street and described the location.

"I know it," Jacob said.

The men all rushed downstairs, leaving me with Mukovski. "Thank you," I told him. As we started down the stairs, I said, "Those two-shilling editions you printed. Are those volumes licensed? Do you pay the author and translator?"

"Of course we do. It would be against our principles not to pay the workman. Those books were all written by Russians living in this neighborhood. Why?"

"I own a bookshop. I liked some of the stories I saw in your office. Who distributes your books?" I knew which of my customers loved fiction. I thought I could try to sell a few copies and see if they proved popular.

"We do it ourselves. No one will handle our work. We are outcasts. Immigrants."

"I'll be busy today, but come by Fenchurch's Books near Leicester Square tomorrow at opening time and bring some samples of your work. Preferably fiction."

His lower jaw dropped open and then slammed shut. "You're making fun of us."

"Come by Fenchurch's Books tomorrow morning and see if I'm making fun of you."

He studied my face for a moment and then gave one sharp nod of his head.

There was one more thing I needed to know. "Do you know if a young woman named Nadia Andropov is staying with a family around here?"

He hesitated. Finally he said, "Yes. They live on the second floor in the back, above the printing presses."

So Nadia would have known Ivanov and Griekev. Was she as wary of them as Mukovski seemed to be?

CHAPTER EIGHTEEN

I caught up with Blackford by his coach. "I want to talk to the family Nadia has been living with."

"Do you know where they live?"

"Thanks to Mukovski, yes. Second floor in the back."

We found their rooms, but only an old woman and two children were there. The old woman spoke no English, but the children, a boy and a girl in worn but clean clothes, sounded like any other residents of the East End.

"Do you know Nadia?" I asked.

"Who wants to know?" the boy, the younger of the two, replied. His jaw jutted out mulishly and he fisted his small hands on tiny hips.

Blackford reached into his vest pocket and came out with a half crown. "This wants to know."

Both children's eyes lit up. The boy said, "And one for my sister."

"For everything you know. Everything," I said.

Blackford produced the coin's mate, but held on to them tightly above the boy's reach. The girl stayed behind the young-ster, half-hidden by the door.

"She lives in the building and is comrades with the thief," the boy said.

"The thief?"

"Griekev."

"Are they good friends?"

"Seems that way."

"She doesn't live here?" I pressed.

"Where would there be room for the likes of her? She has her own space. We just pretend to be her family if anyone comes snoop-ing around," the boy continued.

"Why would anyone come snooping around?" Blackford asked.

"You have, ain't ya?"

"So why are you telling us this?" I asked, genuinely curious.

"Because she left and she ain't comin' back," the boy said. "And your money's too good to pass up."

"How do you know she's not coming back?"

"Took all her things with her. Gave my gran a few shillings and thanked her. Said none of us would have to go back to Rus-sia now."

"You're afraid you'll be sent back to Russia?" Talking to this boy was fascinating although I was confused by the conversation.

"Nobody likes anarchists. Or the poor."

"Princess Nadia is the daughter of an evil prince, and her wicked stepmother, his wife, wants her dead. She has beautiful clothes and jewels," the girl said with a note of wonder in her voice as she twisted her braid. "She let me wear her necklace once."

"Where did she get her beautiful clothes and jewels?"

Both children shrugged their thin shoulders in unison.

We got nothing more out of them for Blackford's two half crowns. We climbed into the carriage with Jacob and rode away, the footmen riding on the back of the coach. We stopped at Scotland Yard while Blackford went inside with the silver lamp to report our findings.

After a lengthy wait, during which I nearly fell asleep, he returned. "The police were most interested in what we discovered," he told me. "Inspector Grantham is organizing a raid on the warehouse as we speak."

"Are we going with them, Your Grace?" Jacob asked.

"We're not going anywhere until I find out how Emma is," I told them. The scowl I gave them must have warned them not to disagree.

When we arrived at my home, we found Phyllida asleep in a chair in the parlor. Tiptoeing past her, I went to Emma's room. Sumner sat on the edge of her bed running his hand over her wrist.

"She looks better, don't you think?" he asked me. His voice sounded like distant thunder coming at me from the side of the bed.

"Her coloring is definitely better. What did the doctor say?"

"He thinks it's a laudanum overdose. As long as she keeps breathing, she should eventually wake up." He finally turned to look at me. "Phyllida had this idea to keep sticking things like onions and garlic under her nose to stir her. Then I started running her hairbrush up and down her arms. Seems to have worked. Her breathing's regular now."

"You've done a good job."

He glared at me. "If I'd done a good job, Emma wouldn't have been in danger."

"She'd be the first one to tell you not to think you're so important. She can take care of herself."

"No. That's going to be my job from now on." He held my gaze. "She agreed, before all this, to become my wife."

If she agreed, then Emma must be very happy about this change to her life. I burst out laughing and crying at once. "Best wishes. Oh, I'm so happy for you! Did you tell Phyllida?"

"Yes. She seemed pleased."

"She gets to be the mother of a bride. She must be over the moon."

Phyllida walked in stiffly, followed by Blackford, and looked from one of us to the other. "All is well?"

"You've heard the good news?" I asked Blackford.

He reached over and shook Sumner's hand. "My congratulations. We'll talk later. For now, Jacob and I need to find out what's happening with the police raid on Griekev and Ivanov's warehouse. I'm certain they're the thieves who robbed the homes of the Marquis of Shepherdston, Lord Walker, and the others."

"I'll go with you, Your Grace. I imagine Georgia wants to take a turn at Emma's bedside."

I patted Sumner's shoulder. "Thank you," I whispered, overcome by his generosity. I'd never had any siblings, but it felt like I was gaining a brother by marriage.

"You can both go if you want. I can stay with Emma," Phyllida said.

"I don't mind staying, and you need some rest. Jacob can represent the Archivist Society as well as I can." I turned to Blackford. "You'd better get moving. If Ivanov or Griekev goes back to their hideout for a second load, they'll learn we were there and they'll move everything out of their warehouse before the police arrive. The Russians will escape to steal again, or even to flee England." By the time I finished speaking, I was shoving the two men from Emma's room.

Blackford gave me a bow. Sumner gave me a wink and hurried his boss away. Then I pulled up a chair to Emma's bedside. "Do you want to sit here, Aunt Phyllida?"

She did, and I sat on the edge of the bed. "Georgia, when Emma recovers, we're going to have to plan a wedding." Her narrow face widened to accommodate her smile.

"Yes, but while she's recovering, I'll need to hear what she learned and saw at the anarchists' hideout."

"Are they anarchists or are they thieves?"

"Both. The two groups made a pact that was mutually beneficial. We disrupted that in rescuing Emma, but the thieves have yet to be caught."

"And it was the thieves who—" Phyllida made a gesture toward Emma's sleeping figure.

"Yes. They're the ones Blackford, Jacob, Sumner, and the police are going after now."

"I hope they catch them." Phyllida's tone was as grim as I'd ever heard her use.

We had a half hour wait before Emma finally shifted in bed and opened her eyes. She looked from Phyllida to me and whispered, "What happened?"

"Do you remember the building in the East End?"

Her lids started to close, only to jerk open as she shoved herself into a half-sitting, half-leaning position. "You rescued me?"

"Sumner got us. We all went and rescued you."

"Have you caught Griekev? He's behind the thefts and the plot against the visiting Russian grand duke."

"He's moved his stolen goods out of the building you were in, but Mukovski told us about a warehouse he has a few blocks away. The police have probably already raided it."

She nodded and slid back under the covers. "I'm so tired."

"I'm not surprised. Getting engaged and being kidnapped all in one day must be tiring."

When Emma's eyes flew open once more, it was to see me grinning at her. "Sumner told you?"

"Yes."

"I would have told you after the investigation was over."

"I know."

"You're not angry?"

"Why should I be angry if you're happy? You've always been meant to live a full life. A lucky life. But you'd better hurry and recover or Aunt Phyllida will have your wedding planned before you get a say in anything."

Phyllida laughed, a sound we seldom heard even after all these years that she'd been free from her brother. "I will not. But I do have a few ideas," she added.

"Fine. Just not today." Emma's eyes drifted closed. "Someone is telling Griekev what to do."

"Wait." I shook her shoulder. "Emma, he has a boss?"

"A partner. I don't know who. A woman, I think. I heard her voice once. Someone smarter than he is."

Then the only sounds in the room were Emma's soft snores and a gentle sigh of relief from Phyllida and me. After a few minutes, we rose and shuffled to the kitchen. I was drooping from weariness, and Phyllida appeared too stiff to move.

"Would you be a sweet girl and make some fresh tea? My old bones aren't letting me get around like I want to this morning," Phyllida said.

I put the kettle on and said, "You can't imagine how relieved I am. I think you and Emma have earned a nice rest this morning. After you both get some sleep, you'll feel much better."

The look she gave me was uncharacteristically hard. "And

you, Georgia? Don't you deserve some rest?" She lowered herself slowly into a chair, and I brought the sugar and milk to the table.

"Once Ivanov and Griekev are in custody and we've eliminated the danger to Princess Kira, I'm certain I'll sleep for a week. Today, I need to arrive at Hereford House at my usual time. At least I can bathe first."

"Could you fix breakfast before you leave? There's some bread and eggs in the icebox."

Phyllida was looking thinner and paler than usual after her ordeal. My heart ached for her as badly now as hers must have hurt for Emma during the night. "Of course."

I opened up the tin-lined wooden box, pulled out what I needed from above the block of ice, and began a process Phyllida had spared me for years.

I hated to cook, but she enjoyed it, and life in our house went smoothly when we stayed with our God-given talents.

Apparently the day was going to be as topsy-turvy as the night had been. I juggled the various tasks as well as I could, Phyllida exclaiming when I dropped a hot pan and when smoke rose from the eggs. Finally, I placed our breakfast on the table and sat down with her as she poured me a cup of tea.

Taking a long, grateful sip, I set down my cup and watched Phyllida's nose twitch as she sampled a forkful of eggs and bread. "It's too bad your mother never taught you to cook."

"She tried. I wasn't a good pupil. I'd rather have been working with my father in the bookshop."

"I've been teaching Emma to cook," she said with studied nonchalance, studying her plate.

"For how long?"

"A few months. We thought it might be a good idea. Sumner

had been calling on her despite there not being an investigation to serve as an excuse."

I ran my mind over the past few months. Sumner dropped by the bookshop regularly, but I had always thought it was to check out the newest releases. He seemed to be a fan of Mrs. Hepplewhite. Emma started running all the household errands, but I had thought she was merely being helpful.

They had been courting, and I was so wrapped in a cocoon of book shipments and ledgers that I'd never noticed. Perhaps because every time I saw Sumner, my thoughts immediately traveled to Blackford. I often wondered where he was.

Knowing it would bring me no comfort, I never asked.

I sent Phyllida to bed after breakfast, did the dishes, bathed, and dressed, all while moving lethargically. Guilt almost made me wear a work corset pulled loosely rather than wake Phyllida to help with a dressier one. In the end I woke her because I needed to look tidy. My clothes would mask my sleep-starved state.

I glanced up once to see the duke's folding knife sitting on my dresser. I hugged the handle with my hand, remembering Blackford's efforts the previous night for Emma and loving him for his determination. I slipped his knife into my pocket, hoping for an early opportunity to return it.

Despite my weariness, I was dressed in time to check on the bookshop before I had to leave for Hereford House. It seemed fitting somehow that I had to wear a waterproof cloak and put up my umbrella against what appeared to be the start of a daylong rain.

When I went to retrieve my ledgers, Charles Dickens, our neighborhood cat, was curled up in my chair in the office. I walked over to him and found myself faced with his slit-eyed stare. His look dared me to move him as much as any words could.

I put a hand on his bottom to shove him out of my way and discovered he could somehow change his body mass to become too heavy to move. He seemed to weigh twenty stone. Then he reached out one back foot and scratched my wrist with his claws.

I jumped back, sucking on my wounded hand while Dickens gave me a haughty look that clearly said, *I was here first.*

I picked up the ledgers and carried them out to the counter in the shop, turning on the lights as I went. A moment later, I heard a knock on the door despite the Closed sign hanging in plain sight.

Walking over, I was about to shout that we were closed when I saw Blackford in the door's glass panel. I quickly opened the door to him and said, "Emma's awakened."

He walked in and shut the door behind him. He shook off his hat and coat and then peeled them off before dumping them on the umbrella stand. Taking a deep breath, he let it out and let his shoulders slump. Looking haggard, his clothes streaked with coal dust, and his eyelids drooping, he said, "I know. I was just there. I'm afraid I bring bad news, Georgia."

My heart stopped beating. Despite our best efforts, Emma had died. I had failed her. My legs started to crumple. Tears slid unstopped down my cheeks. "Emma's dead?"

Blackford grabbed me by the shoulders before I could collapse on the floor. Then he wrapped his arms around me and held me close. "Wait. Georgia. No. Emma's all right."

I looked up at him, stunned, confused. "But you said you were just there and were bringing bad news."

"I misspoke. Forgive me. I'm just so tired and—" He shook his head.

I looked at Blackford, surprised to see him in such a state. The man never looked ruffled, yet this morning he looked like he'd been beaten up and run over by a wagon. Whatever the bad news was, my heart ached for him more than myself. Wrapping my arms around him, I couldn't stop myself from using his name rather than his title. "What's happened, Ranleigh?"

The duke didn't blink at my use of his surname. He didn't shy away from my embrace. My actions were overly familiar, but he clearly needed a friend. Blackford appeared to have used up the last of his ducal reserves.

After a moment, he stepped back, peeled off his filthy fawn leather gloves, and took my bare hand in his. "We recovered all the stolen goods from the warehouse. The police have taken custody of them. But after a short fight, two policemen have been shot. Griekev and Ivanov escaped. The police, Sumner, Jacob, and I gave chase, but they vanished."

I gasped. "How are the policemen?"

"Not badly injured. Expected to live. Ivanov is not the good shot we believed him to be after killing Robert the footman at Shepherdston's. But nothing will save Ivanov now. Sumner is hunting him down."

"Good heavens. We still have to worry about Sumner."

"He'll be all right."

Didn't Blackford understand the danger? "Ivanov has a gun."

"So does Sumner."

I couldn't see this ending well.

Blackford pulled me close again and I snuggled against his shoulder. He spoke, his mouth near my ear. "After questioning, the police learned the anarchists at the house where Emma was held have no plans to hurt anyone. They have no interest in bothering Grand Duke Vassily or Princess Kira. They don't believe in violence. They're very happy to be in the safety of England. They admit there are a few radical anarchists in England, but they don't know them or their plans, if they even have plans."

"Do you think Griekev and Ivanov are behind the threat to the grand duke?"

He nodded, his eyes closed, as fatigue rolled off him like fog off the Thames.

"Emma said Griekev has a partner who's smarter than he is. A woman. But so far she's not told us anything more. When she wakes again, we can ask more questions."

"In the meantime," Blackford said, "I'll talk to the grand duke."

"No, you won't. You and your footmen need to go home and sleep for a few hours. Then you'll be able to deal with whatever threat arrives at the door of these Russians." I spit out the last few words. My temper was not to be trusted when I was tired. "And to rescue Sumner if necessary."

I softened as I looked into his sleepy dark eyes. For an instant, I pictured those eyes looking at me across a pillow. Shaking off my daydream, I said, "Remember, we still have until tomorrow to find out what Griekev and his fellow criminals have planned for the grand duke. Emma learned the date and time of the attack, just not what is planned. You have time to sleep."

"My valet will appreciate a chance to tidy me up before I descend on official London again." His smile wiped away the weariness in his eyes.

"Did Sumner tell you what happened to Emma in the East End?"

"Sumner got in with the anarchists, bringing Emma in as his wife. He claimed to have gotten into trouble with the bosses at a coal mine up north. Then he worked as muscle for me. Said he stole my boots." He grinned for an instant.

"They stayed in a room in that building, and Emma managed to talk to most of the people. Sumner passed out leaflets for the cause at first and then was used as a thug by Griekev to force vegetable merchants around Covent Garden to pay protection money."

"So they managed to get into a position to find out what was going on."

"Except they didn't. Griekev kept everything to himself. Mukovski appears to be harmless, interested in intellectual arguments to change the world. Sumner says Mukovski puts everything up for a vote in the group. Griekev doesn't tolerate anyone disagreeing with him. That man is a pirate captain."

"But Mukovski admits he made a deal with Griekev."

"Which he once described to Emma as making a deal with the devil." Blackford yawned behind the back of his free hand. I still snuggled against him, both of us so tired we were holding each other up.

"Why did they take Emma prisoner?"

"They must have discovered she'd overheard Griekev talking to a woman about an attack on their targets. And they could be sure Emma told Sumner. They took Emma prisoner and tried to throw Sumner in the cellar, probably to keep him imprisoned until they completed their plans. He escaped immediately, but they must have thought holding Emma would keep him silent."

I now had a hand under Blackford's elbow, supporting him. "I guess they didn't count on Sumner having a lot of people willing to help him save Emma. We listened to his story. And we acted."

I glanced at Blackford and watched his eyes drift closed. I knew I had to do the right thing. "This isn't getting you into bed, Ranleigh. Go home. Get some sleep. You and your men."

He nodded, his eyes still closed. "They followed me loyally today. I must reward them."

"You must. But first, reward them and yourself with sleep."

"And then I'm going after Griekev personally."

"Why?"

"This may come as a surprise to you, but I have pirate ancestry."

I bit back a smile. "Not really, Your Grace."

"I believe I'm the only one capable of stopping a pirate like Griekev. Not the police. Not the Archivist Society. Me. So far he's won every skirmish, but I intend to destroy him. He can't be allowed to blow up the safes of my friends and steal Gainsboroughs."

To me, Blackford sounded like a pirate on the right side of the law, and I couldn't have loved him more for his determination.

He left his dirty gloves stuffed in his pocket as he dropped my hand and picked up his hat and coat. "What will you do?"

"I'll be at Hereford House if you need me." I had to ask before he left. "Does Sumner make enough to support a wife?"

"You'd be surprised how much money he has. Emma chose better than she knows. Unless he's already told her." He opened the door of the shop, making the bell jangle. "Good night."

I looked out at the carriage, where the coachman and footmen looked like a band of worn-out brigands. They huddled under their caps and jackets as the rain fell. "Good night."

CHAPTER NINETEEN

BLACKFORD rode off in his coach, and I began to check over my bookshop ledgers. I was still at it, fighting to concentrate on the figures, when Frances came in. "What's happened with the Russians?" she asked as she took off her hat and gloves.

"The anarchists aren't our problem. There's been a group of burglars who've hidden among the anarchists, living in the same tenement with them. These thieves have been behind the big robberies in London."

"The Marquis of Shepherdston?"

"Yes, and several other thefts, all just as daring."

"Have they been caught?"

I filled her in on all that had happened during the night.

"Good heavens. Policemen shot." The shock on Frances's face must have mirrored my own when Blackford told me. Then she blinked and said, "I'm glad Emma will be all right. I know how worried you were."

"Everything's fine now." I'd let Emma tell her about the wedding.

It was her news to share. "I have the ledgers as far along as they're going to get today. I'd better get over to Hereford House. With Griekev and Ivanov on the loose, the princess might still be in danger."

"Oh, you don't think so, do you? Why would successful burglars want to attack a foreign princess who doesn't have a household they can rob? You said yourself they're not anarchists."

Something bothered me about what Frances said, but I was too tired to figure it out. I carried the ledgers back into the office to find Charles Dickens had disappeared. When I reemerged, Frances had put up the Open sign and had begun dusting. I put on my hat and gloves, said good-bye, and walked to Hereford House.

The cool rain forced me to hurry, pumping blood to my brain. If I didn't think about how many hours separated me from my bed, I might make it through the day without bringing shame on myself by collapsing.

I entered the front hall to find the servants busy giving the area an extra-good cleaning. "What's going on?" I asked the butler.

"Grand Duke Vassily is coming for a private luncheon with Princess Kira, the dukes of Sussex and Blackford, and Her Grace. Then the Russian ambassador and his lady were added. We are having something of a state occasion."

I wished him good luck and went into the back hall to take off my hat and gloves. I had just set them down on the empty table when Amelia Whitten came breathlessly in the back door, pulling a hat pin out of her hair. "Gracious. Where have you been?" I asked.

"I don't answer to you," she snapped and set down her things.

Then she opened the secret doorway in the hall and disappeared up the steps.

Grand Duke Vassily was arriving on a surprise visit to Hereford House today and Miss Whitten had disappeared on an errand without Lady Daisy. I wondered where I could find the three Russians I found suspicious.

I stopped dead in the hallway as I realized all four possible accomplices of the burglars in the Duchess of Hereford's house were women. Griekev had been meeting with a woman just before Emma was taken prisoner. A woman who seemed to be his partner. Or his boss.

While it didn't make sense that Princess Kira would be behind attacks on herself, the attacks had been against Lidijik the guard and Lady Raminoff the chaperone, not Princess Kira. I didn't know what she could gain by their deaths, but I knew I needed to find out.

I raced up the secret staircase, but instead of entering the nursery, I headed for Princess Kira's room. She looked up when I entered.

She greeted me with, "You should knock."

"Where is Mila?"

Princess Kira waved a hand in the air. "She went out to get a new ribbon for my dress. She burned the other one with an iron this morning, clumsy girl. When we get back to St. Petersburg, I will dismiss her."

"And Nadia?"

"She had a meeting with Grand Duke Vassily this morning at the embassy. I don't know what good that will do," she added with a sniff, turning partially away from me.

"Did you two quarrel?"

"Of course not. I'm on her side. I told her that when we get back to St. Petersburg, I'll ask the tsar to give her the honors she deserves."

I began to think the princess lived in a fairy tale where she had more influence than she did in reality. "Did you ever think she might not go back to St. Petersburg? Not even to be proclaimed a princess?"

She opened her mouth but then shut it without making a sound. Frowning, she rose and walked over to look out the window.

"Have an enjoyable luncheon," I said and left the room. Once again avoiding the front staircase, I went in search of Mary, who was now in place as Nadia's lady's maid. I found her in the basement, mending a gown of Nadia's. I glanced around to make sure none of the other servants were within listening distance. "What time did Nadia leave this morning?"

"As soon as she and the princess finished breakfast."

"How did she seem?"

"Seem, miss?"

"Was she in a good mood? Is she invited to the luncheon today?"

After a moment, she shook her head. "No. Mila told me Nadia wouldn't be invited because the Russians don't want her there. And when the princess said she had to get ready for the grand duke's luncheon, Miss Nadia said she was speaking to the grand duke this morning. Then she added that she didn't expect to be invited to the luncheon after this meeting. I got the impression she didn't think her talk with the Russian gentleman would go well."

"They were speaking English in front of you?" Apparently neither of them cared if they were overheard by the servants.

"Yes. I don't think they consider Mila or me important enough to worry about whether we could hear them."

"Did they argue?"

"No, miss. The princess said it was just Russian stubbornness and Nadia's standing doesn't matter in England, and Miss Nadia said it matters everywhere. She put on her hat and gloves and left a few minutes later. She hasn't returned, or she would have called for me."

"And the maid, Mila?"

"I don't know if she's come back yet. She would have left from the servants' entrance to get a replacement for the ribbon she burned. You could ask the housekeeper if she's seen either Mila or Miss Nadia."

"I will. Thank you. And let me know as soon as Nadia returns."

I found the housekeeper dealing with the linens in the tiny closet just behind the butler's pantry. "I don't have time to worry about the back door today," she told me. "Not with a last-minute luncheon on top of the formal dinner we're hosting."

"Last minute?"

"This morning the princess decided she wants to discuss some details of her marriage to the duke with the Russian ambassador and the tsar's uncle, who's in town. She begged Her Grace to host this luncheon, and Her Grace, being the kind woman she is, said yes. And then apologized for the extra work she's put on us."

"She is a nice woman," I agreed.

"Yes. And she let me know we won't have to put up with much more of this. Apparently Grand Duke Vassily will take the Russians home with him in a few days. We all say 'amen' to that."

The princess would be leaving in a few days. If anyone wanted to kill her in England, they'd have to hurry. And three possible links to Griekev and Ivanov had all gone out this morning after this luncheon was planned.

I felt like I had been thrown upside down into a Russian snowdrift.

Hurrying out the back door, I dashed across the back garden to the coach house and cornered the first footman I saw. "Did you see the Russian maid Mila go through here this morning?"

"Yes. She went out almost an hour ago. Haven't seen her come back."

"And Miss Whitten, Lady Daisy's tutor?"

"She went out and came back already."

"Was she carrying anything?"

"Not her, no. The maid was, though. She carried out a bundle with her."

"And have you seen anything of the princess's sister, Nadia?"

"Not either of the Russian ladies. Not today."

"Have they gone out this way recently?"

"They've sneaked out together a few times and asked us not to tell Her Grace. We figured she has enough to worry about, and you never can tell what the quality wants to hear from us. Or even what we're supposed to notice."

"Where did they go?"

"A couple of times, they had us give them a ride to church. One of them funny Russian churches. Not a proper English one."

"Is that where the Russian maid keeps going?"

"Not her. She's smuggling food out. I've seen her give a bundle to a raggedy-looking boy a couple of blocks away. I was on my way to a public house on my afternoon out, so I had time to linger. The boy opened it partway right there on the street and, as I knew who she was, I watched. Part of a loaf of bread and some ham, as well as I could see."

The groom squared his shoulders. "I told the butler about that. Wasn't right, stealing from Her Grace. She's a right generous lady, is Her Grace. Ain't right taking advantage of her like that."

I thanked the groom and went back into the house. I headed

straight for the nursery, where I found Miss Whitten and Lady Daisy playing a counting game. "We need to talk."

"No, we don't." The tutor turned her back on me.

"You can either talk to me or talk to the authorities. Your choice."

Amelia Whitten frowned and pursed her lips together. After a moment, she said, "Lady Daisy, would you go find your nursery maid and stay with her until I call you?"

"May Millie play our game?"

"Of course. You may teach it to her."

The girl ran off, blond hair flying behind her.

Amelia Whitten swung around to face me, her fists on her hips. "Now, what is it you want to say to me?"

"Someone in this household has been helping Ivanov on his mission against Princess Kira. You are one of those suspected."

"I've had nothing to do with him. I wouldn't want to have anything to do with him." The shudder that crossed her face couldn't have been faked.

"Why did you slip out of here this morning after coming to work?"

"That is none of your business."

"You won't be able to give the police that answer."

"Fine. You aren't the police."

"But she is working under my direction, and I am your employer, Miss Whitten. Please answer her question." The duchess stood in the doorway to the nursery, her arms folded over her stomach.

We both curtsied.

"I'd rather not answer, Your Grace."

"Then I have no choice but to fire you without a reference. You may be the one bringing danger to my household, and I can't risk the life of my daughter on what you'd rather not do."

Fire rose in Miss Whitten's eyes. "You'll fire me anyway. At least this way I can keep my dignity."

"Your dignity?" I asked. "I wouldn't ask if it weren't important to rule you out as the danger. What's wrong?"

She slumped down onto a stool. "I have a little boy. He's nearly three. My mother keeps him for me. She's been ill lately, and I've been going round to check on the two of them."

I faced the duchess. "I'd like to verify this if Your Grace doesn't mind."

She nodded, and I turned to the governess. "Let's go over there, if your mother doesn't mind visitors. You can tell them I'm a friend come to call if you'd like."

"Miss Whitten," the duchess said, "if this bears out, there will be no more talk of your leaving." She left the room in the direction from where we could hear Lady Daisy's laughter.

We went downstairs, put on our hats and gloves, and headed out the back door. "It's shorter this way," she told me.

We caught an omnibus and rode it perhaps a mile to an area of small homes and shops. Smaller and older than the ones in my neighborhood, the buildings' brick walls were dark with soot. Papers and leaves in the rain-soaked gutters gave it a neglected air. Miss Whitten stopped in front of a narrow house in the middle of the block and let us in with her key.

Inside was even darker and more neglected looking than outside. There was a threadbare rug on the entry floor and, through the open parlor door, I saw once-expensive furniture now worn and faded. "Is that you, Amelia?" a woman's voice called from the room.

"Yes, Miss Mary." Miss Whitten led the way into the room.

I followed her to find a little boy on the floor, playing with some wooden blocks and tin soldiers, while an old lady watched him and darned a stocking.

The boy jumped up and ran over to hug Amelia Whitten around the knees. "Mama."

The room was cool, but the draperies were thrown open to let in the watery light of the dreary day, along with the sounds of traffic in the road. Amelia bent down to pick up the boy and tweaked his nose. He appeared clean, well nourished, and well behaved.

"This is my son, Andrew, and this is Miss Mary Harper."

"I'm a boarder here," the old woman told me, as if that answered all my questions. "I'm watching Andrew while Agatha rests. Her cough seems worse, Amelia. You might want to check on her."

"You play," Amelia said to the squirming toddler as she put him down. "I'm going to check on Gram."

She left the room and Mary Harper said, "Sit down and bring me news of the outside world."

Never good at starting a conversation when all I wanted to do was sleep, I said, "Autumn is settling in. Before we know it, it'll be Christmas season." Not brilliant, but at least I sounded coherent.

"Do you work for the Duchess of Hereford like Amelia does?"

"Yes. I'm her secretary. Hers and the Princess Kira, who's visiting from Russia to meet her intended, the Duke of Sussex." Well, she wanted news. I might as well give her the long version since I'd be waiting a few minutes for Miss Whitten.

"You get to see all sorts of important people."

"I do. Do you get to watch Andrew often?"

"I have lately, with Agatha being so ill."

"Are you family?"

"I have no family. Just a small income and a need to live somewhere. They've welcomed me in, and we've found we suit each other quite well."

"Are you the only boarder?"

"No. There's Miss Dawson, a clerk in a shop. She'll be here in time for dinner."

I glanced around. "Has the house been in the Whitten family for a long time?"

"I believe Amelia grew up here."

Andrew came over and showed me one of his tin soldiers before running back to continue his game. It made no sense to me, but I'd not spent much time with children. It appeared to make perfect sense to Andrew.

"He's such a joy," Mary Harper said quietly so the boy wouldn't hear her.

"Who's his father?" I asked.

"A young scholar who made an advantageous match and left Amelia in the dust. He denies all responsibility."

"Coward."

Mary Harper nodded. "Exactly. But that doesn't help Amelia. She's the one to face ostracism and loss of her employment."

"I don't think the duchess will do that. She's already said she won't hear of Amelia leaving."

Mary Harper turned a sharp gaze at me out of faded blue eyes. "Does she know about the boy?"

"She does now."

"She sounds like a good one, your duchess."

"She is, but she's hardly my duchess."

Amelia came downstairs and said, "My mother seems to be resting quieter now. I'd better get back." She walked over and ruffled the boy's fair hair.

"We'll be fine here," Mary Harper said.

"I'll see you tonight, sweetheart," Amelia told her son.

He grinned up at her. "'Bye, Mama."

We started back the way we'd come, Amelia keeping still as we traveled. Finally I couldn't bear the silence any longer. "You have a lovely child."

"Thank you."

"It can't be easy."

"It isn't. And now with my mother being so sick—"

"What ails her?"

"Lung disease, influenza, her heart. We're not sure."

"She hasn't seen a doctor?"

"Doctors cost money. Money we don't have."

"Your father didn't leave you much?"

"He died young and left us nothing but debts."

On that gloomy note, we continued in silence to Hereford House. After we took off our wet outerwear, I followed Amelia upstairs and left her in the nursery while I went in search of Mila, Nadia, and the princess. I found the maid fixing Princess Kira's hair in curls.

"When you get done there, I need to speak to you, Mila." At least Mila spoke English.

"Once the princess is ready to go downstairs for the luncheon."

"Of course." I sat down on a side chair, its seat upholstered in a blue-patterned fabric. "Has Nadia returned from her appointment at the embassy?"

"Not yet. She's upset at being excluded from today's luncheon." A bright smile crossed the princess's face. "I'm going to ask to have her in my wedding party. The ambassador and Cousin Vassily are going to yell and threaten."

Clearly she was looking forward to the uproar she'd cause.

I shook my head. "What would Lady Raminoff have said?"

"She'd be against it, of course. She says Nadia can be anything she wants here in England, but she can't be a princess when the royal family is around. Lady Raminoff was on Nadia's side as long as the Romanovs weren't being embarrassed."

"Nadia didn't think so?"

"Nadia thinks that people either want her to be a princess or are against her."

"That must make her hard to get along with."

"No. Nadia is so full of life. She's not afraid of anything. It makes her fun to be around." Princess Kira gave me a smile that made her eyes glitter with mirth.

"If she weren't afraid of anything, she wouldn't have run when her mother died." Aggravating the princess seemed to get me more answers than if I were respectful.

"Her mother was killed, and those same men tried to kill her, too. But she hid until she could escape to England. She's so clever," Princess Kira said, pride and defiance filling her voice.

"You are ready, Princess." Mila stepped back and lowered her head.

The princess, dressed in more jewels than an Englishwoman would feel was proper for luncheon, left the room. I shut the door behind her and turned to Mila. "Now, why are you stealing food?" I asked.

In a burst of speed, the lady's maid dashed past me, threw open the door, and ran down the secret staircase.

CHAPTER TWENTY

*B*LAST. I took off down the dark, narrow stairs after Mila, furious about all this exercise after a night of no sleep and much running around. Where did she think she'd run to? She was a Russian subject, only recently arrived in this country, and leaving again soon with Princess Kira.

She took off out the back door and across the garden, her half boots splashing in the puddles. I followed, shouting to the men in the carriage house as she approached, "Stop her! Stop that woman!"

Mila ran through the open door and inside the building. When I reached it, panting, I discovered there was no one inside and the door to the alley was open. I hurried over, holding my side over the pain that was stabbing me, and looked out. No one was in sight.

I leaned against the door frame, gasping in air and wondering where she was headed. Would she go to the tenement where Emma had been taken hostage by Griekev and his accomplices? Was she the woman Emma had heard?

Why else would she have run?

And why had I chosen to wear an outfit that required a tight corset on a day when the first thing I had to do was chase someone young and fit?

I needed to call Sir Broderick and have someone check to see if Mila was spotted in the area. If she were the inside person helping Ivanov, she wouldn't come back now. So where was their attack going to take place?

Then I remembered the hunt for a lady's maid for Nadia. That had allowed us to add Mary to the household to help me watch the Russians. Perhaps now Mary could help with the princess as well, until a new lady's maid was found.

I walked back to the house, still trying to catch my breath and ease the pain in my side while hurrying to avoid the rain. Miss Whitten's hat and gloves sat on the table next to mine in the back hall. At least I'd eliminated her as a suspect.

Ahead of me I saw Nadia cross the front hall heading toward the formal entrance. She wore her coat and hat. Had she returned with the grand duke after their meeting, or were they not on speaking terms? Had she caused an unpleasantness in the dining room? "Nadia. Wait."

She ignored me as she increased her speed to escape. She grabbed an umbrella out of the stand before she rushed out the front door and shut it behind her. Where was Nadia's lady's maid, Mary? And Kendrick, the butler?

I headed for the back stairs, only to meet Mary coming up with the repaired gown in her hands. "Where did Nadia go?"

The girl shook her head. "I haven't seen her since I spoke to you earlier."

"If either Nadia or the princess leaves, find out where they're going and let me know." With Mila's defection, I needed to know why Nadia had left the house so abruptly.

I retraced my steps and then cut down a side hall to reach the butler's pantry behind the dining room. I'd give a footman a message to give to the duchess during the next course and then I'd hurry next door to phone Sir Broderick. We needed to find Mila before she disappeared into the crowded streets and neighborhoods of London.

And learn how things stood between Nadia and the rest of the Russians.

The butler's pantry was small even when the butler and several footmen weren't carrying dishes through it. Now they were just beginning to change courses and several men rushed past, on their way down to the kitchen or into the dining room. All of them carried trays and a few of them muttered curses as they dodged around me.

Seeing the butler, I said, "I need to get a word to the duchess." He gave me a glance. "Not now. Get out of the way. George, take that downstairs," he said as he moved into the dining room.

I had to duck under a few trays before I reached the protection of the entrance to the linen closet. Still, one of the footmen clipped me with a tray full of dirty dishes and we both had to juggle to keep from spilling food and china.

In an effort to move out of the way temporarily, I opened the door and stepped backward into the small, unlit closet.

A sparkling light caught my eye. Had some fool set a lighted lamp in here? No, the light crackled as it marked a line along the floor. Heat came up my skirt as I realized the light was a fuse. I bent over to peer deeper into the closet and saw the flame rush toward a bundle of dynamite sticks.

Oh, dear Lord. Dynamite.

I stared at it for what felt like an hour, my mouth moving but making no sound. I was mesmerized by the sparkly light. The damage done to the houses by the dynamite thieves raced through my mind.

No. It couldn't happen here.

"Get out!" I screamed. "Dynamite."

I frantically tried to jerk the fuse out of the bundle, but the metal tube the fuse ended in was crimped. I couldn't budge the wiry cord and I couldn't tear it with my hands. The butler came up behind me, demanding, "What—?"

Why wouldn't they just run? "Get everybody out. The house is going to explode." I was screaming and I could hear voices talking over me in a Babel of conflicting orders. People shoved against my back while I listened to footsteps running in different directions. I wanted to run, too, but I was trapped by the people behind me.

I heard a footman say, "Her Grace asks—"

I thought of Blackford, the duchess, Lady Daisy. An instant ticked off as the burning fuse snaked toward the dynamite.

I felt as if I were in a dream. Everything was in slow motion. I pulled the duke's knife from my pocket, opened it, and sliced through the fuse cord just below where it went into the crimped metal tube. I tossed the fuse on the floor as it burned my hand.

The pain woke me up. I stomped on the cord and kicked the dynamite sticks away as I sucked on my singed fingers.

Turning around to face the crowd in the butler's pantry, I found myself staring at Blackford as he shoved the last of a group of curious servants out of his path to reach me. He picked me up by the waist and swung me out of his way to see the bomb.

"Did you cut the fuse, Georgia?" he asked, removing his still-open knife from my uninjured hand.

"Yes. I don't think it'll blow up now." My words came out in little gasps as I struggled to catch my breath. Looking down, I could see scorch marks in the wooden floor where the fuse had burned.

"It won't." He pocketed the knife as he turned to the butler and said, "I think you might want to send some of these people downstairs."

The butler dispatched the footmen with various orders while Blackford held me up with both hands firmly gripping my shoulders. I started to shake. I blinked away tears. I had almost died.

Someone had tried to kill all of us.

"We n-need to find out who was in here." My voice was now a whimper.

"We will. But first, you need to sit down." Blackford moved me into the dining room and sat me on the closest chair. Then he pressed a wineglass into my hand. "Drink this."

I took a sip, swallowed, and then tried to take a deep breath. I felt a little less shaky as Princess Kira demanded, "What is she doing in here and what is going on?"

"You were almost blown up. I cut the fuse," I snapped. "Oh, and your maid left shortly before all this happened, when I accused her of theft."

"Mila? Mila tried to blow us up?" the young woman said and dropped back into her chair. Sussex sat next to her, holding her hand.

"No. She couldn't have. She wasn't here to light the fuse." Then it hit me. "But Nadia was."

"No. No. No. Nadia would never hurt me. We're sisters."

I shook my head, fury in my tone. "Silly girl. Haven't you seen the way she looks at you? She hates you."

"Where did you see Nadia?" Blackford asked me.

"She was walking out of the front door when I was coming in here to try to send Her Grace a message."

"No. Nadia wouldn't do anything like this. She just wants to be treated like the aristocrat she is. Her great-grandfather was Tsar of All the Russias," the princess proclaimed.

"Perhaps. But she is still a bastard," the Russian ambassador said. "Her mother caused all sorts of trouble for the royal family. Making demands. Wanting honors."

"Is that why she was murdered?" I asked.

He nodded. "I suspect so."

"They should have given her the honors," the princess shrieked at him. "They should never have killed her. And they tried to kill Nadia."

"An arrangement might have been reached," the ambassador said, lowering his tone and speaking calmly. "But Marina wouldn't listen to good counsel. She was always headstrong. Putting on airs. Embarrassing your parents, Kira."

"But to kill her? And Nadia, too?" The princess's voice was barely above a whisper. She seemed to have wrapped herself in a blanket of numbness to muffle the blows to her beliefs.

"Not Nadia. I was instructed to give her every assistance when she arrived in England. But she is too much like her mother, I fear. She makes demands to be treated as a princess. She says it is her right." The ambassador shook his head, sounding aggrieved.

"You might have warned us before I invited the girl to stay in my house," the duchess said, her posture as rigidly stiff as Blackford's when he was angry.

"I fear she has joined the anarchists," Grand Duke Vassily said to the princess.

"I won't believe it until she tells me herself," Kira said, pulling her hand away from Sussex and wrapping her arms around herself protectively.

Blackford was still hovering over me. "Do you think she's the woman Griekev and Ivanov have been working with?" I whispered to him.

He glanced at the princess, who was cringing away from a hurt-looking Sussex. "It would make sense. They, rather than the anarchists, have been carrying out robberies using pistols and dynamite. Someone would have had to show her how to set the fuse."

"Unless she's been involved in the other explosions and already knew how to build a bomb. She could have smuggled the parts needed into the house a little at a time. Nadia and Kira have been sneaking out to the Russian Orthodox church with some frequency."

Blackford frowned. "No. The church is firmly behind the tsar. They wouldn't help the anarchists or criminals."

"But you don't know what goes on in the congregation during service," I told him. I turned to the princess. "Princess Kira, does Nadia meet with anyone when you slip out to go to church?"

"How did you—oh, the coachman. Of course." She could have been discussing the weather in her bored tone. Brushing the air with one slender hand, she said, "There is a young man Nadia talks to. He's quite smitten. Always bringing her presents."

"Has she shown them to you?"

Kira shook her head.

"Do you know his name?"

"Andrei Griekev. He lives quite close to the chapel, apparently—he said across the street—and he and Nadia arrange to meet there."

My tone turned hard. Someone had to talk sense into this girl. "Andrei Griekev is a notorious robber who uses dynamite to break into aristocrats' safes and carries a pistol. He pays anarchists to hide him and his fellow thieves."

Her expression was furious as she stared at me. "How could Nadia know this?"

"From what we've learned, she's been planning these robberies with Griekev."

"No. Nadia wouldn't—" the princess whimpered.

A commotion from the front hall signaled the arrival of a police inspector and a group of bobbies. At a nod from the duchess, Blackford went with her to deal with the police. The grand duke and the Russian ambassador joined them in the front hall. The rest of the women and Sussex stayed in the dining room, waiting silently. Listening.

I stayed where I was, sipping the duchess's very nice red wine and admiring her gray and lavender decor. The dishes matched the colors in the wallpaper and the rug. The draperies used the same fabric as the seat cushions on the chairs. The silver gleamed. The ivory tablecloth glowed in the light of the chandelier, and the ivory lace curtains muted the gloom outside.

I admitted to myself that I'd love to live on such a grand scale. I could understand Nadia's jealousy. What I couldn't understand was her desire to hurt people because they had what she wanted. Or to destroy this perfect room.

Did Nadia think the only thing that mattered was what she wanted? And was that a trait she shared with Kira?

As I glanced over at the princess, I caught her staring at me. I held her stare, and she looked away.

"I'll take the princess out of here while the police carry out their investigation," the Duke of Sussex said.

"That's not a good idea. They'll want to question everyone about what they saw. And what they know," I told him.

"But she's distressed."

"So am I. I found the bomb." And defused it. Something I didn't want to do ever again. My fingers throbbed.

"But she's a princess."

With that pronouncement, the Duke of Sussex became my third-least-favorite person, right after Nadia and Kira. "We would have all been dead, Your Grace. That distresses everyone. Even servants."

My attention was caught by a snort that turned into a cough. Blackford stood in the doorway to the hall. "They're looking for Nadia, but they don't hold out much hope she'll resurface. They think it likely she's headed back to Russia."

I shook my head. "No. She wouldn't go someplace where she's known and not wanted. How much do you think Griekev and she kept from their burglaries?"

"Almost everything was recovered by the police."

"If they had a lot of valuables they could sell to maintain their lifestyle, I would have guessed they'd go to the continent. They could pass themselves off as anyone. But with no money? I'm sure they're staying in London, looking for a way to raise another fortune."

He looked glum. "The only question is how."

A bobby came in and asked the princess and Sussex to speak to the police inspector. They left, and Blackford followed them out of the room. A moment later, I could hear him speak to the Russian ambassador and Grand Duke Vassily.

Mila and Nadia were both missing. I needed to get the Archivist Society looking for them. I rose and slipped around by back halls to the front door, where a helmeted constable stood on guard. "I just need to post a letter for Her Grace. I'll be back in a few minutes," I assured the youngster as I picked up an umbrella and walked past him.

The bobby looked like he should still be in school. Fortunately, he was as green and innocent as a schoolboy. He let me pass without question.

I went out to the sidewalk and walked next door. The butler was getting used to me showing up on Blackford's front step. "Hello, Stevens. I need to use the telephone."

He opened the door farther, a dubious expression on his face. "His Grace is not in at the moment."

"I know. He's next door. I just left him." I walked past Stevens and down the hall to the study. Once there, I picked up the instrument and spoke into the mouthpiece, giving the number.

Jacob answered the phone.

"Get Sir Broderick immediately. And listen in. We need your help, too."

Sir Broderick came on a full minute or two later. "I was downstairs, Georgia. What is going on?"

"Both Mila and Nadia have disappeared, and someone rigged dynamite to blow up Hereford House. I think it was Nadia. And I think she's Griekev's accomplice in the robberies."

"Good grief. I'll have everyone in the Archivist Society on the lookout for both women."

"Nadia probably waited for the house to blow up. When it didn't and the police came, she would have gone into hiding. She and Griekev must be plotting a way to raise a lot of money quickly so they can leave the country."

"Then she'll be dangerous. And Mila?"

"She's been stealing food from the house. Check the Russian community in the East End for some poor immigrant relations of hers. We need to talk to her to clear her, but I don't think she's a danger."

"And if you're wrong?" Sir Broderick asked.

"I don't think I am."

"I'll send Jacob and the others to the East End to look for Mila, Nadia, and Griekev. I'll tell them to report their sightings of Nadia and Griekev to a constable. The sightings of Mila can safely be reported to me if you're sure."

"I am." I thanked him and rang off.

I slipped out of Blackford House and walked next door as if I was doing exactly what I should be doing. An older bobby was on duty in the doorway now and he immediately challenged me. "Are you Miss Peabody?"

"Yes."

He put a forceful grip on my shoulder. "We're trying to find the bomber and the guv wants a word with you."

"Tell him you found me, and all will be well." At least I hoped so.

Not releasing his grip on my shoulder, he dragged me at a quick trot into the house. "Sir. Sir! I found the woman who escaped."

CHAPTER TWENTY-ONE

"GOOD lad." The inspector came into view around a corner. Inspector Edward Grantham—Eddy to his grandmother Lady Westover—stopped and blinked when he saw me. I had a half second's fear that he'd give me away before he said, "Miss Peabody? If I could have a few minutes of your time?"

"Of course, Inspector."

I shook off the constable's grip and followed Inspector Grantham to the morning room, where Blackford and another constable waited for us. As soon as he shut the door, Grantham turned to me and said, "Georgia? You're the one who cut the fuse and kept everyone in this house from being killed?"

I nodded. I wasn't sure if I could think about that moment even now without losing my breakfast.

"Well done. Where did you learn about bombs?"

"I've read about them. I've never actually seen—" My first view of the sticks of dynamite came back to me again and I dropped into a chair.

"She's still looking pale. As soon as you're done with her, I'm taking her home in my carriage," Blackford said.

I gave a sigh of relief. Now that the danger was past, all my limbs felt weak. I didn't relish the idea of riding home in the rain on an omnibus.

"Yes, of course," Grantham said. "How long has the Archivist Society been involved, and have you involved my grandmother?"

"Not long. We were brought in on the Russian murders by the Foreign Office, and the burglary cases by Lord Shepherdston. Your grandmother doesn't know a thing."

He nodded, and I released a sigh. If he thought the Archivist Society had involved her in anything dangerous, he'd forbid her from ever working with us again. "Tell me what has happened here, starting with this morning."

I skipped the visit I paid with Amelia Whitten and started my story from when I entered the princess's room. When I finished, Grantham allowed Blackford and me to leave and we headed for his coach house.

"We'll take the ordinary coach," Blackford told his coachman. "After I see you home, I'll stop round Sir Broderick's and tell him to alert the Archivist Society."

"I called him already. Stevens let me use your phone. And if he asks, tell him you knew I would call from your house."

Blackford didn't trouble to hide his smile. "Stevens won't ask. I think he secretly admires you for the work you and the Archivist Society perform, even if he's shocked that a lady would put herself at such risk."

"That's because I'm not a lady. I'm an ordinary person, just like he is."

"No, Georgia. Stevens and I agree. You are a lady."

He sees me as a lady. I could have danced around the coach house. My heart did a waltz in my chest as a smile spread across my face. "Thank you, Your Grace."

"Don't thank me. Nature made you one of the great ladies in England."

Heat burned my cheeks. I must have been blushing the color of a ruby. I could barely contain my desire to hop up and down in a most unladylike manner. Instead, I gave him a regal nod, and he helped me into the coach.

I was amazed at how sunny a rainy London day could be. We congratulated each other on being alive after our brush with explosives, and then he gave my hand a squeeze. I will save my glove for all time in remembrance of the thrill that shot through my body.

"Do you think the Duke of Hereford will return to London now?" I asked.

"If he doesn't, I will ride out to his estate and drag him back," Blackford said with some heat.

"Especially since—" I stopped, remembering my promise.

"Yes?"

"I promised not to say."

"That she's increasing?"

"You know?" I felt a rush of warmth throughout my body at discussing such a subject with a man. Blackford was more observant than I thought.

"I've seen a great deal of her lately. It's been hard to miss. She needs Hereford here, not those Russians."

"When does Princess Kira go back to St. Petersburg?"

"Only God and the Russians know that." His tone matched the duchess's whenever the subject of Princess Kira's departure was mentioned.

"Let's hope it's soon. Nadia and Griekev need money to escape in style, and the princess is foolish enough to help them in their scheme. Princess Kira still believes in her sister. You can see it in her eyes."

"Help her escape in style." Blackford stared out the window of the carriage for a minute. "Why wouldn't they just escape?"

"Ivanov would. We know Ivanov killed the Russian soldier on the train and the footman of the marquis. We'll hang him if we get the chance. Has Sumner found him yet?"

"Not yet," Blackford said.

Another shovelful of worry landed on my shoulders. I'd hoped Sumner had already returned safely. Shaking off my concern, I said, "Nadia and Griekev would go to prison for the robberies, not hang from a noose. But life without money, without the trappings of an upper-crust existence, would be as bad as jail for that pair." I watched Blackford consider my words.

Finally, he nodded. "I wish you weren't right, Georgia, but I fear you are. Ah, we're here. I want you to go straight to bed and get some sleep."

He helped me down from the carriage, no great feat from his ordinary coach, but he made very sure I had my legs under me before he let me go. We walked up to the flat and I used my key to open the door.

I turned then and said, "Thank you, Your Grace."

"Thank you, Georgia."

We stood there, looking into each other's eyes, gaining a closeness I hadn't expected to feel when I left home that morning. We'd nearly died together. Now our lives would always be intertwined.

"Georgia. You're back. Emma's doing so much better. Oh, Duke, I didn't see you there." Phyllida came up behind us, opening the door wider.

She curtsied; he bowed. "See Miss Fenchurch gets some rest. She's had a harrowing morning. Ladies." He tipped his hat and walked off.

"Harrowing? Georgia, what happened?" she asked, shutting the door.

"I'll tell you later. Right now, I need to get some sleep. Could I get you to undo my corset?" I walked toward my bedroom on shaky legs.

In five minutes, I was undressed, in bed, and asleep.

WE WERE DRESSED and finishing our dinner of roast chicken, vegetables, and rolls when I asked Emma for what felt like the twenty-seventh time, "Are you sure you feel up to attending the meeting at Sir Broderick's tonight?"

"Yes. A nice walk in the evening air and then a meeting to figure out how to catch the people who nearly killed me. What could be better?" She gave me a hard look, which was reinforced by her bruises. When Emma was determined, there was little point in arguing.

"Should you go out tonight, Georgia?" Phyllida asked. "You've had very little rest, and Blackford said you had a harrowing day. One I haven't heard about yet. How did you burn your fingers?"

I shot Emma a stare when she opened her mouth and she shut it again. "It's not important now."

Phyllida gave me a steely look. "So it was important then."

"You've been hanging around the Archivist Society for too long. You've developed a suspicious mind."

Emma turned laughter into a cough.

"I'm waiting."

I made it look like I had given in. "There was a hot piece of wire. Not knowing it was hot, I picked it up and burned my hand."

Phyllida didn't look like she believed me. "And you're still certain you should go out tonight?"

"Emma and I will both go and take care of each other."

"I don't like this, but I've learned to accept it. Come on, let's clear the table so we can get these dishes done." Phyllida rose and carried the roast platter out.

We'd followed her into the kitchen with our hands full when we heard a pounding on the front door. "Now, who could that be?" Phyllida asked, her apron forgotten in her hand.

"I'll see," I said and set down the dishes I carried. I rushed down the hall and opened the door to find Grace Yates standing in front of me.

"Grace, has something happened at the bookshop?"

"No." She shook her head and tried to catch her breath. "I've been sent to get the Archivist Society together early."

"What's happened?"

She grabbed my arm and gasped, "Princess Kira has been kidnapped."

"If she's disappeared again . . ." I grumbled. The princess was still capable of ruining her future.

"The Russian ambassador just received a ransom letter asking for ten thousand pounds in jewels."

I stood in the doorway staring at Grace, my mind refusing to accept her words. "Ten thousand?"

She nodded.

Good heavens. Griekev and Nadia had found a way to raise a fortune for their escape. "Does Blackford know?"

"The duchess sent a footman to his house as soon as they

realized the princess was missing. Soon after, he was called in by Whitehall when the Russian ambassador asked for their help."

I gazed at Grace for a moment, taking in the new danger. "We'll meet you at Sir Broderick's."

Grace hurried off and I went back to the kitchen. Emma took one look at my face and pulled off her apron.

"What's happened?" Phyllida asked. When I told her, she said, "The poor girl. You both have to go," and returned to the dishes.

Emma and I put on cloaks, hats, and gloves, said our good-byes, and hurried out into the night. "All right," she said when we were a half block from home, "what happened today?"

I filled her in on everything. When I reached the lit fuse on the dynamite, her eyes widened and she grabbed my arm, but she didn't say anything to slow the memories I struggled to put into words.

By the time I finished my tale, we were knocking on Sir Broderick's door. Jacob answered and took our cloaks. "We're in the study tonight," he said.

"Why? Is Sir Broderick unwell?"

"No, but that's where we've always held our counsels of war. He doesn't want the parlor tainted with this business."

I had known Sir Broderick longer than the rest of the Archivist Society. My heart sank. "He doesn't think this will end well."

Jacob looked from one of us to the other. "No."

When we walked up the stairs, we found Sir Broderick in his usual spot in front of the roaring fire. Frances sat on one of the sofas, scone crumbs on her front. Dominique was serving tea to Adam Fogarty. There was a sizable group of Archivist Society members, some of whom I'd not seen in some time. I walked around, greeting old friends, while Emma headed straight for Sumner.

"Who's he?" I was asked more than once.

My answer was always, "Mr. Sumner, a former military officer and an employee of the Duke of Blackford."

"He looks like a villain," someone said.

"Only if you're on the wrong side of the law or you're rude to Emma."

"They have an understanding?" one of the men asked, disappointment in his tone.

"Yes."

Several men groaned. I knew Emma was beautiful, but I didn't realize how popular she was in the Archivist Society.

The one who asked if she had an understanding with Sumner said, "Well, if he was an officer, he must be well educated and come from a good family."

That had never occurred to me, and my lack of insight surprised me. Once again, I was reminded of how my mind immediately went to Blackford whenever I saw Sumner.

Seeing him now, I wondered where Ivanov was. Unfortunately, this wasn't the time to ask.

I glanced around the room. "Where's Mrs. Hardwick?"

"Gone to visit her sister who's ill."

That explained a meeting with all of us crowded into the study. Mrs. Hardwick was the only person who'd been able to convince Sir Broderick to expand his physical horizons.

"Shall we begin this meeting?" Sir Broderick said in a loud voice as he clapped his hands.

We all obediently sat down, except for Adam Fogarty, who paced the back of the room. Emma crowded onto a sofa with Sumner and Jacob. I watched several male faces fall. Emma was definitely a favorite of the men in our group.

"At five o'clock, a message arrived for the Russian ambassador, asking for ten thousand pounds' worth of jewels in exchange for the release of Princess Kira, currently on a visit to London to meet her fiancé, the Duke of Sussex. They immediately confirmed that the princess had disappeared from Hereford House, where she is a guest. The Duke of Sussex hasn't heard from her and has no idea where she is."

"Is the princess's safety worth that much?" one of the group asked.

"In light of our shaky relationship with Russia and the princess's royal connections to the tsar, whatever the ambassador can't raise, the British government will have to."

"Do we know for certain Nadia and Griekev are behind this?" I asked.

"Not for certain, no. But because the police took custody of the goods they'd stolen and Nadia's relationship with the princess, they are thought to be the kidnappers."

Sir Broderick looked around the room and continued. "Nadia Andropov and Andrei Griekev are believed to be the masterminds behind the 'dynamite burglaries,' and Nadia is the princess's bastard sister."

"Do we know where they might have taken her?" Jacob asked.

"We've checked the two places where we know they had been living and hiding their loot, and they aren't at either one. They probably had already created at least one more hideout in the East End that we're unaware of," Sumner said.

"No. It's near the Greek chapel where Russian Orthodox services are held. Probably within sight of it," I said.

"Why do you think that?" Sir Broderick asked.

"One of the servants at Hereford's said Princess Kira and Nadia would sneak out at night and go to the church where the services are in Russian. Princess Kira would pray—there certainly aren't any services late at night—and Nadia would meet with Griekev. The princess told me that's where she met him. She said Griekev lived practically across the street."

"Where's this Greek chapel?" someone asked.

"Welbeck Street. West of here, just past Cavendish Square."

"Nadia and Griekev could have invited the princess there without arousing her suspicions." Sir Broderick looked around the room. "It's certainly one place to focus our search."

"Is there a deadline for delivering the jewels?"

"Dawn."

"Can it be done that quickly?"

"Yes. Victoria has commanded the government to save the princess by any means necessary."

"Do we know if the princess is still alive?" Sumner asked.

"No. But everyone is proceeding as if she is," Sir Broderick replied.

"Nadia hates Kira. I suspect the princess will die as soon as her half sister gets her hands on the jewels. We have to get her back before the jewels are handed over," I told them.

"Are you certain?" Sir Broderick asked.

I thought of the look I'd seen Nadia give the princess from the top of the stairs. And she'd made no move to rescue the princess from the dynamite. "Yes," I said. "I'm certain."

CHAPTER TWENTY-TWO

"IF you think Nadia will kill the princess, then we need a small group to scour that neighborhood," Sir Broderick said. "We can't wait for the ransom to be paid and the princess released."

Several of the men, including Sumner, volunteered. Emma and I did, too.

"Ladies, I don't think—," Sir Broderick began.

"We've been part of this from the beginning. We're going," I told him.

"You have your knife, Emma?" Jacob asked.

She gave Sumner a smile. "Of course."

"Before we go, we need to have Blackford do something for us in these negotiations," I said, and everyone turned and looked at me. "We don't know which house they're in. We need to have one of them depart after we're in position to see which house they exit."

"By all means, Georgia. Call him. He's at Whitehall."

I picked up the telephone and asked for the Foreign Office. It took the man on duty in the Foreign Office some time to track down Blackford, probably because the halls of government were full of dukes, but finally his forceful baritone came over the line. "The Duke of Blackford here."

"It's Georgia. I'm at Sir Broderick's. We think we know where Nadia and Griekev might be hiding Princess Kira, but we need you to get one of them to leave the house in a half hour. That way we can pinpoint the exact building."

"Griekev isn't at any hideout. At least we don't think he is. He has us passing written messages through a lad, and from the speed with which one of the replies came back to us, we think he's somewhere close to Whitehall."

"Is it your turn to respond?"

"Yes."

"Wait fifteen minutes, and then send a message saying you want proof they have the princess and she's alive. Ask for her hat. Do you know what she was wearing when she was taken?"

"No."

I tried not to sigh into the telephone. I still found it amazing the duke wouldn't think of something I considered important. "Call your house and have someone find out. Mary Thomas is acting as the princess's lady's maid and she should know."

"I'll do that. And Georgia, be careful."

"We will. Remember, don't send the reply for fifteen minutes."

We took a late omnibus west on Oxford Street and walked north from there. This was a neighborhood of middle-class shops, homes, and respectability. Streetlamps were numerous, their glow shimmering on the wet pavement. There was no fog to hide our movements. No one was on the street but I could see lights burning behind many curtains.

We walked silently in groups of two or three, obvious to

anyone who glanced outside. I kept quiet when all I wanted to do was shout out my fear. What if this didn't work? What if Griekev had lied about living here? What if he had another hideout somewhere in London?

All our hopes were riding on this one place. This area I had insisted we watch. I wrapped my arms around myself to fight the cold burrowing deeper inside me. If anything happened to the princess, it would be my fault.

I'd have been the one to misdirect the search. The Russians would blame me, the British government would disown me, Blackford would consider me a fraud. And I would have failed and caused another death.

I wanted to cry out, to discover if anyone else thought this was a good way to proceed. But it was too late. We were committed to my plan. I stayed silent.

As we approached the church, we began to separate, slipping into alleys or shadowed courtyards where we could each watch different buildings. I'd almost reached my spot when I caught movement in an alley.

The movement became a shadow and dashed out of the alley toward me. Beside me Jacob moved his hand in such a way that I knew he held some sort of weapon. And I stood my ground, waiting for the blow to come and fisting my hands. But instead of striking as the shadow came near, I saw Mary Thomas peer into my face. "Miss Georgia?" she said, exhaling a relieved gasp.

"What are you doing here, Mary?"

Rain dripped off Mary's hat and her cheeks looked chapped with cold. "The princess told me not to tell anyone when she left with Nadia. I thought you'd wonder where they went, so I followed them. So far as I can tell, they're still in there. What are you doing here, miss?"

"Nadia and a man called Griekev kidnapped Princess Kira and sent a ransom note to the Russian embassy. We knew Nadia used to meet Griekev down the street at the Greek chapel, so we thought he lived around here."

"Kidnapped?" In the light from the streetlamp, I saw her eyes widen.

"Which house did they go in?"

"I'm not sure. I was too far away. I took an omnibus until their cab turned off on a side street, and then I had to follow by foot the rest of the way. I saw their hired carriage pull away, though, and I heard them arguing before a door slammed. They must have gone into one of the houses on this side of the street between this alley and the corner."

I glanced at Jacob. "I'll watch from across the street," he said and hurried off.

"Griekev's been told to bring her hat as proof he has her. He'll have to go to where they're hiding her to get it. Then we'll know which house," I told Mary. "Do you want to go home and get out of the rain?"

She looked like a drowned pup, all big brown eyes and water dripping from her clothes. "No sense in that now. And I want to see this through." She sounded more like a guard dog.

We hid in the alley between a newsman's shop and a confectioner's, knowing the Greek chapel was a half block farther on our side of the street. From my post I could see the houses across the street, and I knew Jacob had squeezed in between two houses from where he could watch my side of the road.

All we could do was wait silently for Griekev to return as the cold in the alley seeped into my half boots and through my dark cloak. Fortunately, I had slept during the afternoon or my eyes would never have stayed open. I stomped my feet from time to time to keep my blood circulating as every muscle stiffened. I was cold and bored. Mary kept shivering, but she refused my offers to send her home.

Twice I heard boots clomp along the sidewalk. One set belonged to an old man who went in the doorway next to a glass shop. A moment later, I saw a light go on in the rooms above. No one left that doorway. The other set belonged to a man who went into a doorway on my side. When he didn't reappear, Jacob signaled that all was well.

What if Griekev had refused to get Whitehall the proof they requested?

I heard another pair of boots moving quickly. I held still as the footsteps stopped nearby. When they didn't resume, I wondered if I had missed the sound of a door opening and closing. Mary grabbed my arm in a fierce grip and inhaled deeply. Finally, a man hurried past me muffled in a workman's coat, cap, and scarf. A moment later, I heard a door shut.

Mary let out a loud exhale. I watched Jacob, waiting for a signal.

Seconds dragged on into minutes, and then I heard a door shut so softly I nearly missed it. Then the speedy footsteps sounded again as the man in the cap and scarf passed. This time he was carrying a small satchel. He didn't stop and wait this time, but continued on until I could no longer hear his steps.

At that moment, Jacob came out from his place in the shadows and I came out to meet him. "Third building down," he whispered.

I glanced at the house with two steps up to the door and a bay window on one side. "We need help to guard the back."

"I'll go," Mary said and vanished into the alley.

Jacob said, "I'll get Fogarty," and walked down the sidewalk. I waited where I was, watching the house for any sign of someone trying to slip away.

Jacob was back within two minutes. "Sumner and Emma have the back along with Mary."

Adam Fogarty walked up to join us. "Have the house?"

"Yes. Can you pick the lock?" I asked.

"On the force we were more about knocking down the door."

"I can do it," Jacob said. "I've been practicing on more than just my accounting ledgers." I could see his smile in the light of the streetlamp.

The three of us tiptoed to the building. The ground floor was a tobacco shop. A door to one side of the bay window led to the upper floors. Jacob pulled out some thin, oddly shaped pieces of metal. He bent over the lock and a moment later he turned the handle and let us in.

The stairs in front of us were in darkness and the building had the gloomy silence of emptiness. A lantern sat on the bottom step. Jacob put away his tools and struck a match. Then he gestured up the stairs.

We walked near the wall, but one of the stairs still squeaked in protest, the sound echoing around us. So much for surprise. Above us somewhere I heard an answering creak.

No longer worrying about a stealthy entrance, we hurried up one flight. There were two rooms, both empty. Up to the next floor. The front room was empty. The door to the back room was locked.

Adam didn't wait for Jacob's lock-picking skills. He went at the door with his shoulder and the door swung open. He stumbled to a halt as Jacob and I rushed in behind him and collided in our efforts to stop.

The room was lit by two delicate lamps decorated with flowers painted onto the milk glass shades. I could clearly see Nadia standing over Princess Kira with a shiny revolver in her hand.

The princess was bound to a straight-backed chair and gagged. There was a look of terror in her eyes.

"Don't come any closer." The pistol was now aimed at the three of us. It looked huge.

I held out a hand to her, fighting off the urge to faint or scream. "Nadia, stop this before something goes wrong."

"You will address me as Princess Nadia."

"Where are you planning on going? France?" As a question, it wasn't much, but hopefully we could keep her talking until we could think of a way to rescue the princess.

"What do you care?"

I shrugged, trying to look unconcerned while I hid my shaking hands. "I don't. I've just heard the Russian aristocracy is very popular in the highest circles of French society."

"We are. And I am demanding my rightful standing as a great-granddaughter of Nicholas the First. If Kira can be a princess, so can I." She swung the gun back toward the princess's head again.

I nodded. It would cost me nothing to agree with her. "It makes sense. You have the same father, and he's the one descended from the tsar."

"Did you know my father and his wife had my mother killed because she embarrassed them? Kira's mother, that bitch Sofia, tried to have me killed, too, she was so angry that I existed, but I was too smart for her. For all of them."

"You've been clever all along, Nadia. But you've run out of luck and now would be a good time to start negotiating."

"There's nothing to negotiate."

"Who can award you the title of princess? Is it the ambassador? Grand Duke Vassily? The tsar? Someone needs to make your position official." I wasn't sure how that worked, but I was willing to bet Nadia didn't, either.

"They won't do it."

"You're holding Kira. Of course they will. As long as she's alive and unharmed, they're going to present the title to you." It sounded good. Right now, that was all I could hope for.

"And once it's done, it can't be undone." Nadia smiled and put the barrel of the pistol against Kira's head.

Kira's eyes begged me to do something.

"You don't want to double-cross these people. Honest dealing will get you a lot further," I told her.

"Why should she stay alive and unharmed? Her mother killed my mother. Her mother tried to kill me. Perhaps she should lose her well-loved daughter instead." Hatred simmered in her eyes. The same hatred I'd seen when she looked at Princess Kira in Hereford House.

"Think back, Princess Nadia. Do you really think Kira's mother loves her? I think she's been disappointed by having a daughter who paints."

Nadia nodded. "You're right. Kira's mother has always been a stupid woman. Everything is for appearances."

"Alive, Kira's your means to get your title and passage to France. Dead, there's no reason not to hang you." I kept my tone relaxed, as if I were discussing the weather. But my stomach trembled and my knees thumped together.

"Bring me the letter awarding me my proper title, and I will let her go. Otherwise, Griekev will be back with the jewels soon. Once we have the jewels, no one will care if my title is genuine or not. And I will have no need to spare her life." She spoke the last with a royal sneer.

"Jacob, go back to Sir Broderick's and telephone to Whitehall. Tell Blackford what we need and tell him to bring the letter as quickly as possible." I hoped Jacob would tell Blackford all and alert Sumner and Emma in the back alley.

"I'll hurry." He left the room and we heard his feet clattering down the stairs. Then the front door banged shut.

I walked farther into the room and sat down on the bed. "We have a little wait, so we might as well be comfortable." Now Nadia couldn't watch both Adam and me at once. She had to move her head to glance between Adam standing by the door and me on the opposite side of the room.

Nadia swung the pistol toward me. "I didn't invite you in."

Now was not the time to upset her. I was in a vulnerable position. "No, Princess, you didn't."

"Move over there."

"I'm comfortable here." I saw anger flare in her eyes and hoped I could calm her. "You'll like France. The middle class there is not as independent as the shopkeepers here. That's what I am, you know. A bookshop owner."

"You lie."

"No. I was brought in to try to help Kira learn English. You both had us fooled. You speak our language very well. Where did you learn it?"

"I sat in on Kira's lessons with her tutor, and we practiced between ourselves for years. In English, we could speak to each other without anyone understanding us in the countryside. The miserable, boring countryside." The large, heavy pistol now hung down by her side, but she watched both Adam and me closely.

"You and Kira both hated life in the country. And you each had what the other wanted."

Nadia's eyes narrowed. "What do you mean?"

"She had a title. You wanted a title. You had the freedom to become whoever you wanted to be. She wanted that freedom to become a painter. The only reason she's marrying Sussex is because he'll let her paint as much as she wants."

"He's a poor excuse for a man." There was that sneer again.

"His mother's called a dragon by everyone who knows her. If you want to make Kira pay for having a title, make sure she marries Sussex. The dowager duchess will make her life miserable."

Kira swung her head toward me, her eyes widening from fear to shock. Apparently, no one had possessed the nerve to tell her about her fiancé's mother.

When she turned back to look at Nadia, her half sister smiled coldly. "You didn't know? Neither did I, but it seems fitting somehow. That title you never cared about, the title that smoothed your way through life, is finally going to cost you. It's about time."

We heard the front door open and close below us. Adam started to pace, stomping his feet.

Guessing what he was doing, I said, "It sounds like Jacob is back. Adam, is your leg bothering you again? He was injured several years ago, and his knee stiffens up on him. It's the damp London is famous for. You're smart to go over to France. They have better weather. Especially in the south."

We could hear Jacob coming up the stairs, even over Adam's footsteps. When Nadia didn't respond, her vision glued to the doorway, Adam said, "We have miserable weather here. Everyone I know has stiff joints."

Since most of the people he knew were policemen who had at one time walked patrol, I believed him.

Jacob entered by himself. I couldn't see anyone else on the landing, but I had to hope help was there. "Blackford's coming to negotiate. Nadia gets either the papers making her a princess or the jewels."

"I want both."

"Sorry. The Russians say you can have one or the other. Your choice."

She turned to Kira. "I should just kill you now."

"Then you won't get either," I said, making an effort to keep my voice calm.

Nadia faced me, the gun pointing at my chest, her finger on the trigger. "Maybe I should kill you instead to show them I'm serious."

My heart was beating wildly and I had a terrible time trying to speak while my entire body trembled. "Oh, they believe you're serious." I certainly did. "Otherwise they wouldn't have come this far with their offer. But it's nothing to them whether you kill me or not. Perhaps you could try negotiating. You might be able to get both."

"What do you mean?" She lifted her finger from the trigger and I took a deep breath.

"Get the title and part of the jewels as a reward to see you to France."

Her finger went back on the trigger and time seemed to slow. I watched her eyes blaze with fury and madness as she aimed the gun barrel at me. "All my life I've had to settle for Kira's castoffs. I had to worm my way into her lessons and was looked down upon by the servants. Now it's my turn. I want it all. And now is the time to prove I'm serious in my demands."

CHAPTER TWENTY-THREE

LOOKING down the barrel of the pistol into her furious gaze, I was certain she was going to shoot me. My first thought was who would take over Fenchurch's Books. I wanted Emma to have it, so that she'd have independence if anything happened to Sumner. I should have written a will.

It was a little late in the day to worry about that.

My second thought was that I wanted to see Blackford one more time. Would he get there before I died?

Then we all turned toward the doorway as what sounded like a herd of men entered the building and started walking up the stairs. "We're the negotiating committee," Blackford called up to us.

Once more I felt relief fill my body as the breath I'd been holding slowly escaped.

For the first time, Nadia seemed unsure. Then she pointed the pistol at the doorway and waited.

Blackford entered the room first, walking a few steps toward her and blocking her view of the doorway.

Nadia pointed the gun at his chest, her finger still on the trigger. "Stay away from me."

"Very well." He paced toward the window so he was out of her line of sight if she looked at the doorway or at me. "I'm the Duke of Blackford. I'm the negotiator between you and the grand duke. I believe you two have met."

Everyone turned toward the doorway, where Grand Duke Vassily stood. I thought it was very brave or very stupid of him to show up here. She was more likely to kill him than anyone else.

The sneer returned. "Oh, we have met. The grand duke knew of the plot to kill my mother and me. He'd rather see me dead than given the title of Princess Nadia. He's always looked down on us."

"You're a bastard," the grand duke said.

Oh, brilliant. I quickly replied, "That's not her fault. And you're not helping. Just leave."

"Gladly."

As he turned away, Blackford said, "Get back here. We are negotiating so no one gets hurt."

The grand duke took one step into the hall before I said, "Coward."

He whirled around and marched back into the room toward me. "Peasant."

I hopped off the bed and faced him. I lacked the height to look him in the eye without craning my neck, but that didn't diminish my fury. "No, I'm not. I'm a shop owner. And I'm brave enough to come here to try to help both Nadia and Kira. Which means I'm doing your job."

"I don't negotiate with anarchists."

"There are no anarchists here. Except for Adam, Jacob, and

me, everyone has aristocrats for fathers. These are exactly the people you negotiate with."

"Very well." He turned and faced Nadia. "I have the proclamation styling you Princess Nadia. You may have that or you may have the jewels."

"I want it all." Nadia's eyes glowed as the pistol pointed at the grand duke's heart from a distance of a few feet. Her finger was on the trigger.

He stood soldier straight facing her. I was wrong. He was no coward.

"Perhaps a portion of the jewels and the proclamation. We know it was Ivanov who killed Princess Kira's guard on the train, killed Shepherdston's footman, and shot the two policemen in the raid on the warehouse for your stolen goods," Blackford said. "You have nothing to fear, Nadia."

"You said nothing of Lady Raminoff's death." Nadia stared into Blackford's eyes.

"In Ivanov's absence, we can assume he killed her, too." Blackford glanced over at me, and his expression convinced me that Nadia was the one who had killed Lady Raminoff.

"Ivanov has already left the country," she said. "I doubt he will come back."

"Returned to Russia?" Grand Duke Vassily asked.

Nadia smiled. "Perhaps someday, when we are free of the tsar and the Okhrana."

I couldn't tell from Blackford's expression if that was true, or if Sumner had killed or captured the Russian.

We heard more footsteps on the stairs and then a man came into the room to stand by Nadia. His cap and scarf were gone, letting me see his blond hair and thin face. "You must be Griekev," I said.

"Yes. Are you the one who pulled the fuse out of my bomb at Hereford House?"

"Yes. It was quite impressive, hidden in the linen closet like that. If it weren't for my being in the wrong place while the staff was busy with lunch, your bomb would have made the house a pile of rubble."

He smiled grimly. "Bad luck."

I thought it was wonderful luck. "Where did you learn so much about dynamite?"

"I was an engineering student in St. Petersburg. That's where I met Nadia. It was love at first sight. I was in student demonstrations for change and saw how brutally the Cossacks put down peaceful marches. After the attempt to kill Nadia, I helped her escape from Russia and then followed her."

"And used your knowledge of dynamite for robberies."

"We helped ourselves while we helped the anarchists."

That made me wonder why they hadn't targeted the duchess for one of their thefts. "Were you the one who freed Ivanov from the basement of Hereford House?"

"Yes. I was supposed to meet him. When he didn't show up, I went looking for him. It wasn't hard to guess what happened."

"Were you planning to rob Hereford House?"

"Rob them? No, although it wouldn't have been a bad idea."

He pulled a massive revolver from his pocket. "I'd like to stay and chat, but we must leave. Nadia, get what you want from their coats and let's go."

Nadia handed Griekev her gun and then walked up to the grand duke. She quickly found the proclamation in his inside coat pocket and glanced over it with a smile. Then she walked over to Blackford. "You must have the jewels."

He opened his coat so she could reach the inside pocket; she pulled out a reddish cloth pouch.

She peeked in, smiled, and said, "Let's go."

"Wait." I had to know. "Lady Raminoff was on your side," I said to her. "Why did she have to die?"

"She caught me talking to Ivanov in the stairwell. And she saw the dynamite he handed me." Nadia took her revolver back, gave me a smile, and walked out the door.

Griekev walked backward, watching us all. "Too bad you won't be around to stop us."

Then he dashed down the stairs.

Grand Duke Vassily was the first to move, pulling a pistol from inside his coat while dashing out the doorway. A second later, a roar shook the house, followed by a scream.

Blackford was already racing out the door when the sound staggered his steps. I followed him to find Griekev lying on his stomach, head down on the stairs, a stain on the back of his coat. Vassily still held his pistol ready to fire again while Nadia bent over Griekev's body, sobbing.

Griekev grabbed one of Nadia's hands and groaned out some words in Russian. She murmured back to him, kissing his ear.

I stood and watched as his grip on her hand went slack.

"You killed him. Now we will all die." She infused the words with pathos. If an actress proclaimed those words with such feeling onstage, the audience would rise to its feet in admiration.

There'd be no applause here. Everyone was probably as terrified as I was. "There's a bomb in this house, isn't there?"

"Yes. And I will shoot you all rather than let you defuse it. You have only a minute. Say your prayers." Nadia's grief made her sound determined and tragic.

"No!" Vassily screamed and aimed at Nadia. Blackford moved as a second roar made me put my hands over my ears. Plaster in the ceiling over Nadia's head sent a shower of pieces flying and then floating down on her and Griekev.

"We will all die," the grand duke cried.

"No, we won't. Pull yourself together, man. Sumner put out the fuse as soon as Griekev came upstairs," Blackford snapped.

Nadia cradled Griekev's head, sobbing, murmuring what sounded like endearments in Russian.

"How do you know?" Vassily stared at Blackford with wide eyes in his pale face.

"He was the man I talked to before we came inside." Blackford sounded calm, but I saw the hair along his collar turn damp and curl. This was the only sign Blackford ever gave of nervousness.

I was turning away to walk back into the bedroom to free Princess Kira when I saw Nadia raise the pistol to her head.

"No!" I screamed and shut my eyes.

A third shot shattered the air in the stairwell. I opened my eyes to see Nadia sprawled on the landing, the gun held loosely in her hand and a small, dark hole in her temple.

My footsteps were much heavier when I returned to the bedroom to take the gag out of Princess Kira's mouth. Adam had already begun to cut her ropes. My throat was dry and my stomach churned.

"What has happened?" the princess shrieked hoarsely as soon as the cloth came out of her mouth.

I shook my head.

"I want to know." As soon as Adam had one wrist loosened, Kira pulled at it until her hand was free.

"No, you don't," I told her.

"Please. You can't protect me forever."

Adam worked on the other wrist while I said, "The grand duke shot Griekev in the back. Nadia shot herself. They're both dead."

"No." Her scream was nearly as loud as the gunshots, and more heart wrenching.

When Adam Fogarty freed Princess Kira's other wrist, she sprang from the chair and stumbled on stiff legs to the hallway. She looked down the stairs at Nadia cradling Griekev, blood spilling out beneath their bodies.

Tears slipped down her cheeks. She turned on Grand Duke Vassily and loosed a waterfall of Russian on his head. She finished with English. "You have no honor."

Then Princess Kira turned to me. "Would you accompany me back to Hereford House? I wish to speak to the duchess and then I want to speak to Arthur. The Duke of Sussex."

"Of course. Blackford, may we use your carriage?" I asked.

"I wish to return to the embassy first," Grand Duke Vassily announced in strident tones.

"We'll let the ladies leave first. It's only right that we be the ones to speak to the police," Blackford said. "You're the only person still alive who fired a shot." Speaking quietly in my ear, he added, "I'll be busy for a while. I'll see you later."

The Duke of Blackford escorted Princess Kira down the stairs as we carefully stepped around the bodies so we wouldn't interfere with the crime scene or bloody our skirts. The princess stopped when she was next to Nadia's body and I saw her lips move. I was sure she was praying for her half sister. Then she bent down and stroked her hand before moving on.

As Blackford passed, I saw him bend down and pick up the pistols and the bag of jewels. I wondered if he'd provided some of the glittering stones.

I followed the princess out, grateful to escape the stench of death and gunpowder. Blackford put us in his carriage and gave instructions to his coachman. Then we set off, bouncing on the hard seats of the ancient carriage as we rode the short distance to Hereford House.

"You are certain Nadia took her own life?" the princess asked.

"Yes." The image her words brought back nearly made me physically ill. "I saw her."

"She loved Griekev. They both thought the robberies were great fun."

I shook my head. "They were dangerous. And how do you know?"

Kira smiled her answer. "The danger was part of the thrill. Griekev was charming. He was dashing. People couldn't help but love him. He rescued Nadia after my mother tried to have her killed. And all this time, I thought it was my father who hired the assassins." She shook her head. "Then Griekev spirited Nadia out of the country. He followed her a day later."

"And then began his series of robberies with dynamite. People were terrified."

"They never meant to hurt anyone."

"Your guard, Lidijik, might disagree."

She stared into the darkness outside. "Nadia wanted to spend time with me. We all came from my father's estate, and she knew Lidijik would recognize her and report her to the embassy. She'd be deported to Russia and killed, either on the way there or after she landed. My mother would see to that. Ivanov killed him and took an epaulet and a button so tailors could copy Lidijik's coat. Then Ivanov could replace him, and Nadia and I could spend time together safely."

"And you find that acceptable?"

The princess gave me a defiant glare, but I stared back at her.

Finally, she slumped and said, "No. I was just so happy to see Nadia again. To know she was alive and safe."

"She could have been, if she hadn't wanted a title and a fortune in jewels."

"No. All Nadia wanted was the title that my father denied her. Griekev decided to demand jewels to fund their new lives."

There was something I needed to know about Kira. "Were you a willing party to your own kidnapping?"

She gasped and grabbed my wrist. "No. You have to believe me. I thought we were just running off to church so Nadia could see Griekev. Just as we had before."

"After Nadia tried to kill you with the dynamite?" Was Kira innocent or stupid?

"The plan was for her to run in and stop it. To make it look like she saved my life from anarchists so my father and the tsar would be forced to recognize her. You found it too soon."

"There was only a few seconds left when I cut the fuse. She had already left the house. We were all only a few seconds from death at Nadia's hand."

"No!"

Was she completely blind to Nadia's faults? Or did everyone around the Russian royal family act so deceitfully? "Perhaps Nadia thought if your father lost you, he might recognize her as his daughter. Or maybe she just wanted vengeance for the death of her mother."

"No." She began to cry. I didn't try to comfort her. She needed to find her own way to understanding Nadia's betrayal.

CHAPTER TWENTY-FOUR

WE arrived at Hereford House and entered the mansion, where the duchess hugged the princess and said how delighted she was the young woman was safe.

While the princess tried to apologize for all the trouble she'd brought on their house, I approached the well-dressed man standing to one side. "Your Grace?" I asked.

"Yes, I'm the Duke of Hereford. Are you Miss Peabody or Fenchurch or something?"

That seemed to describe my life. "I am."

"Blackford sent for me after you saved my home and family today. Thank you."

"You're welcome." At the moment, my primary thought had been saving myself, but he didn't need to know that. "I've enjoyed working with Her Grace."

"She seems quite pleased with your work. But I suppose you're going back to your regular employment?"

"I own Fenchurch's Books, not far from Leicester Square."

"Blackford's recommended it to me a time or two. I must stop by."

"We'd be honored to serve you, Your Grace." I'd be happy to have another aristocrat spend good money in my shop.

"Excuse me. Hereford, could you send someone for Sussex? The princess would like to speak to him, tonight if possible," the duchess said.

"Of course, my dear. If you'll excuse me?" Hereford gave me a bow and walked away.

I was invited to take tea in the parlor with the duchess and the princess while we waited to see if Sussex could be reached. All I wanted was to see Blackford tonight.

I took my time in drinking two cups of tea while I waited. None of us said a word. I was about to give up and go home when the parlor door opened and the butler announced the dukes of Blackford and Sussex. The princess rose and hurried over to Sussex. He looked surprised and delighted at the change in the way she greeted him.

Hereford turned to his wife and suggested she retire after such a distressing day. Blackford came over to me and said, "I'll give you a ride home if you're ready to leave."

"More than ready, Your Grace. Has Mary made it back to your house?"

"Yes. Sumner and Emma saw her safely home and told her she'd helped avenge her brother's death in stopping Griekev and Nadia. She was pleased to have played a role."

I smiled in response. Mary might become a part of the Archivist Society. She certainly had good instincts for the work.

We said good night to our hosts and walked out into the rain. Once again, I began to shiver from the chill air and my exhaustion. Blackford had to help me into the carriage. I had no reserves of energy left for climbing into the monstrous vehicle.

"What happened with Grand Duke Vassily?"

"Nothing. I took him to the embassy before I collected Sussex."

I stared at him in horror. "He shot a man in the back."

"He's a diplomat. He can do that." When my expression didn't change, he took one of my hands in his. "Remember Count Farkas? Grand Duke Vassily has the same protection. We hope diplomats won't go around shooting and stabbing the populace, but they can. It's called diplomatic immunity. All we can do is ask them to leave."

"Will he?"

"Oh, yes. Inspector Grantham was having a nice chat with the ambassador and the grand duke when I left the embassy. At any rate, the negotiations he's involved in will wrap up in a day or so and he'll have no reason to be here."

I considered his words in silence. "What about the princess?"

"What about her?"

"This has been a shock to her. I think she sees the world differently now. Do you think she and Sussex will still get along?"

"Perhaps better. You saw the way she greeted him tonight. There's nothing like an enthusiastic greeting by his loved one to strengthen a man's ardor."

I looked at Blackford and raised my eyebrows. "Is that all it takes?"

His expression turned serious as he leaned closer. In the darkness of the carriage, broken only by flashes of light as we passed streetlamps, his eyes took on a possessive glow. He took off his hat and angled his head so my hat brim was out of his way as his face came ever nearer.

I was pulled toward him as if he were a magnet before our lips finally met. My hands slid up his shoulders without conscious thought on my part. Pressure from his arms pushed me snugly against his chest. The brandy-flavored kiss gentled and lengthened.

Excitement rushed through my veins as his words, "strengthen a man's ardor," echoed in my brain.

Maybe this time he'd see me between investigations. Maybe this time he saw me as duchess material instead of as a mistress.

He broke off the kiss but his arms stayed around me. His voice rumbled breathlessly as he said, "I find the more I do this, the more I want to."

I smiled at him almost like a conspirator. "I'm glad you find it agreeable." Then I laid my head against his shoulder, my eyes squeezed tightly against my tears. "Oh, Blackford. I could have lost you today."

He held me in a protective embrace. "I could have lost you, too. And I don't want to ever lose you."

The carriage stopped and a thump came from the driver's seat.

"You're home," he said with what I almost thought was a sigh. Perhaps the sigh was mine.

I glanced out through the gap in the curtains. "Yes."

"I'll see you tomorrow if you can tear yourself away from the wedding plans."

Wedding plans? Wedding plans! Oh, goodness gracious—and then I realized he meant Sumner and Emma. I hoped he didn't see my expression sink before I said cheerfully, "I'm sure I can find time for you, Your Grace. You'll come by the shop?"

"I hope to." He gently helped me out of the carriage and walked me to my door. "Good night, my brave Georgia. I hope you sleep peacefully tonight."

"Thank you, Blackford. I hope you get some sleep as well."

"I will, now that you've rescued us from the threat of burglars with dynamite and Russians with vengeance on their minds."

"And Ivanov?"

"He won't hurt anyone ever again."

His somber tone told me Ivanov's fate. "Is Sumner in trouble?"

"No. While Sumner was chasing Ivanov, he lost sight of him. He came around a corner, wondering which way the Russian had gone, just in time to see Ivanov go down under a fully loaded beer wagon's wheels. He died within moments." Blackford put a final kiss on my forehead and walked away.

I went inside to find Emma and Phyllida discussing the wedding.

MUKOVSKI WAS MY first customer the next day. I looked at him blankly as he walked into the bookshop with a package under his arm. He set it on the counter and opened it to reveal a dozen different two-shilling paper-covered novels.

Then I remembered our conversation the morning before in his print shop. He waited silently while I perused them, checking quality and the Russian community's knowledge of English. I'd seen much worse by native Englishmen. Frances came in and looked over my shoulder before choosing one of the volumes and beginning to read.

"What do you think?" I asked her.

"This one's quite good."

I turned back to Mukovski. "What kind of a discount do you give bookshops?"

He looked at me blankly. Finally, he said, "I sell them for a shilling."

I paid only a little more for the two-shilling copies I bought from regular distributors. "Fine. I'll buy them for a shilling each and contact you in a few days if we get any demand for them."

We shook hands, I paid him, and we shelved the volumes, minus the one Frances was reading. From her interest, I felt certain she'd sell any number of that story to our customers. I suspected I'd be contacting Mukovski soon.

Blackford came by the shop near lunchtime. I was on my own except for Dickens and was waiting on two customers at once. The duke glanced at some magazines that prominently proclaimed the engagement of the Duke of Sussex and Princess Kira while I transacted my business. Then he walked to the window box and petted Dickens. Dickens rolled onto his side and stretched, knocking over a display of mathematics texts.

After the second woman left with her purchases, I turned to the display and righted the books. "Your Grace."

He gestured to a magazine covering the engagement of the princess. "If they only knew."

Dickens kicked the books over again and stretched out so I had no room to set up the display. I gave up and put the books back on the shelves. "I thought the whole point was that they wouldn't know."

Blackford followed me. "True. Princess Kira has convinced Hereford and some others to put her up until the wedding so she doesn't have to go back to Russia. Sussex has been helping her twist some arms. And I understand the queen has thrown in her support by keeping the dowager duchess busy as one of her ladies-in-waiting for a full year."

"She'll have to meet the dragon sometime."

"The consensus is they shouldn't meet until after the honeymoon."

"Oh, my." Sussex's mother certainly had a reputation. "I hope someone has taken the princess off the hands of the Herefords."

"News of the duchess's condition has been whispered about and a few of their friends have stepped in to help. The Herefords are going to their country estate so the duchess can have a long rest and paint in solitude."

"What about Daisy's governess, Miss Whitten?"

"She decided to stay in London."

"She has to. Her mother is ill and she has a young son."

"She's won a scholarship to London University for teacher training. She'd started her studies before she became a mother. Now she'll be able to live at home and in a year or so, she'll be a fully qualified teacher with a good salary."

"Can they afford the loss of her income for that long?"

"The scholarship came with a small stipend. I imagine they'll manage."

I didn't know if Blackford was paying for all this, but he'd certainly arranged it. Behind his austere facade was a kind man, and I loved him, even if I didn't always understand him. I was certain Amelia Whitten would never suspect who was behind her scholarship and stipend.

After I watched Blackford play with Dickens for a moment, I asked, "Will the Russians let the princess stay here?"

"As far as the Russians are concerned, the princess can stay here and paint forever. Particularly after her father found out she'd been seeing her illegitimate sister. The Russian ambassador has released funds to pay for an English lady's maid for the princess and to cover her dressmaker's bills. I suspect Prince Pyotr was pressured by the tsar into providing more support for his daughter."

"What about another chaperone to replace Lady Raminoff?"

"Whichever English aristocrat has her visiting will supply the chaperone. It's felt at Whitehall and Balmoral that we've had enough Russians visiting lately."

"What about Mila? Did she ever return to Hereford House?"

"No. One of the Archivist Society members found her in the East End with her family, and no one is looking for her since Sir Broderick spread around the news that she's no danger to anyone."

"Why was she stealing food?"

"No one in her family had a job. Now a couple of her brothers have jobs in a warehouse."

"Do we have you to thank for that, Your Grace?"

Instead of replying, he said, "The family left her behind when they escaped Russia, planning to have her join them later when they raised funds for her passage. That's why she jumped at the chance to come here with Princess Kira. Mila had planned to abandon her from the start."

Then he gave me a wide smile. "I understand Emma's wedding will be next week?"

"Yes. Sumner bought a license and our local vicar has set the date. You'll be there?"

"Yes. I wouldn't miss it. But I have to leave for America the next day."

"You what?" My heart fluttered in my chest, unable to work properly. My vision narrowed until all I could see was Blackford's face.

"You remember the night at the Austrian embassy when I was called away from our waltz by some business partners?"

How could I forget? "This business requires your personal attention so soon? What about winter storms? Won't you have a rough voyage at this time of year?"

"Fortunately, I'm a good sailor. And my investments require my attention now. I have several in the States and in Canada and I can't let them go for too long between visits."

"How long will you be gone?"

"I should return by spring."

"Oh." My heart was in my left half boot. My mood was under the floorboards.

"You'll have the entire Archivist Society to keep you busy on investigations and you'll have to replace Emma in the shop. Your life will go on much as before here in London while some of us are traveling."

I gave him what I hoped appeared to be a brave smile. "I'm just jealous. Emma and Sumner are going on a wonderful European tour, spending the worst of the winter in Egypt and Greece. You're going to the New World, with cowboys and Indians and paddle-wheel steamers. Phyllida and I will have to make our own fun here in dreary, cold London."

"Did Emma tell you Sumner's pseudonym?"

"That Sumner is Mrs. Hepplewhite? He's the best-selling gothic novelist in London. Perhaps the most popular writer of light fiction of our time." I couldn't hide my joyous smile. "Emma said he'll spend his time discovering new gloomy castles and writing more stories. More importantly, he'll be able to support a family. I was so relieved when she told me."

If he couldn't have supported Emma, I'd have choked him. And then brought him into the bookshop because I couldn't stand to see Emma as disappointed as I was when my fiancé died.

The postman walked in and handed me the morning delivery. I scanned the envelopes quickly, stopping when I found one with a Danish stamp. I recognized the handwriting.

Something in my expression must have told Blackford, because he said, "Is it Count Farkas?"

Nodding, I slit it open and read.

My dear Georgia,

I've had word of my Bible in Copenhagen, so I'm afraid I've had to leave your beautiful city. I hope you've had a chance to consider our conversation.

I've never had anything but admiration for you.
Hopefully we can one day be friends.

Yours truly,
Count Farkas

I handed Blackford the letter and said, "Friends? Is he out of his mind?"

"Promise me you won't do anything about him until I return from America."

"I won't go looking for him. If he comes looking for me, I make no promises."

"Fair enough. That thought alone should make me hurry back."

He grinned at me and I returned the smile. I'd take anything that would make Blackford hurry back, but I especially relished the idea of trapping my parents' killer with Blackford at my side.

AUTHOR'S NOTE

The marriage of Princess Kira and the Duke of Sussex would not have been unusual in the late Victorian time period. Two of Victoria's granddaughters married into the Russian royal family. The tsar's mother, the former tsarina, was the sister of the Princess of Wales. One can look at the meeting of the queen and the tsar in September 1896 as nothing more than a granddaughter, Nicholas's tsarina, showing off her infant daughter to the baby's great-grandmother. It is hard for us at a distance to remember these were family visits as well as state occasions.

Anarchists were the bane of every European monarch's life. Queen Victoria was the target of at least seven attempts on her life. None were successful due to good luck and the loyalty of her quick-witted subjects. Others weren't so lucky. Tsar Alexander II of Russia and the wife of Emperor Franz Josef were both killed by anarchists. One of Victoria's granddaughters was a target of anarchists on the day of her wedding to the King of Spain and ended up with a blood splattered wedding gown.

As the most feudal and repressive rulers in Europe, it is no surprise that the aristocracy in Russia feared anarchists the most. The attitudes I've given my fictional characters were representative of the Russian upper crust and the immigrants in the squalid East

End. Fortunately for Britain, the immigrants were able to turn their anger and frustration toward social and economic reform. Reformers in Russia were not so lucky in that their government, made rigid by fear and tradition, could not adapt.

Due to German bombing in World War II and gentrification, little of the East End described in this story still exists. The land where the homes of the Duke of Blackford and the Duke of Hereford are situated is now occupied by luxury hotels. Today one needs to search to find any of the London Georgia Fenchurch would have known so well. I've used old photographs, books, and museums as well as visits to various neighborhoods to find the buildings, furnishings, transportation, and fashions I've described. Any mistakes are my own.